You Are Not Alone

By Stacy Eaton

Dedicated To:

The Domestic Violence Center of Chester County:

For all that you do to help the victims of domestic violence, thank you.

Foreword

A word from the author:

Twenty years ago, domestic violence wasn't spoken about. Even ten years ago, people didn't sit around the dinner table and discuss it. These days, we are finally seeing it discussed, but that is only because of serious events by famous people that have brought it to the news and to our focus.

It's time to stop hiding behind closed doors and to start having these conversations in public. It's time for victims to know that they are NOT ALONE and that they can have happy, safe, fulfilling lives. They do not need to tolerate the mental, verbal, sexual, or physical abuse that they endure day in and day out. They can find help, they can have a life. They can have happiness and love, real love. They just have to decide it's time—and then reach out to someone who can help.

US National Domestic Violence Hotline Number: 1-800-799-7233 or visit their website at: www.thehotline.org.

National Coalition Against Domestic Violence: www.ndvh.org.

Chapter 1 - Trinity

It wasn't that I didn't like to do these seminars, I did. I mean, who better to educate people on this topic than a person who had gone through it firsthand, right? If it weren't so damned mentally exhausting to relive the memories, then standing up in front of the crowd wouldn't be so bad—maybe.

I unscrewed the cap of my water bottle and put the bottle to my lips. The cool liquid slipped into my dry mouth, and I swished it around softly for a moment as I glanced around at the audience in the large auditorium.

About a hundred and fifty people sat in dark burgundy theater-style chairs, some bouncing slowly on the seat hinges, others leaning on the armrests holding their heads up with their fists as they tried to keep their eyes open and listen to the monotonous speaker on the main floor below them.

Most of the people in attendance were male, although sporadically interspersed through the group were women. A tingle of fear snaked down my spine. Many years ago, it was people similar to these from whom I had been hidden, or they had simply ignored the signs they had seen. No, I had been hidden.

I closed my eyes tightly and clenched my jaw. Not all of them had ignored the hidden knowledge, I said to myself as I screwed the lid back onto the clear plastic bottle and let it rest on my lap. The secret truth had been solidly hidden behind the well-groomed walls of the house in which we had lived. No one had known the awful truth, or if they had, they'd ignored it. It wasn't until the fateful night that anyone actually saw the product of the horror that I'd lived in every day for several years. Some didn't believe it even after they heard the facts and saw the many bruises on my body.

I blew out a slow steady stream of air. My attention was drawn back to the stage area of the auditorium. The male speaker was just finishing up his segment; the audience appeared to understand this as they began to fidget even more, as if to make a run for it at the first chance. They knew that when he was done droning on, they would get a break to eat the catered lunch that was provided before the afternoon segment began—my segment.

My phone vibrated in my suit jacket pocket, and I slipped my hand inside. The number on the screen was from my coworker at the shelter and I made my way to the door. I would take my call in the hallway so as not to disturb the end of the lecture.

I glanced over my shoulder at the speaker. Yeah, it was a lecture, and there was no wonder these guys were falling asleep. I would be too if I had to listen to this guy talk about the legal aspects of dealing with victims and prosecuting suspects with as much excitement as a bullfrog sitting on a rock in the rain. I pushed open the door and slipped out into the hallway as I tapped my screen to answer my phone.

"Hey, Brooke, what's up?" With my phone to my ear, I walked down the corridor of the hotel's corporate area. The dark red carpet under my feet cushioned my steps as I approached a glass balcony that overlooked the main entrance two floors down. Glass, chrome, and highly-polished dark wood sparkled below. A man sat in a chair reading a newspaper, his closed briefcase beside him.

"You're not speaking yet are you?" she asked quickly.

"Would I answer the phone if I was?"

She laughed on the other end, "No, well, you never know, you might if you thought it was important enough."

The doors down the hallway opened and the attendees starting converging on me. I stepped away from the balcony edge and into a corner so I was out of their way. I learned a very long time ago: Never step in the way of hungry men and their food, especially when the food was free.

"Actually, they're just breaking for lunch. I'm up right after. Why I always get stuck with them after they are fed is beyond me. It's so much harder to keep them awake once they have full stomachs."

The men and woman staggered past, some alone, some walking in groups. More than one person mumbled about the speaker putting them to sleep. I smiled and turned my back to them, pushing the phone closer to my ear so I could hear Brooke's reply over the loud movement of people.

"Trinity, we all know that they put you on in the afternoon because you keep them awake!" Her soft laugh flowed through the line, calming me. "Nothing like a beautiful woman with a sexy voice to keep them tuned in."

I shook my head, "Yeah, that's me alright." Not, I thought to myself.

"Oh, let's not go there again. You know you are a beautiful woman. Did you forget to look in the mirror this morning?" I heard a metal drawer being closed through the speaker of the phone; she must have taken her purse out so she could head to lunch.

I decided to ignore her statement. "Did you need something?" I was trying to get her attention back to why she had called and off of me.

"No, I didn't need anything. I wanted to check on you." Her voice grew softer, "I know how you get when you have to do these talks."

She did know me well. Brooke Patterson and I had been friends for almost ten years, and it was to her that I turned when the demons reared their ugly heads and tormented me. Not only were we friends, but we were partners in business. Both of us had lived through years of intense circumstances and had come out alive. We spent all our time now trying to educate people so that they could help others who had lived like we once had.

Our nonprofit organization was called "You're Not Alone", and we worked with victims of domestic violence. We had started it about eight years ago, and it was the largest organization in the tri-state area.

It was because of what Brooke and I had lived through personally that we were able to do so well with the organization. We weren't just people who had learned through college courses, we had lived through the horror firsthand.

"I'm fine, Brooke, I appreciate that, but I'm fine." I turned back around as the hallway quieted. Only a few stragglers meandered towards the food.

I watched one man walk by, his cellphone in his left hand, the pointer finger from his right hand sliding over the screen. He had strong forearms that peeked out of the rolled-up sleeves of his dark green dress shirt. I glanced up at the side of his face as he passed and sucked in a sudden breath.

The curve of his jaw, the angle of his nose, the short cut of his brown hair, all brought back a memory so suddenly, that I froze while only my eyeballs traced his path to the stairs. My feet froze in place while my heart galloped like a horse from a burning barn.

"Trinity, are you alright?" Brooke's voice reached my ears, but I couldn't speak. "Trinity? Trinity, are you still there?"

The man disappeared down the stairs and still I found myself stuck in place, stuck in a memory.

Brooke's shrill voice in my ear yelling my name finally broke me out of my startled daze, and I shook my head to clear it. It couldn't be him, it couldn't be.

"Yeah, I'm here," I cleared my throat of the sudden emotion that had lodged there.

"What happened?" she all but yelled in my ear.

"Nothing," I cleared my throat again, "nothing. I dropped the phone, sorry." I closed my eyes, willing my heart to slow down again.

"Oh, okay. Well, you sure you're alright to do this?" Her voice was back in its normal friendly range.

I swallowed, "Yes, I'm fine. It's just another lecture, no big deal."

"You keep telling yourself that." She laughed and we said our goodbyes after I told her I would call her when I was done.

I hit the button to end the call and scanned the area. Other than some employees bustling into the lecture hall to clean it up, I was alone. No, not alone, I was just by myself for the moment. I thought about going down to where they were serving lunch, but I rejected it.

I was usually a bit uneasy before I spoke, and now my empty stomach seemed to be roiling after that memory had passed through my mind.

I glanced around the hallway, intent on finding a peaceful place where I could gather my thoughts. I saw the door down the hallway and quickly entered the women's restroom.

Inside, I found exactly what I needed, and I sank into a deep burgundy chair in the sitting area. Closing my eyes, I took a few deep breaths.

On the back of my eyelids the memory flashed again, only this time it was with the pulsing flash of amber ambulance lights around me. The strong solid chin, the thin pointed nose, the soft green eyes set back behind thick eyelashes blinked with the lights of the emergency vehicle. He wasn't looking at me as my eyes opened, he had turned so I only saw his profile for a moment before it was replaced with other people and darkness sank in around me again.

I felt my pulse ticking quickly in my throat, the pain from that moment so long ago almost as alive as the memory. I lifted my hand and allowed my fingers to slide over my throat. I took a shaky breath to shove away the pain.

That was ten years ago and far away from here. There was no way that could be him.

Chapter 2 - Gavin

"Aren't you going to eat, Gavin?"

I glanced at Noah and set my phone down.

"Yeah," I took a bite of my baked chicken and tried not to think about the text message I had gotten from my sister.

Noah and I were seated at a table with seven other guys. Some were from our department and a few were from a police department next to us. We all knew each other, and the comments about this morning's slug of a speaker were firing back and forth over the table.

Listening to what the guy had been saying was like trying to swallow peanut-butter-coated bread without a drink. It was good when you first bit in, but then it started to thicken and clog your throat, blocking off the oxygen and putting you into a boredom-induced coma. I was not the only one who was having trouble not nodding off, and normally I paid attention at these kinds of seminars.

I had grown up with domestic violence in my house. For years, my mother had been a victim, and as my sister and I grew, we watched it and became victims to the abuse ourselves. It was one of the reasons I had become a cop.

"All I gotta say," Derek Wilson, one of the newer guys from our department started to talk then took a bite of his potatoes and continued speaking with his mouth full, "is if this afternoon's speaker is anything like this morning's, I'm not gonna make it."

There was shared laughter and a few murmurs of the same around the table. Even I had to agree, as much as I didn't want to. Derek was not one of my favorite people. His brash attitude towards others was well known in our area, and he had been called into the chief's office more than once for complaints against him.

One of the other guys spoke up, thankfully after he had swallowed his food, "Naw, I hear it's a woman. She's gonna tell us her story."

"Great!" Derek threw out loudly. "Just what we need, a crybaby chick talking about how some guy beat her and she couldn't get away from him."

A few people glanced around the table; it was one of those statements you knew was wrong but could be humorous to the right people. This table was not filled with the right people.

"You know what, Derek, you can be a real ass," Noah said before he took a bite of his roll and glared over the table at him.

"What?" Derek sputtered.

Noah glanced my way as I set my fork down on my plate; suddenly I was not hungry anymore.

Noah was one of the few people I had ever told about my family. He knew how I felt about abusive men and how I felt about female victims. I pushed my chair back from the table and stood.

"Not all women can get away from their abusers. Did you not listen to a thing they said this morning?" Noah tossed the words back at him as I stepped away from the table. I walked away before I could hear Derek's response.

I found the nearest door and walked out. As the sun beat down on me I looked around. Derek was a bastard, and I shouldn't let it bother me. He wasn't the only one who thought such things. So many people thought that victims of abuse could just walk away but chose to stay. I knew it was different. I knew how hard it was to make that step to leave.

I glanced at the door as Noah walked out. "Ignore him, he's just an asshole."

I chuckled quietly, "Yes, he is."

"Do you know anything about this organization that is talking today?" I turned to Noah as he spoke. "I know you have worked with a few of them."

I shook my head. "No, I've heard of them, but this is the first time they have done any seminars in this area."

Since I had moved back here two years ago, I spent time volunteering with some of the shelters in the area. I did the manual labor they needed, helped stock shelves, and once in a while would escort some women who needed the protection. Most of the time, I avoided the women, not because I wanted to, but because they were leery of me and just about every other man around them. Sometimes I made a friend and they saw that not all men or police officers were jerks.

We were dispatched to more domestic violence calls than people realized. They would come in spurts, sometimes a few in a day, and then we could go a day or two without them, but one thing was for certain, they were never the same and they were always dangerous for everyone involved.

We followed a group of people back into the auditorium and found our seats. I was calmer and told myself that Derek was just an unfeeling crackpot that shouldn't be doing the job. Noah and I sat back down, and I cracked open a bottle of water I had snagged before returning.

On the stage floor there were a few people milling around getting ready to get started. I looked over each of them wondering which one was today's speaker. None of them looked like they would be entertaining in the least. Noah sighed next to me, and I slid a side glance at him as he laid his head back in the seat, bouncing slightly in the chair.

I grinned because I knew he was thinking the same thing I was. More people filed in and found their seats, and we chatted while the people below on the stage kept glancing up at the door. They were probably waiting to see if everyone was inside.

A few more minutes went by, and then one of the women below called out to get our attention. She asked us to get seated before we began. The ones left standing slowly found seats and cast their attention forward.

"I hope you all enjoyed your lunch. We are about to get started on our afternoon segment. I know that some of you thought this morning was long," she gave a warm laugh as did many of us, "but I think you are all going to find this afternoon much easier to get through." The brunette woman speaking smiled up and around the room as she stood at the podium and spoke into the microphone attached.

"Now, if everyone is ready, we are going to start. We'd like to welcome You're Not Alone here today, and we hope that you all get something out of what you hear. For this first part, I need to make sure everyone is seated and stays there for a few moments." She took in the room visually, as some of us glanced at our chair neighbors with raised eyebrows. The woman appeared happy with our lack of questions and nodded. Within two seconds the lights went out.

Muffled movements filled the room along with several, random comments. Throwing a bunch of cops into the dark without telling them could amp up their stress levels quickly.

"Relax, everyone, just sit back and relax. The lights were supposed to go out. Everyone, I'd like you to welcome, Trinity Morris, co-founder of You're Not Alone."

The name Trinity rolled through my head, and I looked around. Emergency lights cast long shadows around the room. The stairs that led down to the main floor were illuminated with dim green lights. I looked over my shoulder, a woman stood at the top near the door, the outline of her body hidden in the shadows.

"Thank you, Susan, and thank you to all of you who are here today. As we begin this afternoon, I want you all to take a moment and sit back in your seat. Close your eyes and allow the darkness to flow over you."

Her voice was soft and husky as it floated through the room from the speakers. I looked around, and it appeared most people were doing what she asked. A few people, like me, were looking over their shoulders, but they turned around and finally appeared to sit back. I forced myself to look forward. My eyelids closed when her voice continued.

"Clear out of your mind all the things that you have to do, all the things you were talking about with your co-workers just now. Pretend you are in a small dark box, there is no light and you are alone."

I heard soft footsteps in the back of the room. I tried to focus on what she was telling us to do, but I felt the urgent need to open my eyes and look for her. I clenched my lids and tried to listen to what she was saying.

"Inside your mind, I want you to envision your biggest fear. Maybe you are afraid of snakes or spiders. Maybe your biggest fear is falling from up high or being sucked under by a huge wave." She paused for a moment, and I hung on her every word, picturing my biggest fear inside my mind.

"Everyone is afraid of something," her natural voice was moving lower, not the amplified one that came through the speakers, but the one that came directly from her mouth and went into the microphone. I tried not to picture her, and fought to keep the image of my fear in my head, but it was slowly changing to a memory deep inside.

A woman, her voice dangerously husky, her eyes frightened, but still strong. She sat on the witness stand, dressed in a dark gray turtleneck sweater and told her story.

I knew I was jumping at straws here. The possibility that it could be the same woman named Trinity that I knew was too farfetched. That had been over nine years ago and a thousand miles away. I forced the image out of my head and back to my fear as she continued.

"Now, you're in your box and the biggest thing you fear is right in front of you, staring you in the eye, daring you to run, but there is no one who will help you, no one to stand beside you and help you face your fear. There is no one to fight your fear with you." She paused and then very quietly added, "You are alone."

I wondered if others had noticed their hearts beating faster, or if mine was the only one.

"How do you feel?" she asked quietly to the room. From the direction of her voice, she appeared to be below now.

A female voice near the front answered, "Afraid."

"Afraid. Okay, anyone else? What do you feel?" she asked again, and I shivered at the sound of her husky voice as if it had just been whispered close to my ear.

"Anger," came a male voice from the right side of the room.

"Okay, good, anger, what else?"

"I want to punch its lights out." A wave of subdued laughter passed over the group.

She sounded like she was smiling when she answered. Were we ever going to turn the lights back on? I didn't want to face my demon any longer.

"Now, think about what you feel right now, and know that this is what a victim feels like every single day." The room was silent for a moment. "The victims feel alone, afraid, angry, and like they have no one to talk to, no one that will ever understand what they are feeling."

The loud release of her breath carried through the large room, and I shivered again. "The next time you deal with a victim of domestic abuse, remember this feeling, remember this moment and know that this is what a victim feels like," she paused after the next three words for effect, "every…single…day. Then try to find a way to help the victim."

The room was silent for about ten seconds, giving us time to think about what she had said. When the lights clicked back on, everyone blinked multiple times and tried to clear their vision. I fought harder than everyone there to get the first glimpse of the speaker.

As my eyes finally cleared enough to see her, I sucked in my breath. Her long auburn hair cascaded over her shoulders; a cream-colored blouse with a high neckline covered the pale skin on her neck. The chocolate suit jacket she wore made her look dignified and professional. She stood tall, her shoulders back, her chin up, facing us all as we looked down at her. Her eyes scanned the theater, and my heart skipped a beat as they slipped over mine and then bounced back. As I looked into her face and saw her eyes, I knew it was her, and her mouth opened slightly. She had just recognized me, too.

Chapter 3 - Trinity

A long time had passed since I had allowed myself to think about what had happened to me ten years ago, and when jagged pieces of memories broke through and surfaced, I normally tamped them down.

While this particular memory surprised me, the memory itself was not an unhappy one. The person I had visualized was a responding officer to yet another violent session with my husband.

I had met this officer just once before this particular night. We had attended a social gathering and he had been a rookie cop, a young guy fresh out of the academy, maybe twenty-two or twenty-three years of age by his looks.

While he wasn't all that much younger than I was, maybe three or four years, his eyes had the look of someone much older. His face was young and handsome, filled with strength and excitement to do the job behind the badge, yet his green eyes held a sadness and knowledge that had drawn me to him. Of course acting on such a thing would have been a bad idea with severe consequences.

It was a rare event that I was out of the house in the first place. My husband, Brenden, did not often allow me to accompany him on social outings. He said that I would be bored with all the shop talk between him and the other guys.

I knew the real reason, though: He didn't want his fellow co-workers to see the marks that he left on my body. I mean, how would the lieutenant explain all that to his men?

I stood up from the chair in the restroom and walked to the mirror. The image that reflected back did not show the same woman that I had been back then.

The night that I had seen that rookie officer again, I had been twenty pounds lighter, too thin to be healthy. I also had burn marks on my arms, and I could barely breathe because my windpipe had been crushed by my not-so-loving husband's hands.

The rookie had burst into the house and found me on the floor. Brenden, his superior officer, was still straddling my hips, depriving my body of oxygen. The rookie had tackled him before he and his partner wrestled Brenden into submission, placing him into custody.

He had picked up my almost lifeless body and carried me out to the responding ambulance. Of course, I didn't remember any of that firsthand, my knowledge of the event came from reading the police report.

What I did remember personally was a set of strong arms holding me closely, and an emotional male voice begging me to hold on, apologizing over and over for being so late.

He had laid me down on the stretcher and slid his arms out from under me, I opened my eyes long enough to see his eyes and the profile of his face.

That moment I would never forget. That was when I had gained my freedom, and my life had finally started to move forward.

I blinked out of my memory as the door behind me opened and two women walked in. One was dressed in a button-down purple shirt with jeans and hiking boots, the other wore a pair of tan cargo pants and a light blue polo. I assumed they were attendees at the conference and had finished up lunch.

It was time to put the memory aside and get ready to speak. I walked over to the sink, turning the faucet on to wash my hands as much as to wash away the memory. I listened to the women talk about an accident they had recently handled and joked about the driver who apparently had been intoxicated.

Not a laughing matter if you asked me, but I had learned in my years that cops dealt with tough situations differently than other people.

I was drying my hands as they finished up in the stalls and came out to wash up and primp a bit before heading back out to the hallway.

I stared into the mirror for just a moment longer telling myself that, yes, I was a beautiful and strong woman. That was something that Brooke and I had been doing for many years: Taking a moment each day to look in the mirror and remember we were lucky to be alive.

After a quick application of lip gloss, I slipped the tube back into my pocket and picked up my water bottle: show time.

A few people were still milling around in the hallway, so I stood back and waited until they entered. Once the majority of people were inside, I slipped in the back door and pinned the microphone to my jacket lapel.

Beverly stood below and was getting the group ready. She nodded to me, and I gave her a thumbs-up to let her know I was ready.

I started my seminars differently than most people. Turning the lights off and putting the audience in an uncomfortable position got their attention, and got it fast.

To get things started I wanted them to put themselves in a place where they had probably never been. I asked them to close their eyes and allow the darkness in, to put aside all thoughts and just be.

As I spoke, I slowly moved along the back and down the steps, being careful to follow the small lights set into the floor so I wouldn't fall.

I asked them to envision their biggest fears. Some people would take this as a joke, but many would allow themselves to really reach out and pull this exercise in. They would feel the fear, would face that one thing that scared them more than anything else.

I moved to the main floor, speaking slowly and softly. I knew my voice was husky. Thanks to Brenden crushing my vocal cords, I had gone through multiple surgeries to get my voice to be as strong as it was now.

"How do you feel?" I looked out over the room. The emergency lights gave me enough illumination that I could make out the bodies, but not the facial expressions. A woman up close answered me, and then a man added his thoughts.

I was not offended when someone threw in a bit of humor. Fear and humor often ran hand in hand, and by the comment, I knew that it was time to move along.

I exhaled a bit heavier than I had planned, always nervous about turning the lights on and facing this many people at one time.

"The next time you deal with a victim of domestic abuse, remember this feeling, remember this moment and know that this is what they feel like," I swallowed and paused, "every...single...day. Then do your best to try and find a way to help them."

I allowed the words to sink in and, like usual, the room was quiet. I raised my hand to someone in the back room to signal they could turn the lights on, and I blinked along with the audience as the bright fluorescent lights flickered to life.

I scanned the room as everyone's eyes adjusted and directed their attention on me. As my eyes skimmed over the group, almost all the people were relaxed in their seats, but one man caught my attention because he was sitting up in his seat, leaning forward, staring at me intently and blinking.

My heart skipped a beat as I realized that it was indeed the rookie cop whom I had thought about earlier. Why was he here? How had he come to be working in this area? How long had he been up here?

Our gazes locked, and he seemed just as surprised to see me as I was to see him. Two, three seconds passed before someone cleared his throat, and I tore my eyes away from him.

"Good afternoon, my name is Trinity Morris, and I am one of the founders of You're Not Alone." I smiled out towards the crowd and tried to focus on what I was supposed to do. My heart still beat in a quicker rhythm than normal, and I fought to control it.

"The purpose of our organization is to help victims and families of abuse realize that they are not alone and that there are people who are willing to help them. We work very closely with the local county agencies and give them extra resources and more options to the clients that they help." I took a few steps as I talked, picking up a pen off the podium to have something in my hands.

"We also spend a lot of time trying to educate law enforcement and other emergency responders to what can be done to help the victims and their families.

"I know that everyone in here has been to at least one domestic violence call, right?" Practically everyone in the audience nodded. Those that didn't were probably not police officers but support staff or others who worked with victims.

"I bet some of you have even witnessed abuse in your own homes." I looked out over the crowd, some people were looking at me intently, some looked away. I noticed that the rookie looked up at the ceiling briefly before bringing his attention back to me.

I laughed gently, "Don't worry, I'm not going to ask you to raise your hand and share your story." I looked down at the floor and tapped the pen in my left hand.

"In fact, I'm not even going to share my story with you, and, trust me, I've got one hell of a story."

A variety of expressions filled the faces in front of me, some surprised, some thankful, some confused.

"What I want to do is show you what it is like to be a victim, and I want you to have some idea as to how to deal with the victims when you come to a point where you feel you can help them."

"We are going to do another exercise, but this time I need a few volunteers." A few hands went up right away, and I smiled because they had no clue what they were in for.

"Thank you for being so willing to help," I smiled. "How many of you are carrying your handcuffs with you right now?"

About half the class raised their hands along with quite a few eyebrows. "Of those of you who are carrying them, how many of you want to volunteer?"

I heard a snicker come from about halfway up, a man making a joke about me being into bondage. I locked my jaw briefly and ignored the comment.

His hand was one of the hands up, "Know that what I am asking you to do is going to be hard. It's going to be difficult and make you uncomfortable. It might embarrass you in front of your peers, and it might make you angry."

A few of the hands started to go down. People didn't want to be embarrassed in front of their peers, and I understood that and had no hard feelings towards them.

"You will also be asked to sign a waiver." Several heads turned to look at the people sitting next to them, and a few more hands went down. Nervous laughter floated through the theater.

I pointed to one man who looked to be in his late thirties, maybe early forties. "Would you like to come up and volunteer?"

"Sure," he started to stand.

"Thank you. If you have a firearm with you, hand it to someone you trust and then bring a friend down with you, please." I watched him slap the guy next to him on the shoulder before he unhooked his holster and handed it to another guy before they started heading down.

"Okay, I need two more," I scanned the room and pointed to a young woman. "How about you?" I asked. She smiled and looked at the guy next to her.

"One more," I looked towards the middle and saw that the man who had made the comment about bondage still had his hand up. "You," I pointed to him and watched his smile widen, it gave me the creeps.

I looked away from him, "Okay, each of you bring yourselves and your partners down here. Don't forget to pass off your gun and bring your handcuffs."

The audience murmured as the volunteers started to descend towards the stage. I walked over to a table and waved the three over.

I pulled out three sheets of paper and asked them to read and sign them along with their partners. I explained to them quietly, keeping my hand over the microphone to keep it from being broadcast, that we were going to do a very hard exercise. The form they were about to read was a waiver saying they wouldn't sue me or charge me or my organization with harassment or anything else and that they could stop at any time.

There was an air of nervousness that hovered around the three of them, but they all read the form and signed it, allowing their partners to sign as witnesses. I signed on the last line as each of them finished.

"Alright, if the three of you would line up here," I directed them to stand in front of the podium. "I want to talk to your partners for a moment."

I brought the three closer, all men, and told them that they were not to get involved, but if they saw their partners in trouble, they could reach out to them and steady them, or if the person asked to be let out, they could step in and uncuff them. They moved to stand about three feet behind their partners.

The audience watched as we set up, hushed conversation continued around the room until I walked back up to the front.

"I want you to know that you can stop at any time. If you get angry or frightened, all you have to do is say, 'Let me out,' and your partner will release you." I smiled reassuringly at them until I reached the guy on the end who was smirking and eyeballing my chest. What a pig.

"Before we get started, tell me your names. Let's start here on the left."

"Zach." He was dressed in brown slacks and a cream button-down shirt. He was most likely a detective by the look of him.

"I'm Emily," the woman in the middle stated before I could ask. She was shorter than the men, but not by much, she was one of the women from the bathroom earlier.

"Hello, Emily—and you are?" I looked to the last man.

"Name's Derek," he said and placed a lecherous smile across his lips that I instantly wanted to smack off.

"Derek, okay. Thank you all for volunteering. Now, what I want you all to do is hand your handcuffs to your partner."

Each of them pulled their handcuffs from where they stored them and handed them back to the people standing behind them.

"Put your hands behind your back, and your partners are going to cuff your hands." Zach and Emily turned to their partners while Derek winked at me and then glanced over his shoulder, putting his hands back.

We all waited while the partners bound them. Derek made a comment to his partner not to put them on so tight. His partner ignored him, and I fought not to smile at his helper.

When they were done, I walked to the table behind them and pulled up the corner of a dark gray tablecloth. Under the cloth were the things I would use for the exercise. I pulled out three blindfolds and passed them out to the helpers.

"Put these on them and make sure they are tight enough that they can't see anything."

"Whoa, she really is into bondage," Derek wise-cracked as his partner put the mask over his face. There were a few laughs from the group watching, but most people ignored his comment, for which I was grateful.

Once the blindfolds were in place, I pulled out three sets of ear muffs, not the fuzzy kind to keep your ears warm in the winter, but the noise-cancelling kind people used on planes to sleep. I wanted to block out their hearing completely.

With the blindfolds on, all three of them stood taller. One of their senses had already been taken away and a second one had been hampered. As the assistants walked up to the volunteers, I explained that I was cutting them off for a while so they wouldn't know what was going on.

It didn't take a psychiatrist to explain that these three people were now a bit uncomfortable. I turned to the audience and glanced around, they were watching quietly with barely-concealed curiosity to see what would happen next.

"Domestic violence is not just about physical abuse. It's about mental and sexual abuse, too. It's about controlling someone, about making them feel like they are nothing without the abuser in their life.

"These volunteers are about to go through a series of small abuses, but because they can no longer hear, see, or use their hands, the abuses will seem much more intense to them."

I stood in front of Zach. He was staring straight ahead, his shoulders back, his feet planted securely on the floor. I reached up and shoved him in the right shoulder hard one time.

He immediately went off balance and tried to compensate, moving forward slightly. His body grew tenser than before I shoved him. He turned his head, waiting for something else to come, searching for the threat. I walked away and lifted up the cover over my things. I pulled out a long feather and heard a chuckle from somewhere in the audience.

When I approached Zach from behind, I took the feather and very carefully touched the back of his neck with it. He jerked his neck away and almost stumbled. His partner grabbed his arm to steady him and he yanked himself out of the guy's grasp. Right now, he didn't know who was friend or foe.

Other than a mild grunt from his jerk forward, he had been quiet. I stepped to the side of Emily and swiped the feather down the side of her neck. She jumped and squeaked, but otherwise didn't move.

I moved around her and stepped up behind Derek. He was making a fatal mistake, a cocky look on his face and his knees locked. I spoke softly to his partner and told him to move to the front of him.

I slipped my foot out of my heeled shoe and stood behind Derek. I nodded to his partner and then I pushed Derek behind the knee quickly. His leg instantly buckled and he started to fall to the floor. His partner and I watched him go down. His partner grinned as Derek started sputtering. He finally leaned over and helped him up. I almost laughed, almost.

Choice words were now spewing from his mouth. I ignored them and moved back to Emily as Derek got back on his feet. His earlier grin now replaced with a scowl.

I scanned the audience, taking in the laughter from his peers before I continued.

I shoved Emily's shoulder and she jerked back but caught herself, immediately resuming her stance. Her breathing had become more erratic now, and a light flush colored her cheeks.

I whispered to her partner for a moment, and he looked at me like I was crazy. I smiled and told him he could blame it on me later. He shook his head and leaned forward, lifting one side of her earphones off her head. Loud enough so that most of the class could hear him, he said directly beside her, "You're fat Emily, lose some weight, you make me sick." He put the muff back in place, and her expression tightened and her cheeks turned red. Her partner hung his head. He obviously did not like doing that, I patted his upper arm as I walked past.

She didn't need to lose any weight, she was the perfect size, but that was one of the things that women worried about the most, image. During this exercise, I watched the seated crowd. Their eyes scanned over Emily as she stood there and just about every person looked confused or concerned at that statement. They didn't agree with what had been said to her either.

There was only one person not watching Emily, and that was the rookie. His eyes were trained on me, and I turned to speak quietly with Zach's partner for a few moments.

When we were done, he stood beside Zach and lifted his hearing protection.

"You're never going to make it, you can work as hard as you want to, but you'll fail. You'll never be able to pay for your kid's college education."

Zach's jaw tensed, and he lowered his face unseeingly to the floor. While women worried about image, men worried about providing.

I went back to the table and picked up a long padded stick. A few murmurs trickled through the people watching. I walked to Zach, and hit him in the stomach. He was built nicely, so I knew I wouldn't hurt anything more than his pride.

Zach surprised me and caved after that, calling out that he wanted out. His partner stepped forward right away and pulled off the hearing protection and blindfold. Zach met my eyes with an apologetic expression and a light sheen of sweat on his face.

"I'm sorry, but that was extreme. I couldn't take it anymore." He rubbed his wrists when his partner released him.

"Zach, you did great, don't apologize to me. This is a rough exercise and you did well. We all have our limits," I reassured him and told him to head back to his seat—one down and two more to break. I turned to Derek and studied him. He was a man with an ego, and I would go after that, personally.

Before moving to Derek, I slapped Emily on the back with the padded stick, she yelped and stepped forward, turning to face the source of the assault. Her body was on edge, she would break soon, too.

I moved to Derek and instead of hitting him with the stick, I dragged it up the inseam of his right leg to just above his knee. At first his face showed surprise, but then the ego got the better of him and he opened his mouth.

"Aw, baby, I knew you wanted me."

I ground my teeth. A man like this would never get the chance to touch me, not ever again. My eyes flashed into the audience and landed on the rookie. His jaw was locked and his expression reflected my feelings, fury.

I felt the need to prove a point to this lowlife. Maybe it was because the rookie was here, I wasn't sure, but this prick was exactly what my husband had been. True, it wasn't fair to make that kind of an assumption just minutes after meeting him, but it was so obvious, I wanted to gag.

I stepped behind him, dragging the stick up the back of his leg. I put my hand on his head, letting my nails trail over the short tuffs of his flat top. Arrogance rolled off his shoulders.

I lifted up his hearing protection, leaning in close to his ear but speaking loudly enough that my voice would travel through the speakers.

"You might think you're a man, but you're not, and you could never please a woman like me."

He grunted and turned his head to me, "Wanna bet?"

"Shut up, you prick! I've heard the rumors about how you can't make a woman happy. You just love them and leave them, but even if you wanted to keep one around, they wouldn't have you because you can't please them in bed."

I let the ear muff fall back over his ear and stepped back three steps from him. Like Zach had reacted to being told he could not provide, Derek reacted to me going after his manhood. It was nothing personal, but I knew that he would be the type most affected by this approach.

His face was red and he sputtered, "You're an evil bitch. Let me out of these. I'm not taking this shit."

The audience grew unsettled, and I motioned to Derek's partner to release him. He stepped forward to remove the equipment, a smirk on his face. As soon as the blindfold was off, Derek turned his head to me. He was pissed.

I met his glare and lifted my chin. I was no longer afraid of men like him. When his hands were un-cuffed, he moved to the stairs and back to his seat. His partner winked at me. It wasn't a wink of the sexual variety. He knew I had gotten under Derek's skin and he was enjoying it.

I glanced up into the audience; the rookie was still watching me carefully. His face showed concern and it surprised me. I looked away uncomfortably.

I turned back to Emily. She had small beads of sweat running down the side of her face. By now, she had been standing in this position for over twenty minutes. She had been blind, deaf, and unable to defend herself, but she was tough.

I walked over to her and lifted the earmuffs; she flinched. Her partner untied the blindfold when I motioned for him to do so. After throwing the blindfold on to his shoulder, he pulled out keys to unlock the cuffs. Emily blinked at me and glanced around.

"You did great, Emily. How do you feel?"

"That was the freakiest thing I have ever done. You really got into my head," she laughed sheepishly, "especially with that last comment."

I patted her on the shoulder. "You did great, and just for the record, you're not fat."

She released a strangled laugh and moved back to her seat. I glanced up at the clock. "Okay, why don't we take a fifteen-minute break so those three can calm down, and then we will move forward."

Mumbles of agreement coursed through the air, and people got up and moved up the stairs. Some people grouped around the three volunteers to ask them questions, and I turned around to put away my props.

The exercise had gone well, so why did I suddenly feel apprehensive? Maybe because as the others were starting to move up the stairs, the rookie had started to move down. I busied myself with putting my items back into a box. The sound of his words caused my spine to stiffen slightly.

"Hello, Trinity."

Chapter 4 - Gavin

I sat in awe of what she had done on the stage. In a matter of minutes, she tore down three very strong people, people who were trained professionals that came up against the slime of the Earth on a daily basis, and yet with just a few motions and phrases, she'd had them so uncomfortable that they had exhibited physical reactions with accelerated heart rates and sweating.

I don't think anyone there didn't feel for Emily and Zach and what they were going through. Derek was a different story. Most of the people in the audience were familiar with his attitude and his ego. Seeing him get taken down a notch or two by a woman who knew nothing about him was fascinating.

I watched her as she reacted with Derek. Her face was strong and intense, and I had the impression that she was seeing him as her husband, and I couldn't fault her for it. In many ways, he was a lot like the man who had abused her.

When it was time to work on Emily and Zach, her face softened, almost like she regretted what she was doing to them. I wondered how difficult it was for her to do these kinds of exercises.

The whole time I watched, I not only observed what she did, but how she moved. She had grace and strength in every movement. When I remembered her lying in my arms unconscious, her arms bleeding, her neck swollen, her face showing the early signs of the strikes she had endured, I shuddered.

Not everyone was as lucky as she was, and seeing her here today, I realized that I played a part in the fact that she was. I knew I needed to approach her. She knew who I was, she had recognized me right away, but would she be willing to talk to me? There was only one way to find out.

When she called for a break, almost everyone started heading out into the hallway where they had coffee and snacks waiting for us. I went the opposite way and started down the stairs. She was aware that I was heading towards her, and she turned to shuffle her things around on the table behind her. Did I make her nervous, or was it just the memory that made her fidget?

Should I call her Ms. Morris, I wondered, or should I just call her Trinity? It was how I knew her, how I had thought about her for years.

"Hello, Trinity," as hard as I tried, I couldn't keep the slight tremor out of my voice. Her back stiffened ever so slightly, and she rolled her shoulder up higher before turning to look at me.

"Hello," she replied with a shake in her own voice that had not been apparent during her earlier speaking.

Her eyes were a deeper green than mine, and the dark eyelashes that framed them fluttered as she blinked.

"How are you?" I asked and took a tentative step closer.

She hesitated just long enough that I wondered if the words she spoke were actually true, "I'm very well, thank you. Are you enjoying the seminar?"

I nodded and spoke at the same time, "Yes, I'm glad I signed up for this one. What you did down here was pretty intense. I wish I had volunteered."

She smiled. "I doubt that, about you volunteering I mean, and besides I wouldn't have chosen you." She turned away to resume her straightening.

I stepped up beside the table, toying with the gray tablecloth that lay there with nervous fingers. "Why not?"

The side of her mouth turned up slightly, and she peered at me sideways, "You really want to know?"

Of course I did. "Yes."

She turned and crossed her arms gently over her chest. "I wouldn't have chosen you because I think you already know what it's like to feel like a victim. I see it in your eyes. I saw it years ago when I first met you."

I opened my mouth to speak but closed it again when I couldn't think of what to actually say. A single chuckle strangled through my vocal chords, and I grinned silently at her.

She raised her eyebrows. "Am I right?" she asked quietly.

I glanced away then directed my attention back to her. "Yeah, I guess you could say that. That's very perceptive of you."

"I learned the hard way how to read people. It's how I knew that Emily would be the one that would be concerned about something as silly as her weight when she shouldn't be, and that Zach would be worried about providing for his family."

I added, "Or how Derek is just an egotistical ass."

She grinned and turned back to her table to finish putting away her things. "Yeah, and that, too."

As she turned, her grin faded, and I suddenly wished that I could make her smile again. Her face had lit up, her eyes sparkled. For the first time, she didn't look serious, or afraid.

She glanced up at the clock; I followed her line of sight. We only had a few more minutes before we were to start again. I needed to find a way to get her to talk to me more. I didn't want to just walk away when this class was over.

For years, I had wondered about her, thought about what she had endured and dreamed of the scene I had walked into. Now, here she was standing tall and proud and more gorgeous than I could ever imagine her being. I glanced at her left hand—no ring.

She picked up her box of goodies and moved it back further onto the table.

"So, um, would you be interested in having coffee sometime?" Okay, how lame was that? I wanted to roll my eyes at myself. How old was I, sixteen?

She stopped what she was doing and set her hands flat on the table. I knew what was coming, she was about to turn me down, and my ego felt almost as deflated as Derek's must have.

"I know this might seem odd, but I don't even know your name. I only knew you as the rookie cop, and well, when it came to the trial, I wasn't myself and didn't really pay much attention to anything there, besides Brenden going to jail. I'm sorry."

She looked genuinely remorseful and slightly embarrassed, and I smiled to ease it.

"The rookie cop. Yeah, back then, I was." I held my hand out to her, "My name is Gavin Brooksfield, and I'm a sergeant now, no longer the rookie."

She slid her slim hand into mine. It was warm and strong as she squeezed it to show she was business but not trying to hurt me.

"It is a pleasure to meet you Sgt. Gavin Brooksfield." Both our hands and our eyes lingered just longer than would be considered normal. A loud laugh from the top of the room broke the moment, and she stepped back and looked away pulling her hand with her.

"So now that you know my name, what do you think about coffee?"

"Gavin," she hesitated, and I knew that while there had been a brief connection, she was about to shoot me down anyway, "if you would like to get together to discuss what I do with my organization, then I would love the company."

"Really?" I was happily surprised after expecting a complete shutdown.

She laughed, "Yes, really."

She turned around to the briefcase that sat next to the table and pulled out a business card from the side. "Call my office some time. We can set up a time to have coffee."

I took the card from her and tapped it against my hand. "It's a plan."

She scanned the room and saw it was filling up. I turned from her and mounted the stairs to my seat. Noah smirked at me as I sat down, "Teacher's pet, huh?"

"What?" I feigned nonchalance. I shrugged and avoided making eye contact. "We were just talking." I took a quick peek at him and then at Trinity. She met my glance with a small smile before looking away.

"Yeah, just talking, I saw that. You got the hots for the teacher."

"Whatever, man," I knew he was just teasing me, but it was hitting just a bit too close to home, and my neck started to warm up.

"So what did she have to say?" I turned to him, and he was watching her down by the podium, she was getting her PowerPoint presentation ready. "She is hot, by the way."

"Um, actually I was just saying hello. We know each other. Well, we did know each other about ten years ago." I leaned toward him and kept my voice low. I didn't want to share her personal information with others. "I arrested her husband after he tried to kill her. That's why her voice is so husky. The bastard crushed her windpipe and vocal cords."

"No shit? Huh, I actually think her voice is pretty sexy. Could you imagine hearing that whispered in your ear at night?" He nodded as if he was thinking about it.

I didn't say anything to him, but in the back of my mind, I hoped that one day I would hear just that.

"For the next hour, we are going to talk about what happened in the earlier exercise and also talk more about what you can do to help the victims that you come across." She scanned the room as she spoke, never putting too much attention on any single person.

She was a good speaker and had a great knack of keeping people interested in what she was saying. Many of the attendees here asked questions and at times we got sidetracked by other topics, but she always turned them back to what the main discussion was about.

The longer I sat in the chair, the more engrossed I became, not only in the approach she was using, but in her in general. She was so different from the first time we had met.

I hadn't been with the department very long, maybe four or five months, when I had attended an awards ceremony. Lieutenant Brenden Marks had been receiving a commendation for his years of diligent service. Others also received certificates, but it was because of him that she came.

Our department had about forty-eight officers at the time, and most of them were expected to be there that day. I was reporting for a shift later that day, so I had gotten dressed in my uniform early. I stepped outside to walk around the building to the township meeting hall instead of through the maze of hallways. It was a beautiful day, and I glanced over the parking lot as I moved.

A silver sedan had just parked, and a woman started to get out of the car, but then she began to climb back inside. My feet slowed just to make sure she was alright. She stood up again, glanced at her watch and looked around. Our eyes met fleetingly as hers passed over me. Obviously, I was not the one she was looking for.

I noticed that she bit her lip and she looked nervously around. She was wearing brown slacks and a tan blouse that buttoned almost to her neck. Her long auburn hair was tucked behind her ears, and simple gold earrings glittered in the sunlight. She glanced at her watch again and looked around the parking lot once more, focusing on the main entrance of the Town Hall.

With hesitant steps, she started to move to the back of the car. Always the Boy Scout, I decided that she looked lost and headed over to her to see if I could help. As I approached, she turned to move back to the driver's door again. She must have heard my footsteps and looked up with a startled expression on her face.

"Ma'am," I called out to her, "are you alright?"

"What?" her eyes darted around the parking lot, she squeezed the small purse she held in her hands until her knuckles were white.

"Are you alright?" I slowed my steps as I reached her car. She looked like a frightened cat about to either whip out her claws or turn and skitter away. "You look lost."

She shook her head, "No, I'm just waiting for my husband. He told me to wait here for him." She looked around again.

"Is your husband an officer here? Are you here for the awards ceremony? If so, I can take you in to him." She stepped back from me, her eyes opening slightly larger in an alarmed way.

"Um, thanks, but I will just wait here for him."

The look on her face, and the way she spoke uncertainly, reminded me of someone I knew too well. I tried not to clench my jaw and to remain calm.

"Are you sure? What's your husband's name?"

Her eyes darted up to the door again and then she took a very small step closer to me, "Look, you're new here, right? So you probably don't know this, but you shouldn't be talking to me. Just go back to what you were doing, please."

Fear had crept into her eyes and she said the last of her sentence in almost a plea.

I didn't want to scare her, and obviously the fact that I was talking to her was doing just that. I put my hands up to show her I meant no harm and took a step back to alleviate whatever I could of the fear she felt.

"If you're sure. You're alright?" I asked her one more time.

"Yes, I'm fine, thank you." She smiled slightly, and I began to turn and walk away, but behind her someone's car alarm beeped and startled us both. She dropped her small purse to the ground as she spun toward the offending sound.

So much for the claws, she was the skittered cat, and I had to wonder what caused her to be so frightened.

I stepped forward to pick up her purse. It had fallen open when it fell to the ground. The contents were strewn on the asphalt and I began picking up the items and shoving them back inside. I knew women were particular about how their purses were arranged, but somehow I didn't think she would mind the mess as long as it was all back together.

Just as I stuffed the last of her items inside, I heard a deep male voice, an angry male voice coming from the other side of the car.

"Trinity, what the hell are you doing? I told you to stay in the car until I came to get you."

She turned towards the sound of the voice, and I saw the legs of her slacks shimmy as if her knees were shaking.

"I was waiting. I just got out to stand here so it would be easier for you to find me," she answered him quietly.

All of the items were back inside her purse, but I feared standing up. I recognized the tone of voice being used on her.

"You can't do anything I ask, can you? You're such a stupid bitch." I heard the sneer in this voice.

I took that moment to stand and face the man, my lieutenant, and noticed the sharp look of anger on his face, and then the unsure look he got when his glare met mine.

"Rookie, what are you doing out here with my wife?" he barked at me in a tone I had not heard him use before.

"Sir, I was walking to the hall and saw your wife standing here waiting for you. A horn blared and startled her, and she dropped her purse. I was just picking it up for her." With the words out of my mouth, I slowly held her purse out to her and she took it with shaky hands, never meeting my eyes.

He cleared his throat, apparently trying to calm his anger in front of a witness, "Well, that was nice of you, Rookie. Women can be so jumpy sometimes, I appreciate your assistance." He immediately dismissed me without another word and called out to her, "Let's go, Trinity, I don't want to be late."

She stepped around me, not saying a word or even glancing in my direction. I watched her walk towards him, and he wrapped his hand around the top of her left forearm, as if he wanted to drag her away. I wondered if he had done that to her before and found my jaw clenched so hard it hurt.

They entered the building, and I leaned back against the car with my arms crossed. I had never heard that the lieutenant had an anger issue. No one had ever mentioned that he was an abuser. An egotistical ass, though, that one I had heard. Maybe they didn't know, or maybe like many small departments, they didn't want to face that one of their own had a problem.

I shook my head and glanced down at the ground. A glint of gold caught my eye underneath the chassis of her car. I bent down and picked up a small diamond earring. It must have fallen out of her purse.

I fingered the diamond gently in my hand and slid it into my pocket. I would get it back to her when I could find a safe way to do so.

That earring still sat in my small jewelry box on top of my dresser all these years later. I never found a way to get it back to her safely, and I held on to it hoping that someday I might be able to.

Trinity kept talking in front of the class, and I realized that I would finally have the opportunity to return it to its rightful owner.

Chapter 5 - Trinity

Almost a month later I sat in my office looking at an email from one of the shelters that we ran. It appeared that there had been a leak in one of the apartments, and it had caused some serious damage to that apartment and the one downstairs.

Damn, this was going to cost more money. I rubbed my temple in frustration. Nonprofit organizations ran on very tight budgets, and there was never much of a surplus.

A knock on the doorframe brought my attention up from my computer. Marcy, the receptionist and administrative assistant to our office, stood there.

"Oh no, you have a bad look on your face," she said as she stepped inside.

I sat back in my chair, the springs squeaking slightly as I did, grating my already-frayed nerves.

"Just another issue that needs to be resolved, nothing I can't handle," although I'd rather not have to deal with it, I thought to myself.

"Anything I can do to help?" she asked as she walked into the room.

I laughed, "No, not unless you know a cheap carpenter who can do some quick renovations."

"Why? What's going on?" She sat down in the one chair across from my battered wooden desk.

I laid my head back against the top of my seat, the springs creaking again with my movement. "The New Horizons property had a major water leakage problem in one of the upstairs kitchens. Looks like it caused extensive damage to that unit and minor damage to the one downstairs."

Marcy winced, she knew how tight money was for the organization. "Ouch."

"Yeah, ouch is right, and both the units are occupied. That location is full right now, so I'm not sure what to do. We will have to move the occupants to another location for a little while and find someone who can fix it quickly." I huffed out a quick lungful of air. "Hey, you're not still seeing that guy, what was his name, Bret? Isn't he a carpenter or something?" I leaned forward on my desk, hopeful for a moment.

"It was Scott, and no, I'm not. He was a jerk, sorry." She gave me an apologetic look.

"I know one." Marcy and I both looked up at the door from where the male voice had emanated.

"Oh my," Marcy exclaimed, and I threw her a quick glance before I stood up to welcome my unexpected visitor.

"Sergeant Brooksfield, hello, I didn't expect to see you here today. Did we have an appointment?" I glanced down at my desk calendar, thinking to myself that there was no way I would have forgotten an appointment with him. When I lifted my head, I found he had stepped inside the office.

He smiled warmly at me and glanced at Marcy who openly appraised him from head to toe. I scowled at her rudeness momentarily before turning back to Gavin.

"No, no appointment, I was in the area, thought I would pop in and see if you were free for that cup of coffee."

Marcy stood up quickly, "If she's not, I am."

Gavin gave her an amused smile, "And you are?"

She stepped forward holding out her hand, "I'm Marcy Sherwood, the everything girl here."

Gavin took her hand and shook it once before he released it, much to Marcy's chagrin, "Gavin Brooksfield."

"Sergeant Brooksfield was in my last seminar," I offered by way of explanation when Marcy turned back to me with wide adoring eyes.

"Call me Gavin, please. I'm not at work." He reached across the desk to me, "Good to see you again, Trinity."

My manners took over, and I reached out to take his hand, "Gavin, right. Sorry." Unlike with his shake with Marcy, he held my hand just a second longer than he needed to and smiled into my face.

"So from what I could hear, you need a carpenter? How about I buy you a cup of coffee and you can tell me what you need."

I wiped my damp palm on my hip, suddenly nervous to have him in my office. "Um, I didn't know you were a carpenter. I thought you were just a police officer."

"Just a police officer? Ouch!" He put his hand over his heart and I glanced at Marcy as she giggled at him. "I'm way more than that, but actually, I'm not the carpenter, I have a buddy who is, and I help him out sometimes. I'm sure I could get him to help you out if you tell me what it is you need."

"That's exactly what you need, coffee and a carpenter," Marcy exclaimed and grinned at me, more amusement in her eyes than needed to be there. I struggled to keep the scowl off my face.

"So what do you say?" Gavin raised his eyebrows in question, and I couldn't help but notice the sparkle in his green eyes. I only noticed because it was the brightest thing in my dull office, yeah right.

"Sure, I could use a cup of coffee." I shuffled a few pieces of paper on my desk and reached for my purse, picking up my cellphone and sliding it into the side pocket.

"Marcy, I'll only be a little while. Call me if you need me," I told her as I stepped around my desk.

"Oh, no worries," she winked at me, and I inwardly rolled my eyes. She had matchmaker written all over her face, and I sighed as I passed her. "Have fun, you two," she called out as I stepped through the doorway and Gavin followed behind me.

When we got out of the office, I turned to Gavin, "Sorry about that."

He laughed and I felt it all the way to my stomach. "No problem." When we got to the elevator, I punched the button, and we stood quietly beside one another waiting for it to arrive.

When the metal doors slid open, he gently put his hand on my lower back. Part of me instinctively wanted to move away from the touch, something I had done with everyone that had touched me over the last ten years, while the other part of me suddenly yearned to lean back into the warmth and indulge myself in some human contact.

He made the decision easy as we stepped inside and put distance between us by standing on the opposite side of the elevator. He pushed the button for the main floor, and the doors slid closed.

Our main office was on the fourth floor of an older office building. The elevators were slow, the tile floors were tinged yellow from years of abuse, but the rent was cheaper than the newer buildings, and saving money was everything these days.

When we exited the elevator, Gavin kept a respectable distance, and we passed the few minutes walking to the local coffee shop talking about mundane things like the weather and local news.

After seating ourselves at a table near the front window, I decided it was time to get down to business. While it was nice to see him again—I had only imagined seeing him, what, a dozen times over the last month—I had things to get done, and sitting down for a long chat over coffee was not on my list of things to accomplish, even if it was with a very handsome man.

"So you have a friend who is a carpenter, huh?"

He leaned over his coffee cup and inhaled the scent before he set it back down on the table. I knew from the feel of my paper cup that it was too hot for me to try to drink, maybe it was the same for him.

"Yeah, well he's not really my buddy. He's more like my brother-in-law."

I raised my eyebrows, "And what makes you think he would want to help me out?"

He looked me in the eye for a moment, "Because if I ask him, he will."

Nervous laughter left my throat, "That sure of yourself, huh?"

He leaned back in his seat and glanced around the café, smiling. "No, he's a good guy. He does a lot of help for nonprofits when he can."

I twirled my cup around on the table trying not to think about how wide his chest looked as he sat back in his seat. The thought rattled my mind and I cleared my throat. I couldn't remember the last time I had noticed something like that about a man.

"That's nice of him." I peeked up at him when he leaned forward again and wrapped his hand around his cup. His hands were solid, with long tapered fingers and clean short nails.

I closed my eyes in an attempt to stop the thoughts floating around in my head. How many years had it been since I thought of the way a man's chest looked or how long his fingers were? Thirteen? Fourteen?

"You alright, Trinity?" he asked quietly as he leaned closer over the table.

I caught a whiff of his musky cologne. Internally, I groaned.

I sat up and forced a smile, "Yeah, I'm fine. It's just been a long week."

Gavin was quiet for a moment then asked, "So what work do you need done?"

Thank you, Gavin, for putting my mind back where it needs to be. "Well, it seems we had a leak and I have some major water damage in one of my shelters. It is putting two families out until I can get it repaired."

"Okay, so do you know if the water leak was repaired yet?" he questioned.

"Yes, that I do know. They had to call in an emergency plumber to fix it, but as for the damage to the property, I am not sure of the extent, although from what Mike, the property manager said, it's bad." I winced as I finished speaking.

"Okay, let me give Taylor a call and see what his schedule is like." He reached into his pocket and pulled out his phone.

"Wait," I started to reach across the table to him, but pulled my hand back. He looked at my hand and then up to my face.

"Yes?"

"Has your brother-in-law ever been arrested for anything? He would need to sign a waiver saying he would never disclose the location of this property to anyone, and have a criminal background check done."

He grinned at me, "No problem, he has worked with shelters before. He knows the deal."

Without another word, he punched a few buttons on his phone and put it to his ear.

He chatted casually with his brother-in-law for a few moments before he started to talk to him about the job.

"It's for a friend of mine." He had been looking out the window while he talked but glanced over at me as he said the words.

I smiled as he turned back to the window. I watched him closely as he explained what he knew about the job, stating that he had not seen the damage yet, but knew it probably extended to two units. I found my eyes drawn to the way his lips moved as he spoke.

"Hold on a second, I'll ask." He took the phone away from his ear and made eye contact with me, "Is there any way I can see the units, so I can tell him what he's going to need?"

"Sure, but you would need to sign the nondisclosure statement, too."

"That's not a problem." He went back to talking on the phone, and my cellphone rang. I pulled it from my purse and saw Brooke's name on the screen.

"What's up, Brooke?" I asked when I put the phone to my ear turning slightly in my seat.

"So I hear he's cute," she said with a smile in her voice.

I shook my head and looked down at my cup. "I guess you are in the office now?"

"Oh yes, and Marcy filled me in on the yummy-looking police officer that came in and whisked you away to coffee. Are you still with him?"

"Yes, I am. He's talking to his brother-in-law about doing the repairs to the New Horizons property right now."

"I just saw that email," she sighed into the phone. "How much is this going to cost?"

"I have no idea, but it needs to be done." I picked up my cup and finally took a tentative sip. It was still too hot, I set it back down.

"Yeah, I know," she hesitated and I got the feeling she had something else to say. "I just got a call from Safe Place."

I sighed and lowered my head, I knew the tone of her voice. Something else had happened. "Yeah, and?"

"And it looks like someone tried to break in to one of the units last night. They also cut the security monitor feed so nothing was recorded."

"What?" I said sharply, and Gavin and I exchanged a glance.

"Is there any way you can go over there and check on it? I have a meeting in an hour with Senator Walters about that grant we are trying to get."

"Yeah, I can. No, wait. I don't have a car. Mine went into the shop for work this morning."

Gavin set his phone down and waved to get my attention. "Hold on," I said into the phone.

"If you need to go someplace, I can take you," he offered.

I stared at him for a moment, "Are you sure? It seems like today is nothing but problems, and now I have to stop by another shelter."

"Of course, I'm sure, I wouldn't offer if I wasn't. Besides I need to see the damage to the one place anyway."

Who are you, my knight in shining armor? I thought.

"Okay, if you're sure. Thank you, Gavin."

I put my phone back to my ear, "Brooke, Gavin is going to take me over to Safe Place, and then I'm going to show him the damage at New Horizons."

"Gavin, huh? From what Marcy says, the sexy name matches the body."

I felt the blush rising up my face, "You can't believe a thing Marcy says. I'll call you later." I heard her laughing as I ended the call.

When I looked back at Gavin, he was smiling. My blush grew warmer on my cheeks, and I suddenly realized that he must have heard what Brooke had said on the phone.

"Well, I guess we should get going. Good thing we got cups to go. We can take them with us. Shall we?" Gavin turned to me, and I was thankful that he didn't say anything about the phone conversation.

"What did your brother-in-law say?"

"He said, 'Anything for a beautiful woman.'" He smirked and waited for me to move past him toward the door.

"Yeah, right," I muttered and heard him laugh behind me.

He led me to his car two blocks down, a dark blue Jeep Grand Cherokee and pulled his keys from his pocket. I waited until I heard the telltale sign of the locks opening before trying the handle.

Once we were inside, I looked over at Gavin, he was staring at me. I couldn't read his expression, but his eyes ran over my face slowly and I suddenly realized this was the first time I had been in a man's car alone—in years. He was looking at me as if he wanted something, and I felt my pulse pick up.

"Yes?" I said hesitantly.

His eyes sparkled again, "These places are non-disclosed, right?"

I nodded.

"So you need to tell me where I'm going. Which way?"

I relaxed as I realized that he was only waiting for me to lead the way. Once I gave him a general direction and we got moving, he turned up the volume on his radio, and a country song filled the air around us.

"Oh, you never told me how much your brother-in-law charged." The thought that I was going to let him do it without asking for his prices made me want to smack myself in the head.

"Just material costs," he said as he changed lanes.

"What?" I answered, surprised.

He glanced at me then back to the road, "Just material costs. He knows you are a nonprofit and what kind you are." He smiled and looked back at me. "You can close your mouth, it's not that surprising."

"No one does anything for nothing. How much does he want, really?"

He glanced over at me again and slowed down to stop at a traffic light that had turned red. "Trinity, believe it or not, he doesn't want anything. I'll help him, and it will just be the cost of the materials."

"But why?" my voice shook with emotion.

"Because that's the way we do things. Both Taylor and I have our reasons, and both of us have worked with shelters before." He reached over and pushed a strand of hair away from my face. The urge to shy away from his hand fleetingly crossed my mind, but I controlled it and held still.

I nodded, not sure I could say anything, and he turned his attention back to the traffic that was now moving.

I gave him directions to Safe Place, and as we pulled in, I turned to him, "Remember, you can't disclose this location."

He turned to me after putting the car in park, "No worries, Trinity, I would never do anything to hurt you or anyone you are trying to protect."

His words were heartfelt, and I knew at once that he was telling the truth. I hoped my smile showed the visual gratitude I felt for him as I reached for the door handle.

"So what happened here? You didn't tell me why we were coming here first," he asked as he joined me on the sidewalk.

What, on the outside, looked like just a plain beige stucco apartment complex was a safe shelter for abused women and children. A few years ago, we had purchased it with funds from a grant and refurbished the interior to create thirty small one- and two-bedroom apartments.

"Brooke, my partner, said that last night someone cut the security feed and tried to break into one of the units."

He looked down at me in alarm. "Did they call the police?"

I shrugged as I walked. "I assume so. I don't know the details. That's why I'm here." I dug into my purse and pulled out an identification card with a magnetic strip. There were no words written, just a number printed on the top in black letters. If found, no one would know its purpose.

I slid the magnetic strip through a small machine near the door and the latch released.

Gavin pulled open the door and stood back for me to enter before him. As we stepped in, Mary walked out of a door off to the side of the entrance.

"Trinity, I'm so glad you are here," she glanced at Gavin quickly, unable to hide her disdain for a man entering the premises. "Some of the residents are a bit upset."

"I bet they are. Mary, this is my friend Gavin Brooksfield. Gavin, this is Mary, she's is the property manager here."

I held back the fact that Gavin was a police officer because I knew that many of the people here were leery of men in uniform. I wasn't the only one who had dealt with a bad situation from someone with a badge. Mary gave him a curt nod but did not offer her hand. I held back my sigh.

Mary turned to walk back into the door that led to the office section of the building. We followed behind her. "So what happened?"

Mary glanced over her shoulder. Her eyes hovered over Gavin for a moment nervously. "May I speak to you alone?" she asked politely.

I smiled up at Gavin apologetically. "Sure, let's go in your office."

Gavin didn't seem put off in the slightest and sat down in one of the chairs in the waiting room, crossing his left leg over his right knee casually.

I followed Mary back into her office, and she closed the door. "What's wrong, Mary?" I asked as soon as the door clicked shut.

"That guy is a cop," she whispered as she turned back to me. "I can smell one from a mile away."

"Relax, and yes, he is, but he's also my friend and you don't have to worry about him."

"How can you trust one of them—especially after what happened to you?" She twisted her hands in front of her.

I reached out for her hand, grasping one in mine. "Gavin is the one who rescued me and put Brenden behind bars. If there is one cop I can trust, it's him."

Her shoulders straightened, and she looked me hard in the eye. I saw the moment she began to believe in what I said.

"I promise. He's not going to hurt anyone here. It might be good to have him hear what happened. He might be able to help us."

"If you say so," she answered hesitantly, obviously not truly convinced. "Just do me a favor and be careful with him." The tone of her voice hinted at more than me just being careful of a friend.

"He's just a friend, Mary." I smiled lightly.

She examined my face intently, then appeared to accept my words for what they were and turned to open the door.

"You can come in," she stepped back after calling out to Gavin and moved to sit behind her desk before he stepped into the room.

Gavin and I shared a glance, and I gave him another apologetic smile before we took the two office chairs in front of her desk.

"So what happened?" I asked as we got settled.

She chewed the inside of her mouth as she focused on me, "Last night around midnight, someone cut the security monitor line and got into unit number three through the side window." I knew about the line, but not about the entry.

"They actually got in?" I tensed.

"Yes, they got in, but once they were in there, they neglected to close the window. One of the other residents was coming home from work and saw the window open. She knew we have strict rules about that, and she also knew that the resident wasn't supposed to be home."

I glanced at Gavin, he was listening quietly.

"She came in to tell the security guard and when he went out to check the window, he saw someone climb out and take off running to the back of the property."

"Did you report the incident?" Gavin asked from beside me.

Mary looked at him and then directed her attention back to me, "No, we didn't. The guy was long gone by the time security checked the area, and we checked the unit to make sure there was nothing taken from inside."

"Why didn't you report this?" Gavin was tense beside me, and I almost reached over to take his hand to calm him.

Mary folded her hands on the desk and met his glare with one of her own, "Officer Brooksfield, if you haven't noticed, I don't like cops, and most of the people here feel that you all are worthless. Trinity might trust you, but I don't. If you would just keep your questions to yourself, I would appreciate it."

"Mary," I gasped.

Chapter 6 - Gavin

The words that spewed off Mary's tongue cut me to the quick, and I took a moment to inhale deeply and calm myself before I reacted to them. I heard Trinity's sharp intake of breath beside me and saw her straighten in her chair.

I held my hand up to stop her from saying anything. I needed to defuse the situation myself, and not with anger. Mary was expecting me to react to her harsh words like other men she had dealt with, but I was not like those men.

"You make it quite clear about your dislike for law enforcement, but I can assure you that I am not like the ones you apparently have dealt with." I glanced at Trinity; she sat uneasily in her chair but watched me carefully.

I took a deep breath, this was not how I wanted Trinity to know about me, but I figured if it would help the situation, then there was no better time.

Mary's hands were knotted on the desk, her knuckles white as she waited for an outburst that was not going to come. I leaned forward, resting my elbows on my knees and steepling my fingers together, my head bent, but not hung.

"You might think you know me," I lifted my face to her, "and that is only because all you see is the badge. If you opened your eyes long enough to look behind that, you'd see a man who lived through a young life of abuse at the hands of a man who cared nothing about the people he was supposed to protect."

Trinity's soft gasp lifted the hair on the back of my neck, and Mary shot a quick, nervous glance over at her.

"My father beat my mother from as early as I can remember." I sat back in my seat rubbing the tops of my thighs with my palms, "Maybe if there had been more places like this when I was growing up, my mother wouldn't have become an alcoholic who committed suicide after she found out her husband was molesting her daughter over and over again."

The color drained out of Mary's face and her mouth fell open. "So you putting me into some nameless group, just because you have had difficulty with someone in my profession, is a low blow. I would do anything and everything to protect those that can't do it themselves, especially from abusive men. I am not like my father."

The room was silent as they digested my words. Mary flattened her hands on her desk, obviously trying to decide how to respond.

"I didn't tell you that to upset you." She lifted her head slowly as I spoke. "I told you so you would understand I mean no harm to you or anyone else here. If I can help, then I would like to." My voice lowered as I finished.

"I owe you an apology, Officer Brooksfield." Shame was written as clearly on her face as ink on a newspaper page.

"No, you don't, and please call me Gavin."

Next to me, Trinity brought her hand to her face. Did she just wipe a tear from her cheek?

She avoided my questioning look and spoke to Mary, "Can we get back to the matter at hand, please?"

Mary looked more than thankful that the tense situation was over and sat back in her chair looking more relaxed than she had since we had arrived.

I let Trinity and Mary discuss the issue and only chimed in occasionally. I didn't want to intrude too much on what they were doing, but I did want to offer up any knowledge that I might be able to.

It was decided that the police should be notified and after being shown the window and the apartment, I stood by when the responding officer arrived to take the report. I gave him the information that was needed, and he left shortly after.

Mary seemed more then thankful that I had offered to deal with the officer, and I accepted her shy smile instead of words as just that, a thank you.

Trinity next suggested we move on to New Horizons to survey the damage.

Once back in the car, I moved to turn on the radio and heard a deep rumble coming from the seat beside me. I chuckled as I turned to see the embarrassed smile on Trinity's face and a hand over her stomach.

"Sorry, I didn't have time for breakfast this morning."

"Well then, I guess we need to make a detour and grab a bite to eat before we hit our next stop." As if my own stomach agreed, it growled just as I finished speaking. We both laughed, and I put the Jeep in gear and backed out.

We settled into a comfortable silence after we discussed our options in food between here and the next location. We ended up at a pizza joint, and she all but begged me to allow her to pay for lunch.

"You bought me coffee, and you helped me deal with that situation, it's the least I can do." I allowed her to pay because I understood how she felt.

Carrying the tray with three slices of pizza and two sodas over to a booth in the back, we slipped onto the hard orange benches and dug in.

I watched Trinity pull her slice of cheese pizza back. A long string of mozzarella fighting to stay on the pie pulled tightly then snapped. It hung down on her chin, leaving a line of tomato sauce. She dropped her slice back to her paper plate and picked up her napkin.

I folded my piece in half and bit into mine as she set her napkin back down.

A dot of red still marred her chin and I lifted my paper napkin and reached to wipe it off. My mouth was full of food so I didn't say anything as I moved toward her. She flinched when she saw my hand.

I held my hand still and waited for her to look at me. I forced the mouthful of food I had been chewing down my throat when I saw the stark fear in her expression.

"You missed a spot," I mumbled and moved the last three inches to wipe the rest of the sauce from her chin. She was staring at me when I finished.

The fear changed to embarrassment and her cheeks colored. "I'm sorry."

I set down the napkin and picked up my pizza. Before I took a bite, I said to her, "Don't apologize to me for that."

Trinity resumed eating but with a coiled tension in her shoulders. I knew she wanted to say something, and I had a good idea what it was about. I kept my mouth shut unless I was devouring my lunch because I didn't feel like encouraging the discussion.

Finally, she pushed her plate away, the edge of her crust the only thing left and sat back. "Where is your father now?"

I suppressed the sigh that wanted to escape. I knew it was coming and instead reached for my soda and took a sip.

"State pen."

She lifted the straw out of her cup and then pushed it back down making it squeak. "For how long?"

"Been in almost eleven years, has another twenty before he goes before a parole board. Hopefully, he will die in prison and never get there." I threw my napkin down on my plate to show my disgust.

"You don't want to talk about this, do you?" she asked. The expression in her green eyes was haunted, and I knew she could understand my feelings. If there was anyone I could talk to, it would be her, but I wasn't ready.

"Nope."

She nodded absently, "Okay, then are you done eating?"

How quickly she let that conversation slide, I thought. "Yeah, let's go."

We slid out of the booth, and I discarded our trash before we exited. The wind was blowing towards the front of the building, and Trinity pushed on the glass door, but it started to bounce back at her after a strong gust struck it.

I caught the door with an outstretched hand above her head, just before it could strike her, but my movement left her trapped between my chest and the door. She stiffened, her breath fogged over the clear glass in front of her as she exhaled shakily.

I leaned down just enough so my cheek touched the side of her head. "Trinity, I'll never do anything to hurt you, I promise."

I stepped to the side to get a better grip on the door and pushed it open for her. She didn't turn my way, but I saw her head fall forward and then she lifted her shoulders and shook her hair around her face for a moment before stepping out into the wind.

We climbed into my Jeep, and other than her telling me which way to go, she remained quiet and pensive beside me for most of the trip.

"I'm sorry for keeping you all day." Her voice was calm and the tense atmosphere seemed to have leveled out when she finally spoke.

I smiled over at her, "I'm not."

The corner of her lip turned up. "I assume you didn't have to work today, but you're not on night shift tonight, are you?"

"No, I'm off for a few days." I flipped the blinker to get off the highway.

"Turn left at the bottom of the ramp," she directed. "Well, I'm sure you had other things to do today besides chauffeuring me around."

I made the left when the coast was clear before answering her, "Nope, nothing that can't wait a day or two. I'm glad that I got a chance to help you."

"I am, too. It has been nice to have someone around today." We looked at each other and shared a moment. My heart beat an extra beat when our gazes stayed connected just a moment longer than expected.

"Well, I'm glad that I decided to stop in to visit with you today. I almost didn't."

I heard her shift in her seat, but refrained from turning her way. "What made you stop in today?"

If I told her the truth, I'd spook her, so there was no way I was going to tell her that I had been waiting a month till my days off to run an errand that would put me close to her office just so I could see her. Yeah, that wasn't going to work.

"I was in the area," I shrugged like it was no big deal. "I remembered your business card said your office was in that building, just took a chance that you were there."

"Well, I'm glad you did." Genuine warmth vibrated in her voice and wrapped around my heart. "Turn right at the next street, and it is around the corner."

I followed her directions and we pulled into the lot. "This is a nice place, looks a lot newer than the last building."

"It is. This one we bought for a steal from a bank foreclosure when the developer went bankrupt. We didn't have to do too much to get it finished either, which was a good thing."

We parked and again she pulled out her admittance card to slide it through the machine. This time when we entered, an older man met us at the door. He hugged Trinity casually when we walked in.

"I don't get to see you as often as I would like. You should visit more." He smiled broadly at her and she returned it.

"Thanks, Mike, I wish I could get out more often. If it weren't for problems, I probably wouldn't get out here at all. You aren't making these things up just so you get to see me, are you?" she teased him as she stepped back.

"Now, that's an idea." He turned his attention from her and held out his hand to me, "Mike Withers, and I assume you are Gavin Brooksfield?"

I raised my eyebrows in surprise. "Um, yeah that would be me." I took his hand and pumped it casually.

He displayed a toothy smile with crooked front teeth. "Mary called and told me you were coming. She said you were good people, and if you can get by Mary, well, you're okay in my book."

Trinity shook her head and muttered something I couldn't understand under her breath.

"Glad to hear I passed the Mary test," I joked back.

"That's not an easy feat, let me tell you. Well, come along and let me show you the damage." He walked down the hallway, calling out to someone we couldn't see in an office off to the side that he would be back.

"So the plumber fixed the leak, right?" Trinity asked as she stepped up beside Mike. I trailed behind, glancing around the building as we proceeded.

The hallways were a soft buttercup yellow, the carpet a dark tan. Mike pulled open a fire door and held his hand out to us to precede him. We stepped into a long hallway with doors on both sides.

"Yeah, the plumber fixed the leak. Cost us a bundle to get him out here at night, but it could have been worse. Any longer and the water would have gone through the second unit too and onto the bottom floor."

Trinity's shoulders tensed at the mention of money. I wondered how they did financially and decided it wasn't any of my business to ask.

Mike continued as we approached an elevator. "The clients in the top apartment are away on a vacation. Maria is trying to find work out with her parents in Virginia. They are supposed to be back tonight." The elevator door slid open and we entered. "The clients on two were at work and when they got home, they walked into a mess."

"Where are we putting them for the time being?" Trinity asked as she leaned back against the metal wall. I stood beside her but kept my distance.

"We are going to put the clients on two over at New Start. It's the only place with a room right now."

"Does she have transportation to get her to work? That's quite a distance."

"Yeah, she does have a car, and I wondered if it would be alright to offer her a bit of money from the petty cash to help with gas since this wasn't her fault." He looked at Trinity with an eyebrow raised.

"Sure, that's not a problem. Do we have someone who can move them?"

"Already taken care of, they moved her out about thirty minutes ago. She's going to come back here and get the kids from the nursery and then head over there after she gets off work."

"You have a nursery here?" I piped in, surprised to hear this information.

"Sure we do. With so many young women here, we have to. We keep the children safe during the day, even home school many of them. The older ones generally choose to go to the public schools, but we leave that up to the parents."

Trinity grinned up at me, pride all over her face for what she had built here. I returned it with more feeling than I should have and our gazes locked again.

Mike cleared his throat, and we both turned to him. I felt like a kid who had gotten caught with my hand in the cookie jar. I shifted and crossed my arms over my chest, looking to the white tiled floor just as the elevator door slid open.

We followed Mike down the hall and waited while he tried a couple keys to get the right one in the lock. When the door was open, I held it against the wall and let Trinity go through.

The smell of the water damage already permeated the air with a tinge of mildew, and I knew that within another day or two the mold would be growing rapidly and the damage would be much more extensive.

Trinity groaned as she walked into the kitchen. The clip of her heel on the vinyl tiled floor got my attention and a flash of panic raced down my spine as I stepped quickly to her side, but I wasn't fast enough.

The tip of her heel went right through the damaged floor and she started to fall. I grabbed her arm and jerked her harder than I had intended to keep her from falling. She landed against my chest in a thud.

Her hands grasped my forearms, and my other arm wrapped around her waist, pulling her closer to me. She stood rigid in my arms.

"Are you alright, Trinity?" I let go of her forearm and tipped her chin up with my knuckle. Panic raced over her features, "Are you alright? As soon as I heard your heels hit the floor, I had a feeling that was going to happen. I'm sorry I had to grab you so hard, but I was afraid you were going to fall and hurt yourself."

I felt her lean into me for a moment before she sucked in a breath and pushed away, "Yes, thank you. I should have been paying more attention."

"You two need to get a room," Mike tossed out as he walked into the living room and away from us. Trinity blushed as she backed away. I bit back a smile and tried to stifle a laugh. I really liked this old man.

Chapter 7 - Trinity

Oh Mary, I thought, as she lashed out at Gavin. The fact that he kept his composure and never tried to strike back verbally or physically surprised me. Even after all these years, to hear a man so calmly reply to an accusation like the one she had thrown out left me slightly off balance.

Years ago when I had looked at Gavin, the rookie cop, in the eye in the parking lot, I had seen an understanding that now began to make sense. He had grown up with abuse. He understood it. While my heart tore to hear that he had lived with the level of abuse that he had and that he had lost his mother in such a horrible way, it also made me feel closer to him in a way, more connected. We had something in common. Something other than his coming to my rescue or being the officer to put my husband behind bars. He had been a victim, he understood.

Somehow though, as I sat there and listened to him, the thought that he understood both comforted and scared me at the same time. I was glad that he kept his attention on Mary and didn't look my way. If he had, he would have seen the emotion in my eyes, and me wiping a drop of moisture from the bottom of my lid.

Gavin was a strong enough man to confide in us and put a walking bridge between Mary and him. I could not say that they would ever be friends, but the foundation had been laid that they could work together, if need be.

For a few moments, I had the opportunity to stand back and watch Gavin work. So far, I had seen the rookie cop, the hero, the student, and the victim. Now, I observed him being a man assisting with the stressful situation that had occurred here at the center.

Many of the things that he explained to the police officer went right over my head. They spoke cop lingo, and while I had been married to one many years ago, I had never been given the opportunity to share or learn the talk.

I had been a pawn for Brenden to control. I was the one who received the brunt of his anger after a bad day at work, the woman who was punished for not having supper ready at the exact moment he walked in the door, even if he was three hours late. I was the wife who always had to be ready when his body craved attention and to act adoringly when he felt the need to take me out in public.

I had been his to control, his to command.

As Gavin and I left, we decided to get something to eat, and I sat in the car wondering about what he had said earlier in Mary's office. Had he been a pawn in the grand scheme of the abuse from his father?

I tried not to dwell on those thoughts and instead considered the fact that it had been so long since I had found any enjoyment in the company of a man. I had a few male friends, and I didn't look at every man as an abuser, but the fear from my past kept my emotions under lock and key, never allowing for anything else besides business or simple friendship.

I wasn't lying when I told Gavin at the seminar that I only wanted friendship. I didn't trust myself to choose someone. I wasn't sure if I could ever love another man after what Brenden had done to me. I had hoped that one day I could, but as the years passed, I had never found someone who interested me, or whom I trusted enough.

A nervous flutter wiggled in my belly as I wondered if maybe he might be someone worth trying to get to know. I shook my head and looked out the window. There was no reason to have such thoughts. He would never be interested in a damaged woman like me. I was destined to live my life alone, and I was fine with that.

Lunch turned out to be almost a catastrophe! I couldn't believe that I had flinched when he had reached over to wipe the sauce off my chin. I was mortified that I had reacted that way, but Gavin had taken it in his stride with a simple comment.

After lunch I contemplated the array of emotions I had witnessed during our brief discussion of his father. It wasn't so much anger as frustration and sadness that had covered every inch of his handsome face.

I wondered if he would ever trust me enough to explain to me exactly what he had endured as a child. No victim really ever wanted to talk about it, but most knew that to share the story with someone who could understand helped the damage to heal, if ever so slightly.

I put my head back against the headrest, dwelling for a moment on when we had left the pizzeria. I had put one of my hands on the door to push it open, only to be surprised when it bounced back right into my face. Gavin's quick response kept me from slamming right into the glass.

His chest pressed against my back, and for a moment, I froze. Half a dozen memories flashed through my mind: Brenden pushing me up against a wall, Brenden holding me against my will in the kitchen, Brenden's vice-like hands around my neck. As quickly as the memories came, I banished them. This wasn't Brenden, this was Gavin, and the chest that was braced against me was the one I had admired in the coffee shop as wide and relaxed.

I had blown out a shaky breath as the heat of his body and his warm breath brushed by my ear. He promised never to hurt me. Was there more to his words than what had happened at the moment? Could I trust that? Hadn't Brenden promised those same words, over and over again?

I glanced at Gavin as he drove. He was calm, confident, and comfortable behind the wheel, checking the traffic in his mirrors every once in a while. The music drifted around us casually, and I melted into the leather seat, thankful that he was with me.

As that thought crossed my mind, I wondered if I was keeping him from something. Maybe he was supposed to work tonight and now he would be tired after spending the day driving me from place to place, dealing with problems that had nothing to do with him. Did he regret stopping in my office to say hello?

His words vanquished the guilt I felt, and I was again thankful that he was with me, if just for one day.

The property manager, Mike, was one of the few men that I could call a true friend. For years, we had bantered back and forth and he was one of those men with whom women felt immediately comfortable. When he accepted Gavin so easily, I released a sigh on a muttered prayer, "Thank God."

Mike was a nice guy, and his instincts were normally right on. I trusted him completely. I had seen him gauge a man in seconds, women, too, and figure out the best way to deal with them. Property managers were more than just someone to watch over the buildings. One of their main responsibilities was to know about the clients that stayed on the property.

In the case of shelters, they were also counselors who took every second they could to help the ones who walked through our doors. They gave them support, directed them when they needed guidance, and many times became parental figures in their lives and their children's. They were solid, trustworthy, and they cared.

I wished there were more people like them in the world.

Mike led us back to the elevator and told us about how the problem had been found. My mind thumbed through bank records wondering where the funds would come from to fix everything correctly. I prayed the grant Brooke was working on would come through.

As always, Mike had already taken care of the clients and I had no problem telling him to use some of the petty cash. If I had said no, he would have taken it out of his own pocket. I knew him well.

While Mike was telling Gavin about the children and the schooling that we offered, my heart warmed. There were few shelters in the area that gave so much to the clients that were trying to get back on their feet. Our job wasn't just to get them out of abusive homes, but to also give them a safe place to recuperate and get back on their feet, and that meant for the children, too.

I smiled up at Gavin. An expression spread over his face, one that I had never seen directed from a man towards me and it held me spellbound. When was the last time a man had looked at me with, what, admiration? I didn't think ever.

My cheeks colored when Mike interrupted our stare, and my mind was back in the elevator as I stepped into the apartment. I tried to think back to a time that any man had looked at me with such warmth, caring, and respect and could not think of one since my father.

Sure, I dealt with men every single day in business and life. The men that I normally dealt with could either care less about you, or treated you like an annoying pest that wouldn't go away. The men who would take the time to get involved and listen were few and far between. Yes, listening was something that needed to be done when working in this kind of environment.

My mind was still reeling from the contemplation of what I had seen in the elevator that as I walked into the apartment I barely noticed anything.

I stepped onto the kitchen floor, and my low-heeled shoe started to sink. If Gavin had not grabbed me when he had, I would have twisted my ankle or worse, yet the impact of his hand on my arm, and my body being slammed against his jarred memories long suppressed to rise, and my muscles went rigid.

The feel of his finger under my chin, a single soft sensation that was something so unfamiliar to me, threw me for a loop. I knew what was coming next and I tried not to flinch. My heart began to jackhammer against my ribs.

I held my breath, waiting for it to come. I stared up at him. His anger would grow, his verbal assault would start, and then a slap or a push or even a punch would follow.

To my dawning surprise, as I stood completely still, no anger or repulsion was displayed. His brow furrowed, his eyes turned sad, and even his jaw slacked a bit instead of tensing. My body started to relax and lean into his, and I suddenly realized what I was doing. I pushed away quickly, "Yes, thank you. I should have been paying more attention."

"You two need to get a room," Mike threw over his shoulder as he walking away shaking his head. My cheeks burned with embarrassment. Had it looked like more to Mike than it was?

Gavin chuckled and tried to cover it up with his fist and a cough. He stepped away from me and went to talk to Mike.

With careful steps I moved to the balcony. It was made of cement, so it should be safer than the soft water-damaged kitchen floor. Right now, I needed safe, if just to get my heart beating smoothly again.

I leaned on the railing and looked over the playground. Twelve children were running and playing in the enclosed area. The tan building surrounded it on all four sides and no one on the outside could see that they were here.

Mike and Gavin were discussing building materials and measurements, and it was best that I stay out of their way. The kids below were much more interesting than how many sheets of board would be needed and what kind of linoleum would go on the floor.

After a few minutes, Gavin poked his head out the door to say something but stopped when he looked over the railing.

"Now that is a really cool playground." A grin resonated in his voice.

I sighed, "Yeah, it is."

He cleared his throat, "Mike and I are going to go look at the apartment downstairs. Do you want to come or do you want to stay up here?"

He was giving me a choice? I was tempted to smile, but I squelched it. "I'll stay here if you don't mind."

"Not a problem, I'll be back up once we take a look." Instead of walking away, he stepped closer to the railing and took in the details down below. "That really is a cool playground."

I smiled to myself, and he turned to go back inside. A little boy drove a dump truck through the sand box and a little girl yelled that he was destroying her town. He told her he was helping her make it better.

Yes, here, we were making it better for them. Well, we tried anyway.

The children played below without the knowledge that I was there, although a few of the volunteers had seen me and waved. I observed the children, praying that what little we were offering to them would be enough. Here, the color of your skin didn't matter; neither did the language you spoke. You weren't yelled at for spilling your milk or put to bed without supper.

We made sure children had clothes and food, and we even had a volunteer that sat and read two bedtime stories in front of the fireplace in the large common room every night.

I heard voices behind me and stood up. It was only then that I realized how much my back had stiffened from standing still so long. How long had I been there? I noticed the sun hidden behind an office building a few blocks away. It was late afternoon already.

Gavin's voice carried to me as he talked on the phone to someone. I assumed it was his brother-in-law as he was discussing materials and labor time.

I felt guilty again for pulling him away from other things as I listened and was surprised to realize that he planned on helping to do the repairs.

Gavin stepped out on the balcony. "I talked to Taylor.

We can stop by and get the building materials in the morning. He is calling in the order now, and we can get this all started. I will be coming by here tomorrow to start ripping everything out. Mike said he'd give me a hand, and since it's Saturday, he said there are a few boys around here that would probably like to help."

It was my turn to wear my admiration on my sleeve as he explained his plan. He leaned over the balcony, resting his forearms on the black metal railing. His eyes scanned over the scene below as kids squealed and ran in circles. I noticed small crinkles at the corners of his eyes as he smiled. My hand itched to reach out and touch them.

"We should get everything ripped out tomorrow and be able to put new subfloors in. I will leave it up to you if you want us to come by here on Sunday, the second day will be the really noisy day, putting up the new ceiling and all the drywall."

"You don't have to work on Sunday," I responded solemnly.

"No biggie to me. I told you I was off for a few days, and there is nothing else I'd rather do." He turned back to me, resting his hip on the rail while crossing his arms casually. "Trinity, before you even start with the 'I feel guilty for you doing this,' stop." The words were forceful, but not mean. "I want to help. I have done things like this a couple dozen times for shelters." He stepped closer, and my chin rose so I could keep looking at him.

"This is what I do."

My throat clogged with emotion, and for just a moment, I wondered what it would be like to have a man like Gavin in my life. "Thank you," I finally released through suddenly dry lips.

"No need to thank me," he winked and turned toward the door. I followed him back inside, but he stopped short and I almost plowed into his back.

"Trinity, I'm going to hold on to you, just till we get to the hallway. I don't want you falling through the floor again."

An instant uncertainty coursed through me, but I shoved it aside. So far Gavin had been a perfect gentleman, and the fact that he told me what he was going to do before he put his hand on me just confirmed that.

"Okay," I responded and he slipped his right arm gently around my waist and wrapped a large warm hand around my left bicep. The heat from his hands burned through my clothes, and my heart rate accelerated. How long had it been since a man had touched me like this without trying to control or hurt me? Thirteen, fourteen years maybe, when I had dated Brenden?

We made it out to the hallway without incident, and Gavin released me at the threshold. The warmth from his hands started to dissipate, and I tried to cling to the safe feeling for as long as it lasted.

We returned to Mike's office on the ground floor, and I gave him a hug goodbye.

"He seems like a good man," he whispered in my ear.

I pulled away and flashed a small smile, not wanting to look more deeply into his words. Mike and Gavin shook hands and we moved to exit. Gavin stepped beside me and placed a hand on my lower back as we moved. It was the first time in a long time that I didn't mind the contact.

"So where to now?" Gavin asked after we were back inside his Jeep.

I checked my watch. By the time we got back to the office, it would be after five. Everyone would have gone home, and I would have to figure out how to get a ride home. I checked my phone to see if maybe I had missed a call from the car repair shop, but there were no missed calls. "Damn."

"What's wrong?" Gavin leaned slightly against his door as he twisted toward me, his right hand resting on the back of my headrest. My eyes followed the length of his arm to the point where it attached to his shoulder and then slid over his chest. I suddenly realized that I hadn't answered him, and my eyes flicked up to his face. His eyes locked onto mine, and heat crept up my neck.

"Um," I turned away from the warmth of his emerald eyes and stared out the windshield. If I told him the problem, he would offer to drive me home, I knew he would. Did I really want him to know where I lived? Could I get him to give me a ride to Brooke's place? Would she be available to take me home? Should I even bother her to do it?

"Trinity, what's wrong?" He shifted his hand, and I thought he might touch me, instead he lowered his hand into his lap and fisted his fingers tightly. Tension raced through me at the sight because I wasn't sure if I had upset him or not.

"Nothing, it's just that my car doesn't seem to be ready. They were supposed to call me when it was done, but they haven't called, so I don't know how I'm going to get home," I rambled.

"That's fine, I'll take you home." He shrugged and turned his attention to the car, turning the key, and starting the engine.

"I hate to trouble you anymore than I have already. Maybe you should just give me a ride to the office, and I'll get a ride home," I offered.

He leaned back in his seat. "Trinity," he said quietly. I kept my attention out the front window until he spoke again. "Trinity, look at me, please." I swallowed and turned to face him slowly. "I don't mind taking you home, unless you would prefer that I not know where you live. If that's the concern, just tell me."

How did he have the ability to calm my worries with his simple words? Why was it that after so many years, I felt comfortable in this man's presence? I somehow trusted him, and although I still jumped at being touched and the ingrained fears of my past still floated to the top, I knew that he wouldn't hurt me.

I licked my dry lips as he waited for my answer. His eyes noticed my lips as I did, and his forearm tightened slightly as it gripped the steering wheel.

"Are you sure you don't mind?" My voice was quiet, barely audible over the running motor.

The muscles in his face relaxed, and his lips curled into a breathtaking smile. "Mind? No, I'd be honored to see you home safely."

I turned to look out the passenger window, warmth spreading up my neck once again. "If you're sure you don't mind."

"Nope, lead the way." He put the car in gear, and I gave him directions to my house.

Forty minutes later, he pulled into the driveway of my small Victorian home. "Nice place."

"Thanks." I looked over the house I had purchased nine years ago when I had moved here. The light blue siding added depth and texture to the exterior. The strong façade sported a steeply-pitched roof and dominant front-facing gable. The asymmetrical porch along the front and right side finished the welcoming impression.

I sighed louder than I had intended. Family—this house was made for a family, and I lived here alone. When I had bought the house I had once thought that maybe, in time, I would be able to fill it with a loving family. Yet, nine years later, I still lived alone, well except for my German shepherd, Callie.

I had yet to let my walls down enough to allow anyone to get close to me. Maybe it was because I hadn't met the right person, maybe it was because I was afraid, or maybe it was because I was meant to be alone. I didn't know, but I shook my head and turned to say goodbye to Gavin.

There were questions written in his expression. I didn't understand what they were, didn't know how to interpret them, I was just aware that they were there.

Silence filled the air as we both sat there. Gavin finally broke the awkwardness by clearing his throat and speaking, "Do you have any of those forms here that you need Taylor and me to fill out and sign?"

"Oh, I forgot all about those. Yes, yes I do. I have them on my computer inside. If you can wait just a minute, I can print them off for you." I opened the car door and climbed out, as I turned to close the door, I studied Gavin sitting there silently. He would stay in the car because I hadn't asked him to come in. If I didn't ask him, he would assume I would not be comfortable with having him in there.

Maybe it was time to change my comfort level. "Gavin, if you would like to come in and wait, you are welcome to."

His smile was slow in coming, as if he were weighing my words. "If you don't mind, I'd love to." I nodded and closed the door as he opened his.

Chapter 8 - Gavin

I couldn't remember the last time that I had enjoyed spending my day running around like I had today. It wasn't the errands that I was helping with but the company that I was keeping.

While Trinity wasn't a big talker, and she still appeared jumpy at times, I enjoyed being with her immensely. I found that even in silence, it felt natural, good—almost too good.

I had to remind myself that she had already made it known that she wasn't interested in getting involved with anyone. I could understand that, but after ten years of self-imprisonment, could I find a way to get her to break down the walls she had built around herself? Did I even want to try?

When we arrived at her house, I didn't even want to ask to come inside. If she wasn't going to offer, I would happily sit in the car and wait however long it took for her to get the papers ready. I was just glad that she trusted me enough to allow me to take her home.

We climbed the steps to her front porch, and barking came from inside the house. "You have a dog?"

"Yeah, you're not afraid of dogs, are you? She's good, but I'd move slowly around her. She can be very protective."

"Why am I not surprised?" I chuckled as I waited for her to unlock her door. Before she put the key in the bottom lock, she glanced over her shoulder, scanning the street behind her.

She turned back around and unlocked the top dead bolt, pulling her key out and pushing the door open. A large cream and black shepherd burst out the front door and moved between us. I stepped back slowly to give it more room. The dog's tail was wagging slowly, happy to have Trinity home, but leery of me.

"It's okay, Callie, friend," she said and ran her hand down the full coat of fur on the dog's back. "Callie, friend," she repeated, and the dog's tail wagged faster as her mouth opened and her tongue lolled out the side in a silly dog grin. She sniffed the air, and I put my hand out to her so she could smell me more easily.

She circled me, and I made sure to stand still until the inspection was over. Trinity stepped into the house, "Callie, enough, come." She slapped her leg and the dog scurried into the front door and turned to watch me.

She didn't bare any teeth as I entered, and I assumed that was a good sign. She followed Trinity down the hall as I closed the door gently behind us.

I stood in the hall, unsure if I should follow. Trinity had invited me in, but maybe she just wanted me to hang out here instead of venturing further into her domain.

"Gavin, you can come back to the kitchen. My laptop is in here, I can print out those forms for you." Decision made. I walked down the hall to the kitchen at the rear of the house.

The kitchen had a country feel to it, the walls a soft warm peach color, the cabinets and table all a warm oak finish, with a brown granite countertop. It wasn't a large kitchen, but it was very comfortable looking.

Trinity took off the sport coat that she wore and dropped it over the back of a chair at her table. Her dress shirt looked like it was made of silk and moved with her body as she reached for her laptop and lifted the top. I swallowed tightly and pulled my view from her to look around the kitchen area again.

Off to the right of the dining room was a family room area. A large stone fireplace dominated the far wall, with two large armchairs and a big fluffy couch that had oversized pillows piled on it, filling the space in front of the hearth.

I was tempted to drop down into one of the chairs, but figured if I did, I might not want to get out. That probably wouldn't go over so well. While Trinity was logging onto her laptop, I pulled out a chair at the table. She glanced up, and I stopped. "Do you mind if I sit?" I asked quickly.

She waved away my question, "No, I'm sorry. Please have a seat. This won't take but a minute. I'm sorry to keep you waiting."

"It's not a problem, Trinity. You don't have to apologize." I sat at the table and leaned back on the high wooden dowels of the back of the chair.

She didn't respond. She just started typing. Her house phone rang and she stepped away to reach for it, "Excuse me for a moment."

I surveyed the rooms again; I really liked how she had decorated them. They weren't full of stuff, just tastefully done. All of it looked like it was done to be not only functional but to also appeal to the need for relaxing and enjoying the comforts of home. I could live in a place like that.

Trinity's voice broke into my thoughts, which was a good thing.

"Sorry, Brooke, I just got home. I'm trying to print out the forms for Gavin now so they can start the work." She glanced at me sheepishly as she stopped to listen to something her friend was saying.

"Yes, he's still with me." She laughed quietly and paused, "Yes, he is in my house, sitting at my kitchen table right now." She shook her head and turned her back on me, but didn't entirely conceal the small up-tilt of her lips after she spoke.

"Stop," she laughed louder. "Was there something you wanted?" I heard laughter coming over the phone, and the sound of a woman talking, but I couldn't make out the words.

"I'm fine, Brooke. I will talk to you tomorrow." She pulled the phone from her ear and shook her head as she pushed the end call button on her cordless phone. The laughter cut off when she hung up.

"Sorry about that." She set the phone down and came back to the table, sliding into her seat.

"No worries. Was she checking up on you?" I laid my right hand on the table and noticed that she looked down at it. She moved her focus back to her computer screen.

"Yes, Brooke and I have been friends for a long time. We look out for each other." Her fingers moved over the keys of her laptop as she spoke.

"I assume she was also a victim?" I said quietly.

She paused, her fingers hovering over the keyboard, "Yes, she was."

A mechanical humming noise came from the family room, and I bent my neck to the side so I could see the source. A printer vibrated in the corner on a small table, and a sheet of paper slid out.

As the humming continued, a few more pages printed, and Trinity stood up to get them. I admired her as she walked into the room, taking in the way her shoulders were set so square and how her waist tapered down and then out again at her hips.

I shifted in my seat and scratched the back of my neck absently as I pulled my gaze off her.

She came back as I heard a clunk and saw a door swing open low in the wall as Callie walked through a dog door.

"Do you leave that open when you're not home?" I asked her.

She was looking at the papers as she came back to the table and answered absently, "What, the dog door? Yeah, why?"

"You know, that's not very safe to leave open. That's a big dog door. A small man could come through there."

She set the papers down in front of me, "The door is secure and locked most of the time. The lock releases when Callie gets about eight inches from it. She has a sensor on her collar. Once the door opens and closes, it automatically locks again."

She sat down and pet Callie who pushed her head into her lap.

I raised my eyebrows, "Wow. The technology that they have these days is amazing. I would have never guessed." I picked up the papers and glanced over the sheet in front of me, a two-page document with my name already printed on the top sheet, and a second set that was blank for Taylor.

"If anyone else is going to help you, then they will need to fill one of those out also. I gave you the empty form in case you needed to have copies made." She stood up, and I took the cue that she wanted me to leave.

"Not a problem. I will get them filled out." I had started to walk down the hallway towards the front door and turned to her. Her eyes were at my waist. Huh, could she have been checking me out? Her eyes flipped up to mine quickly, and a light pink color started to fill her cheeks. She just gave me my answer, and I controlled the urge to jump up and shout my excitement.

"How do you want me to get these back to you? Do you want me to email them or fax them?"

"Email them, please, then I can run them real fast. Not that I'm worried about you, but I have to do it for everyone's safety." She stood at the entrance to the kitchen leaning against the doorjamb. "My email address is at the top of the form."

"It's not a problem, Trinity, I get it." I lifted the papers up in front of me. "I'll go by Taylor's now and get these back to you in a couple hours."

She seemed more relaxed now than she had been all day as she stepped forward. I turned to move toward the door, and Callie trotted over and sat beside the door. I allowed her to smell the back of my hand again before I tried to pet her. She licked my hand, and I gave her head a big rub between her pointed ears.

Trinity stopped near the door and put her hand on the knob, but didn't open it. "She likes you. Normally she won't leave my side when someone is around until she knows them."

I wanted to praise the dog. "Well, that's good then, right?"

Trinity met my eyes after she looked at the dog. There was a question in them as they met mine. I wanted so badly to ask her what she was thinking, but I refrained. The sudden urge to pull her into my arms and kiss her almost surged me forward to do just that.

"Yeah, that's good," she said quietly. For a few more seconds, we stood in silence and watched each other. Finally, Callie nuzzled my hand to get another pet, and Trinity pulled the door open and thanked me one more time for all my help.

I stepped out before the urge overwhelmed me. I had dreamed of her for ten years. In some of those dreams, I carried her out of her house in my arms, her almost lifeless body hanging limp. In other dreams, she stood against me and her arms were wrapped tightly around my neck of her own accord.

As I went down the front steps, I wondered if the second dream would ever come true.

Her eyes stayed fixed on me as I walked to my Jeep, and I gave her a wave as I climbed in. She returned the wave and then scanned the area before stepping back and closing the door. I could just imagine her locking the locks as she stood on the other side. Demons still chased her.

* * *

She didn't live that far away from Taylor, and when I rapped on his front door and pushed it open, a lopsided grin was still plastered on my lips.

"Hello?" I called out as I stepped into the entryway. A small squeal came from down the hall, and then little footsteps pattered on the tile floor in my direction.

I prepared myself for the greeting and squatted just as little Peter came flying around the kitchen corner and straight at me. "Uncle Gavin!"

He literally jumped from three feet away, and I scooped up and hugged my four-year-old nephew.

His little arms squeezed me tightly as he practically shrieked in my ear, "Are you staying for dinner? I wanna show you my new police car! Mommy bought it for me today!" He unclutched his hands and wiggled to get down. I let him go and almost tripped when he snagged my hand and started dragging me down the hall.

"Come on, Uncle Gavin! I wanna show it to you!"

"Alright, Peter, I'll take a look at it. You don't need to pull my arm off, though."

"Peter, stop pestering your uncle," my sister's voice reached us as we entered the kitchen.

"I just wanna show him my new police car," he cried as his mother stared him down with her no-excuses look.

"He drives one, Peter. He knows what they look like. Go tell your dad that Gavin is here, please."

"I'll look at your car when you come back." I brushed my hand over his dirty blonde locks, making them even more of a mess than they already were and bringing the smile back that had faded off his face when his mother had told him to leave me alone.

"You staying for dinner, Gavin?" My sister was two years older than I was and had fallen into the family life a lot more easily than I had. She loved being a wife and mother, but I guess when you found the right person, it was easy to move on.

I studied her as she used her hands to flip a salad around in the bowl. "No, thanks. I just need Taylor to sign these forms and get them over to Trinity."

My sister stilled, and her attention snapped to mine. "Trinity? Not the same Trinity?"

"Yes, the same one. Ironically, she only lives a couple miles from here. She runs a series of abuse shelters and does seminars in the area. I saw her at one last month."

"Is she the reason you have a gleam in your eye?" She cocked her hip and rested her hands on the counter.

Taylor slapped me on the back before I could come up with an answer. "No, that's determination to do a job well done," Taylor said.

He winked at me so Greta wouldn't see it. "Yep, that's it."

"You don't fool me, Gavin. Be careful with her, she has gone through a lot," she called out as Taylor and I turned to head to his office in the basement.

The atmosphere in the room changed slightly as I spoke, "We've all gone through a lot, Greta."

She nodded silently and resumed her salad making. I followed Taylor down the steps.

Taylor didn't say anything until we were in his office and the door was closed. "So it really is her, huh?" He dropped down into a battered leather office chair.

"Yeah, I couldn't believe it when I saw her last month. After so many years," my voice faded off as I sank down to another old chair he had in the room.

"Brought back all the memories, didn't it?" He bounced back and forth slowly on the hinges of the chair.

"Brought them back? No, the memories have never gone away. I still dream about them at least once a week. What it did was remind me of what an incredible woman she is." I rubbed my hands together nervously.

Taylor had started dating my sister right before I got out of the academy. We had been best friends ever since we met, and he was the only person I had confided in when I had met Trinity in the parking lot. The only one to know that back then, I harbored a serious crush on a woman I didn't even know and could never have.

"How is she?" His head tilted to the side, and he stopped bouncing for a moment.

"She's good—no, she's great. She seems like she has dealt with it all pretty well. Her business is amazing, wait till you see this shelter. It's nothing like what you are used to working on. She is so confident now—well, most of the time anyway."

"What do you mean?" He started bouncing again, and I leaned back in the chair and laid my hands on the armrests.

"She's confident and strong until I get close to her, then she gets nervous. She flinched when I went to wipe pizza sauce off her face. I felt like an idiot for making her uncomfortable."

"Has she been in any relationships?"

I shrugged, "No idea, we kind of kept the personal talk to a minimum."

"Give it some time, Gavin. She might not have healed enough to let someone in." He sat forward in his chair, "If you care about her, then you need to just give her some time and just be there, be her friend. Let her see that she can trust you, and then maybe she can open up."

"I know." The room grew quiet for a moment, the only sound Peter's feet slapping on the floor above our heads as he ran from one room to the other.

"So did you bring the papers over?"

We filled the papers out in silence and then Taylor scanned them and showed me where he saved them on the computer so I could send them. "I'm looking forward to meeting her. I'm sure she's pretty amazing for you to have held a torch for her for all these years."

"She is, Tay."

"Go ahead and email that to her and then come up and eat with us. I'll be upstairs."

"I already told Greta I'm not staying," I called out as he walked out the door.

"And she probably already put a plate on the table. You're staying." I heard his footsteps on the stairs and shook my head. He was probably right.

With a few quick clicks, I had my email open and thought for a moment before I began. *Trinity, I'm glad I could help out today while you didn't have a car. Here are the forms you wanted from me and Taylor, let me know if you need anything further.*

How tempted I was to write, Can I take you to dinner? However, I resisted and tapped my fingers on the desk for a minute.

We are looking forward to helping out, hope to see you again soon. Oh, my cell number will be below my name, save it in case you need to reach me. Take care – Gavin

"Or if you just want to talk to me, or see me, or anything," I said to the computer monitor as I reread the message and pressed send.

I shut down the computer and put her card back in my wallet. By the time I got upstairs and sat down at the table, my phone vibrated with a text message.

Gavin – It's Trinity. I wanted you to have my cellphone number in case you need something at the site. Thank you for everything, and thank Taylor too.

I read the message twice and then immediately saved the phone number in my contacts. I didn't want to take the chance of deleting her number.

I sent back a quick reply, *You're welcome, anything you need, anytime.*

I set my phone next to my plate and looked up to find Greta glaring at me. "What?"

"No texting at the table." She picked up her fork.

"Yes, mom," I kidded back to her.

My cellphone vibrated again, and everyone turned to me. I reached for it and Peter's little voice filled the air, "Oh, Mommy is gonna yell at you now!"

"Sorry, buddy," I glanced over to Greta, "sorry to you, too, but it's about the job tomorrow. I promise I'll be done in a minute."

Thank you, good night, Gavin, she had messaged to me.

My fingers pressed the buttons quickly, and I said a simple good night back to her. I put my phone back into the holder on my belt and picked up my fork, much to my sister's delight.

* * *

"Dear God!" I woke from a nightmare with a start. It was the same horrendous dream that had been reoccurring for years, still fresh in my mind. I blinked rapidly to clear the sleep from my eyes. It had been the same dream, but this time there was a slight difference. This time when I burst in the front door, Trinity wasn't unconscious on the floor, but fighting for her life. Trinity saw me as I came in the door, her eyes pleading for help. I drew my gun and pulled the trigger.

The strength of my forty-five caliber bullet struck Brenden, and he flew off of her and onto the floor next to her. She scrambled out from under the leg that still lay over her hips. Sobbing, she crawled to me as I stood rooted to the wooden floor. I was so shocked that I had pulled the trigger. My feet felt like lead weights stuck on the sandy ocean bottom, sinking deeper with each passing second.

Trinity staggered to her feet, her neck showing the signs of his hands wrapped tightly around it, but her throat was not crushed as it had been in reality. She threw herself into my arms, breaking me free from the hold that had overcome me.

I wrapped one hand around her, pulling her close, while I used my other to put my gun back into my duty belt holster and secure it.

She squeezed me so hard that I had trouble pulling in air, but I curled my other arm around her just as tightly and held her to me, kissing the side of her head.

I was so thankful that I was holding her in my arms and my eyes were closed so tightly that I didn't notice the movement on the other side of the room. My ears still rang from the use of my firearm inside the small enclosed space that I did not hear the scratches on the wood.

I felt Trinity stiffen and my eyelids flipped up to see Brenden leaning against the wall, blood running down his chest; he was staring at us, his duty weapon pulled and pointed at her back.

"If I can't have her, nobody will."

The sound of the bullet being discharged from the barrel and the feel of Trinity's body thrusting hard against me with the force of the bullet woke me from the dream.

"Dear God!" I exclaimed again. I wiped the sheen of perspiration off my face and closed my eyes, willing my heart to slow.

Where the hell had that change in the dream come from? What did it mean? Was it that now that I had found her, I would lose her again?

I threw back the covers and looked at my bedside clock. It was four in the morning. There was no way I was going back to sleep. I pulled out workout pants and a sweatshirt from my cheapo dresser and put on my running sneakers.

I had to do something to force that nightmare out of my head. Running seemed as good an activity as any, so I grabbed my house key, slipped my cellphone into a pouch I had wrapped around my bicep, and stepped out of my townhouse into the cool early morning air.

As my feet pounded the pavement, the gunshot echoed in my skull. I stopped long enough to hook up my ear buds into my cellphone, put on the loudest, hardest rock music I had in my playlist, and took off as fast I could, the demons hot on my tail.

Chapter 9 - Trinity

"So…is he as hot as Marcy said he was?" Brooke quizzed as she plopped into the chair at my kitchen table.

"Do you want coffee?" I ignored her question, refreshing my own cup.

"You know I want coffee. Now, answer the question." She tapped her fingernails on the oak tabletop to illustrate her impatience.

"He's attractive." I pulled down the mug she usually used on Saturday mornings. The inspirational words on it of "Be the change you wish to see in the world" fit us well.

"Attractive?" she snorted. "The UPS guy is attractive; men with gray hair on their temples are attractive. Marcy said he was hot! That's more than attractive." She put her mug down in front of her, attempting to avoid her eyes.

I sat down, wrapped both hands around my mug, and lifted my thumbs up so I could read the words printed on mine, "Life always offers a second chance…Tomorrow."

Had my Tomorrow finally come? Was Gavin my second chance?

"Spill!" she blurted out.

"Fine, he is very attractive," I groaned. "Okay, fine, he's beyond attractive, he's gorgeous, but it's not only his looks, Gavin is a nice guy."

"Nice guy, huh?" She took a sip of her coffee, wisps of steam floated past her face. "What makes him so nice?"

I shrugged, "I don't know. He just is." Should I tell her about how he dealt with Mary? Or maybe how he saved me from falling through the floor in the apartment, or the way he looked at me and I felt things I had never felt before?

"You need to start talking. I want to know everything that happened, and don't you dare leave a thing out." She pointed a finger at me in warning.

I contemplated her words for a few moments. "Fine," I huffed out, and for the next hour, I shared the entire day, from the moment he walked into my office, until the text message of the night before. I told her how I was feeling, what I was thinking, and what I was wondering, and she sipped her coffee and nodded in understanding once in a while.

When I finished, Brooke sat back in her seat and asked one simple question: "When can I meet him?"

"Why do you want to meet him?" I asked cautiously.

"Because he sounds too good to be true." We both laughed.

I glanced at my watch. "Actually, if we left now, we could pick up some food and bring them lunch." The thought of seeing Gavin ignited a flame in my belly.

She placed both of her palms down on the table, "What are we waiting for?"

* * *

Forty minutes later, with sandwiches and drinks from a local deli in hand, we pulled up to the shelter. I wiped my damp palms on my jeans before I got out of Brooke's car.

I wasn't sure how I felt about seeing Gavin again. It felt like I had a mangled mess of excitement and nervousness all wound up like silly string in my stomach.

Brooke seemed to read my mind—or my stomach—when she said, "Take a deep breath."

The aide on duty met us at the front entrance, and we chatted with her for a few minutes before getting on the elevator. As the elevator moved up, my stomach did the opposite, it dropped somewhere around the area of my knees.

"Why are you so nervous?" Brooke inquired cautiously. She knew me so well. Over the years we had come to be able to read each other's moods almost better than we read ourselves.

"I honestly don't know. Maybe because I spent all night thinking about him, and it's the first time in years that I actually thought about a man in good terms." I leaned my head back against the cold metal wall. I felt tempted to lean my heated cheek to it.

"I get that. I did the same thing when I started seeing Rick. I'd get myself so worked up before I saw him that I would spend the first hour we were together trying to unknot the tension in myself." She rubbed my arm, "Just take it one step at a time. If there is something there, let it come naturally. Don't rush it."

The ding of the elevator rang out, and I tensed. "Relax," Brooke comforted, "I'm right beside you." She winked at me and we stepped out of the elevator.

The sounds of breaking wood, saws, and pounding hammers filled the hallway. At the entrance to the apartment, three young boys sat wide-eyed and cross-legged staring intently into the room.

As we approached, one of them jumped up and ran towards us. "Ms. Trinity, did you see what they were doing to the room?"

"I haven't seen it yet," I replied. "What's going on in there?"

"They are pulling up all the floors!" He spread his hands in a wide gesture, "They even took out the carpet."

"Wow!" I echoed his enthusiasm for him. "You guys are staying out of the way, right? I wouldn't want you guys to get hurt."

He nodded enthusiastically, "Yes. They told us we had to stay out here in the hall, but they kept the door open so we could watch."

"That's great!" I patted him on the head, and Brooke and I peered into the doorway ourselves.

"Oh, good Lord, what a mess," Brooke said under her breath.

Mike spotted us, "Wow, not just one, but both of you. To what do we owe this honor?" He dusted his hands off on his pants.

"Mike, it's so good to see you again." Brooke stepped into the room, being careful to watch where she was walking. All the noise in the room stopped, and I scanned the area but didn't see Gavin.

There were three teenaged boys on their knees, each with a hammer in his hand. I stood beside Brooke trying not to be disappointed that Gavin wasn't around. Was he working downstairs?

From around the corner, a tall man walked out. I assumed it was Gavin's brother-in-law since I didn't know him. He flipped his gaze between Brooke and me for a moment and then turned his full focus on me with a bright smile.

"You must be Trinity." He held his hand out, "I'm Taylor."

I slipped my hand into his calloused one and smiled up into his bright hazel eyes. "Hi, Taylor. It is such a pleasure to meet you. Thank you so much for helping us out. You have no idea how much it means to us that you are doing this, especially over the weekend."

"The pleasure is all mine," Taylor said right before I felt a hand on the small of my back. The touch was light, but I would have recognized it anywhere. I looked over my shoulder and into Gavin's face. He met my gaze and held it for a moment. His hand stilled on my back as he stood by my side. A shiver of excitement rushed through me.

"Are you kidding? Greta would have put him in the dog house if he had refused."

"Greta?" I repeated, looking between the two men.

"My very opinionated sister and his very devoted wife." Gavin grinned.

"You're right, she would have," Taylor chuckled.

"Hi, I'm Brooke Patterson, Trinity's partner." She put her hand out to Taylor and then to Gavin. I watched her profile as she gave him the once over.

Mike asked Taylor a question about something that needed to be done, and they walked away. Gavin turned to study me. I bit my lower lip, afraid to turn and meet his stare.

Brooke, being the good friend that she was, left my side and joined in on the conversation with Taylor and Mike. I chewed the inside of my cheek, waiting to see if Gavin would say anything.

He didn't, and I sucked in a breath and spun towards him, "Have you guys eaten?" I tried to keep my eyes on his face and not let them wander down the wide chest that filled out his t-shirt. I could try all I wanted, it wasn't going to happen. I let my eyes slide down his neck when he glanced at the bags I carried.

"No, we haven't. We were just talking about taking a break. We've gotten a lot accomplished."

"Then it looks like we are right on time." I lifted the bags filled with food.

"You know the way to a man's heart," he grinned, "food."

We shared a laugh, and he reached for one of the bags. Our fingers brushed and our eyes locked for a moment. I released the bag quickly and turned to see Mike and Brooke watching us. I caught the brief glance they shared and turned away so they wouldn't see my blush.

Brooke corralled the troops and we went down to the courtyard to use the picnic tables. Kids played on the playground, and a few volunteers sat and enjoyed the beautiful summer day. A group of women sat at another table, and while they said hello, they kept their distance from the men with us.

Taylor and Gavin both avoided looking at the other table, and I had to commend them for that. They didn't want to appear antagonistic, and I really appreciated their compassion.

I sat down at the picnic table with Gavin beside me. The three boys that had been working with the men found a spot on the grass, away from the adults. Taylor sat on the other side of Gavin, pushing Gavin closer to me.

The urge to shy away from his proximity rushed through me, but when his leg bumped into mine, I didn't feel threatened. In fact, I felt just the opposite. I was intrigued by the way the very spot his leg touched mine appeared warmer than it had before.

The conversation at the table revolved around the work they were doing. Brooke asked questions, and I tried to stay focused, but from time to time, my elbow would bump his, or his leg would tap against mine, and all sense would dissolve again.

We were finishing up, and Taylor was sharing a funny story of another project he had worked on when my cellphone rang. I pulled it out of my purse and looked at the caller ID.

"Damn, it's Marcy." I spun on the bench and got up to take the phone call away from the table.

"What's going on, Marcy?" I walked towards a quiet corner of the courtyard.

"I'm so sorry for bothering you, Trinity, but I just got a call from the hospital. It looks like Tabitha was assaulted again."

"Is she alright?" I glanced back at Brooke and waved her over.

"The charge nurse said she was pretty banged up, but they won't give me any real details. Tabitha said she won't talk to anyone but you."

As Brooke approached, I told Marcy to hold on so I could relay the information. I confirmed which hospital Marcy was in, and we hung up.

"Sorry to eat and run, but we have to go," Brooke announced as we got back. She wadded up her paper and wiped some crumbs to the ground.

"Everything alright?" Mike asked before he popped a chip in his mouth.

I answered him while Brooke threw our trash away, "Not sure, but it looks like Wayne found Tabitha again."

Mike's face hardened and he stopped chewing. "Is she okay?"

"I don't know that yet. She won't talk to anyone but me. We're going down to the hospital now."

"Wait, are you talking about Tabitha Streams and Wayne Drummond?" Gavin shifted in his seat and tilted his head back to look me in the face.

I turned to him in surprise. "You know them?"

"Yeah, I arrested him the last time he beat her up. She refused to come to court to testify, so he got off."

"She what?" I turned to Mike. "I thought she said she went to court."

"She told me she did." Mike looked concerned, and I could understand why. We did our best to protect them, but we expected our clients to not lie to us and to follow through on prosecuting those who harmed them.

"Where did you arrest them?" I turned back to Gavin, suddenly needing to know something.

"Where they live," he answered cautiously, and I searched his face, but it was blank.

"You work for Sandy Hill." It wasn't a question. I clenched my jaw. He worked in the department where I lived, and he hadn't told me. Why?

"Yes." His tone and eyes were guarded.

I glared at him. I wasn't sure why I was livid, but I was. Had he known all along where I lived? He stood up, and I stepped away from him.

"Why didn't you tell me?" I clutched my purse in both hands. Why hadn't he said anything when he dropped me off yesterday?

He shrugged, "It never came up. I didn't think it was a big deal."

Brooke stepped around the table and took my arm, "And it's not a big deal. Let's go, Trinity. We have to get to the hospital."

Brooke's grip broke me out of my interrogation. She stopped and turned around before we got to the door. "Gavin, can you do me a favor?"

I didn't stick around to see what favor she wanted. I needed to put distance between Gavin and me to determine why I was so upset.

As soon as Brooke got the car on the road and heading in the direction of the hospital, she turned on me, "What the hell was that?"

Unsure what to say, I kept my eyes averted.

"Trinity, why are you so angry that he works for Sandy Hill Police Department?

"I don't know. Maybe because he came to my house and didn't bother saying, 'Oh, by the way, I work this area.'" I answered sarcastically.

"So?" Brooke glanced at me then back to the road.

"So? Brooke, he was at my house. He should have told me. Don't you think it is kind of strange that I run into him ten years later, here? What are the odds?"

"What? You think he's stalking you?" Brooke laughed and stopped at a traffic light. I glared at her profile.

"I don't think he's stalking me, but don't you think it is weird that we both end up here, in Sandy Hill?"

"Trinity, I don't think it is weird at all. I think it's fate."

I snorted and turned to look through the glass again. "Fate, yeah, okay."

"Taylor is his brother-in-law, right? And he mentioned a sister. What was her name?"

"Greta, I think," I mumbled.

"Yes, it was Greta, so obviously he came back here to be with them. The question is probably why he was living down there in the first place, but, Trinity, I don't think you have any reason to be angry with him."

I thought about what she said, and it made sense. I had overreacted, which was not normal for me. Ever since seeing Gavin again, there were a lot of things that weren't normal going on in my life—like lying in bed thinking about a man that I barely knew, for hours. "You're right. I guess it just surprised me when he said it.

I've been living here for years, and he works right here, and I didn't know it. I wonder if he did."

"I think you will have to ask him that." As if on cue, my cellphone rang, and I pulled it out of my purse. Gavin's name filled my screen.

I swallowed. "Yes, Gavin," I said as I answered.

"Trinity, are you alright?" Concern filled his voice, and I felt ashamed that I had questioned him.

"I'm sorry, Gavin, I was shocked to find out you worked right where I live."

"Trinity, I'm sorry. You're right. I should have said something to you last night, but I really didn't think it was a big deal."

"And it's not. Let's just put it behind us, alright?" I suggested.

"No, I don't want us to just push it aside. You were upset for a reason, and I want us to talk about it later when we have time."

"You do?" Most men would have said, Oh, great, sweep that issue under the bed and let's move forward. Gavin surprised me.

"Yeah, I don't want there to be any more surprises like that, um..." he hesitated for a moment, "would you be interested in having dinner with me?"

I sat up straighter in my seat. "Dinner?" I choked on my surprise.

"Yes, that thing you do in the evening when you nourish your body," he teased.

"I know what dinner is, Gavin."

Brooke chortled beside me, and I glared at her. She mouthed the words, Say yes.

"When?" I asked cautiously.

"Well, I was going to say tonight, but it looks like you will be tied up for a while, and we just decided to pull a longer day today and then do a short one tomorrow, so what about tomorrow evening?"

My heart rate accelerated, and I switched my cellphone to my other hand. I glanced at Brooke, she was nodding her head up and down dramatically.

I closed my eyes, "Okay."

"Really?" His voice hit a higher note than normal, before his deep voice grew warm over the phone. "I'll call you tomorrow, and we can decide on a time."

I acknowledged him and was just about to say goodbye when Gavin stopped me, "Wait, you got me sidetracked. This wasn't why I called. I mean it was, but Brooke had asked me to look into something."

"Okay, what was it? She's driving, so I'll let her know." Brooke raised an eyebrow.

"Tell her that Wayne left the scene before officers arrived, so he's not in custody."

"Were charges filed? Is there a warrant out for him?" I asked, after I relayed the info to Brooke who was worrying her bottom lip.

"From what I could find out," he hesitated, "no."

"What? If it was bad enough for her to be hospitalized, charges need to be filed."

"I agree, Trinity, but when I was talking to the sergeant, he said that she wouldn't talk to them, and she refused to give a statement."

"If I can convince her, will they file charges?" I held my breath because I wasn't sure I could convince her.

I heard him sigh on the other end, "I'd like to think so, but, Trinity, this guy has been charged six times, and she refuses to cooperate. She has always given a statement and then doesn't show up for the hearings. The department is getting tired of doing all this work, and then she doesn't even bother to show up."

"That's your job," I snapped.

"I know, Trinity, I'm well aware of that, but not everyone looks at domestic violence victims the way I do."

"Who was the responding officer?" I put my head back against my seat and took a deep breath.

"Do you remember that guy from the seminar, the arrogant one that volunteered for your experiment?"

"Of course I do. His name was Derek, right?"

"Yep, that's the one. He was the officer who responded to the call."

"Yeah, and I bet his attitude did wonders with Tabitha," I muttered.

We spoke for another moment and then we got off the phone so I could relay the info to Brooke, which in turn led me to talk about the jerk from the seminar. By the time we pulled up to the hospital, I was determined to get Tabitha to give a statement and to follow through with the charges, even if I had to drag her to the court hearings personally.

Chapter 10 - Gavin

The run had done me good, but even with four miles of pounding on the asphalt, the tense memory clung to the edges of my mind. It felt more like a foreboding threat than a dream in some ways.

I met Taylor at his house, and he followed me over to the shelter. When he got out he whistled, "Nice place, you were right. It is a lot different than the other places I have worked on."

Mike met us at the front door and welcomed Taylor easily. Mike had managed to wrangle up three teenaged boys to help us, and between the six of us, we got all the tools upstairs and started tearing things out. By late morning, the memories of the dream still clung to me like sand at the beach. The temptation to send Trinity a text message just to ease my worries found me with my hand on my cellphone time and time again, but I kept putting it away.

While in the small bathroom, I heard a woman's voice in the living area, and I rushed to wash my hands. An intense wave of relief crashed over me as I took in Trinity's form. Her jeans hugged her hips and thighs while her T-shirt flowed lightly over her back. I liked this look on her.

I slipped my hand onto her lower back, the need to reassure myself that she was there and alright would only be curbed by the touch of her body. I feared she would flinch, but she didn't.

Her eyes flashed to mine over her shoulder, and a look crossed over her face, but it happened so fast, I couldn't discern its meaning.

Her skin was free of makeup, and her hair was down. She looked beautiful and alive as she inspected me. Her eyes flicked down over my chest and a little sliver of heat wound its way through my blood. I feared that if I moved, she would stop her appraisal, and I forced myself to stand still.

Her business partner was a beautiful woman in her own right, but didn't come close to comparing to the beauty of Trinity. Brooke inspected me openly, and I wondered what Trinity had told her.

Lunch was a relaxing event, until Trinity got a phone call. When she had mentioned Tabitha and Wayne, it surprised me enough to blurt out that we had arrested them. I didn't even think about the jurisdiction issue until Trinity asked where I worked.

She was right, I should have told her last night when I took her home. I could have made an offhand comment how we both ended up in the same area after so many years, but I didn't. I saw my mistake as soon as the first sparks flared in her green eyes.

Trinity stalked away, and Brooke asked me if I would dig into the latest incident. I told Brooke I would do my best.

The other sergeant I worked with answered his cellphone on the second ring, "Hey, Gavin, you're off today, why are you calling me?"

"Hey, Coven, I was wondering if you know anything about an incident involving Wayne Drummond from earlier today." I paced the empty corner of the courtyard.

"Yeah, we got a call early this morning. Looks like he beat up his old lady again and then took off. Derek handled the call. Derek said she refused to give a statement and was taken to the hospital to be treated for her injuries."

"Is Derek filing charges on him?" I knew the answer before I even asked the question.

He laughed, "What do you think?"

Anger spread through me. That prick. "Coven, I know it's not my place to say anything, but he should have filed charges. We all know that if we go to an incident and we see signs of domestic assault, we need to make an arrest."

"I know. That is easier said than done, especially in this case. She refused to tell him who did it to her. If we don't know for sure, and she won't cooperate, what are we supposed to do?" I considered that for a moment. "Besides, no matter how many times we arrest that guy, she never appears in court."

Frustration reared its ugly head, and I blew out an aggravated burst of air, "Yeah, I know. Alright, thanks for the information."

"Why the interest, Gavin?" Coven asked before we hung up.

"A friend who knows the victim asked me to find out what I could."

"Well, if your friend wants to help her, she needs to get her to give us a statement *and* get her to show up in court for once."

"If there is anyone who can do that, it's Trinity," I said with a smile.

"Trinity, as in Trinity Morris?" he asked.

I stopped pacing, "Yes, why?" Something in his voice made me curious.

"I didn't know you knew her. I've worked with her before, nice lady—hot, too, but cold as ice. How do you know her?"

Anger prickled down my spine at Trinity being called cold. "I met her at a seminar."

He seemed satisfied with that answer, and we hung up. I brought Trinity's phone number up on the screen and took a calming breath before I pushed the button to call her.

She answered her phone, and I hesitated, I'd expected it to go to voicemail. She surprised me again when she apologized first. A weight was lifted off my mind when I realized she wasn't angry, but that didn't mean I wanted anything else like this to come between us. Unlike most guys, I liked to talk about things and air them out, not cover them over. I had spent too many years just glossing over issues.

While I gathered my courage to ask her out to dinner, I closed my eyes. I felt like a teenager asking the girl I had crushed on all year to the prom. I wondered if Brooke sitting beside her in the car helped influence the decision. I didn't care, I was just happy she said yes.

Right before she hung up, I remembered that there was another reason that I had called, and we discussed what I had learned from Coven. I knew she wouldn't be happy to hear who the officer was, and I seriously hoped she could talk Tabitha into pressing charges.

Mike, Taylor, and I got back to work. Each of us worked one on one with the boys to help instruct them and to give them some personal attention at the same time. It wasn't hard to figure out that they needed a strong male influence and probably had never been told they had done a good job at anything. Even when mistakes were made, we didn't get upset, we explained why it was wrong and allowed them to do it again to correct the problem.

By the early evening, we were all tired, and Greta had sent a message to tell Taylor she had plenty of food and that I should come over for dinner. I bowed out, telling Taylor I'd take a raincheck.

I hadn't decided yet, but I was tempted to swing by Trinity's and see how things had gone. Would that be stepping over the line? Maybe I should send her a text message instead.

I decided that I would drive by and see if any lights were on. If there weren't, I would go get a shower and then message her later.

As I drove down her street, I saw a marked patrol car slowing in front of her house. When I got closer, I recognized Derek. The hair raised on the back of my neck. He noticed my car and stopped beside me.

"What are you doing in this neighborhood?" He hung his arm out the window and thumped his thumb on the door.

"Just checking on a friend. What are you doing over here? You on a call?"

"Nope, just doing some patrol." He snapped the gum he chewed, and it reminded me of a cow chewing its cud.

"Alright, well, have a good night."

He nodded in response, snapped his gum, and pulled away with a heavy foot on the accelerator. I watched through my rearview mirror as he drove down the road and barely slowed down before blowing a stop sign and turning right.

Jerk, I thought to myself.

I glanced at Trinity's house and didn't see any lights on. She must still be at the hospital. I sighed and headed home.

About fifteen times I thought about sending her a message, and it was only after I had showered, eaten, and watched a program on television that I finally allowed myself to send a simple message to see if everything had gone alright.

Trinity wrote back a few minutes later, *Yes, still at hospital. She is going to file a report. Thank you for asking.*

Is there anything I can do to help? I typed back.

Got any Calgon? Calgon? What the hell was Calgon?

I stared at the word for a minute, wondering if she had mistyped and her phone had autocorrect, but I couldn't figure out what she might have been trying to say.

Um…maybe? What's Calgon? I finally typed back.

I could hear the laughter in her written words when she finally answered, *Lol…Calgon take me away. You know that commercial for bubble bath?*

Immediately, the memory of that commercial from when I was a child flashed in my mind, and I could recall my own mother saying that from time to time when I wouldn't behave.

Ah, yes, I remember, and no I don't have any. Anything else?

Not tonight. Not tonight, huh? Maybe tomorrow night I could do something for her. I grinned at the phone.

Okay, well let me know if you need anything before tomorrow night. And dress is very casual tomorrow night, jeans and sneakers casual.

Lol…Okay thank you for the heads up, good night.

I typed a quick good night back to her and took a moment to reread our conversation.

The thought of her in a bubble bath stirred some interesting ideas, and I finally dropped the phone and picked up the television remote to surf.

Chapter 11 - Trinity

Brooke and I met in the lobby and took the elevator up together. I contemplated how to talk Tabitha into giving a statement and actually attending the hearing. If Tabitha didn't do something now, she wouldn't have a chance later because it would be too late. The violence with Wayne was escalating.

We found Tabitha had been put in a room on the third floor. Neither of us spoke as we rode up the elevator and located her room.

I followed Brooke into the semi-private room and past the first bed. An older woman occupied the bed closest to the door, and she watched us as we passed by without a word or a smile. The curtain was pulled to separate the two beds. I gave a strained smile to the woman but said nothing.

Tabitha was staring out the window, the side of her face swollen and purple. I winced inwardly. Her right eye had closed because of the swelling. Her right arm was in a cast up past her elbow and lay heavily over her stomach.

Brooke walked to her left side, and Tabitha startled when she saw her. Tabitha turned to look at the end of the bed and met my gaze. Tears filled her one brown eye, and I might have shared in those emotions if I hadn't been so angry.

I was so frustrated that Tabitha was here, again, and that she refused to talk to the police.

"Why didn't you tell the police who did this, Tabitha?" I spoke from the foot of her bed, not mincing words. There was no reason to ask how she was, we could see that for ourselves. Brooke reached out and took Tabitha's left hand. I knew Brooke was angry, too, but she would be the one offering sympathy right now. I could not.

Tabitha looked away from me, "I don't know."

"That's not a good reason, try again." I tried to squelch the frustration from coming out in my voice, but it was hard to keep my pitch level.

Tabitha shrugged, and I wanted to scream, not at her, I understood how hard it was to talk to the police. I was frustrated at the system.

Brooke asked gently, "Tabitha, why weren't you at the shelter?"

"I have been staying at the shelter, but I had to go see my mom. She needed help with something and someone must have told him I was there," she answered quietly, her eye fixed on her blanket.

"You know you aren't supposed to go back there, not alone. You didn't tell anyone you were going, did you?" Brooke asked her.

She shook her head, and I sighed. "Tabitha, when are you going to understand that we can only do so much to help you? You have to help us."

"I know, but my mom needed my help," she whined.

"We have people who could have escorted you to make sure you were safe. You know we have that available for our clients."

"I didn't think it would be a big deal. I was only running a few errands for her because her car was broken, and I dropped off the medicine and food she needed. I was getting ready to leave when he showed up."

I clenched my jaw in an attempt to curb the irritation that still flowed through me. "What happened?"

She refused to look at either of us, "He was pissed that I disappeared again. I ran up the stairs, but he came after me, punched me in the face and threw me down the steps." She lifted her cast up. "That's how I broke my arm."

"Who called the police?" Brooke asked.

"My mom." She wiped at the tears on her cheek.

"Tabitha, you have to talk to the police," I urged as I stepped around the bed. My anger was now transferred from her and the situation to the dirt bag that put her in here.

Her head snapped up, "But it never does any good!" She shook her head. "He gets off."

Before I could speak, Brooke did, "He gets off because you refuse to testify against him." Her voice was stern but not hard.

"I can't." Tabitha plucked at her blanket.

"You have to, Tabitha," I reached out and touched her leg. "If you don't testify, he will never be held accountable for it. You can't just give a statement and then not show up."

She sniffed, "He said he would kill me if I testified."

"He is going to kill you if you don't." I squeezed her leg and let go.

"Don't you have an advocate assigned to you? They should be there at the hearings with you," Brooke said as she sank into the chair beside the bed.

"I don't like her," Tabitha stated and looked in the other direction.

Brooke and I shared a long glance. "What if one of us went with you, would you go?" Brooke asked finally.

Tabitha looked between the two of us. "You would do that?"

I smiled down at her for the first time since I'd entered the room, "Of course." She finally nodded and I left the room to make a phone call.

An hour later, we sat beside her bed talking about random things when I heard the heavy footfalls of booted feet, the metallic rattle of handcuffs, and a voice that straightened my spine. I stood up as the man walked past the curtain to Tabitha's bed. Tabitha unconsciously shrank from him.

"Oh, it's her again," Derek shot off. "You want to waste more of my time?" His eyes scanned the area and landed on mine. His smirk raised my hackles. "Ah, look, it's goodie two shoes here to help you out."

"Get out of here," I seethed.

"What?" He held his hands up. "I was told to come here and take a statement. She should have just given it earlier and saved us all a lot of work—not that her giving one now will do any good, she won't show up."

"Get out of here," I said again forcefully. "You are not taking her statement." I moved to the end of the bed. Fury raged through me at the audacity of this man. "And if you keep this attitude up, I will have your badge."

Fire blazed from his eyes, and the lines on his face pulled taut. "Don't you ever threaten my job. You're a worthless woman who can't take care of herself, just like her." He nodded in Tabitha's direction. If I were a foot closer, I would have slapped him. Brooke must have sensed it because she put her hand around my forearm to hold me steady.

"Get out of this room, now," I repeated in a voice I barely recognized.

"Worthless," he spat and stalked out.

I released a heavy shaky breath, "I'm going to call down to the station and see if I can get someone else here to take your statement."

"They are all going to be like that. They don't believe me when I tell them." Tabitha's voice shook.

"Not all of them are like that." I wished I could call Gavin and have him come in and take her statement, he would understand. Brooke and I shared a knowing look. I didn't have to say his name for her to know I was thinking about him. I left the room to make another call to the police department.

This time I asked for the sergeant on duty to return my call, and I explained what had transpired with his officer. He asked if I wanted to file a complaint, and I thought about that for only a moment before I replied in the affirmative. He said he would bring the paperwork with him.

When Sergeant Coven entered the room, Tabitha tensed, but she relaxed as she watched us talk around her.

"Ms. Morris, it's good to see you again." He held his hand out, and I shook it.

"Nice to see you, again, Sergeant." I released his hand after a quick shake. "Do you know my associate, Brooke Patterson?"

Brooke stood and held out her hand, "I don't think we have ever met, Sergeant Coven. It is nice to meet you."

"The pleasure is all mine. I'm sorry about your run-in with Derek." He met Tabitha's eyes, "He should not have said those things to you."

"No need to apologize, it wasn't your fault," Brooke said as she sat back down.

"No, it's not my fault, but the officers are trained to handle things differently." He opened his clipboard, pulled out a paper, and handed it to me, "Here is the complaint form, Ms. Morris."

"Call me Trinity, please, and thank you." I took the form from him.

"You're going to file a complaint against him?" Tabitha asked quickly, fear stark in her brown eyes.

"Yes, I am, Tabitha. His behavior here was not right, and he needs to learn he can't treat people, especially victims, like he did."

"He's going to be pissed." Her eyes widened and filled with apprehension.

"That's not something you need to be worried about," I reassured her as I slid the paper into my purse.

Sergeant Coven spoke up, "There is no need for you to worry about that, Tabitha. Now, I brought my camera. I'd like to take a few pictures of you. I know that's uncomfortable for you, but I need to do that, okay?"

He stood at the end of the bed, and Tabitha turned to me, I nodded encouragement and squeezed her knee. Tabitha gave an abrupt nod at Sergeant Coven, and Brooke and I moved out of the way. As I did, I heard a text arrive on my phone.

I took my phone with me as we stood in the corner so the sergeant could work with Tabitha. Gavin had sent me a message, and a little thrill ran through me. We texted for a moment and said goodbye.

When I looked at Brooke, she was grinning from ear to ear. "What?" I asked her.

"Nothing, it's good to see you smile."

I rolled my eyes at her, and she laughed at me.

We stood by for another hour while Tabitha gave her statement. Once they finished, we talked with her for a few moments and said we would be there with her every step of the way, but she needed to help us too.

I arrived home around eight-thirty and fed Callie. I wasn't joking when I asked Gavin if he had any Calgon. I could have used a nice long bath.

With Callie lying beside the tub, I sank into the soft sweetly-scented bath and leaned back. What a day, I thought as I allowed the warm water to relax my muscles.

I was satisfied that Tabitha had given the statement, but I would not be overly happy until I knew she had appeared in court and testified against Wayne. I sighed and sank lower in the hot water.

My thoughts shifted from the incident to the conversation I'd had with Gavin. He told me to dress casually. Where was he taking me that I should wear jeans and sneakers? Was he a cheap date and were we hitting one of the local fast food joints?

I tensed as I realized that he had the control on this. I had no idea where we were going. Should I call him and ask him? I pondered that for a few moments. No, I had to start trusting, and he seemed like the type I could trust—but what if he wasn't?

I picked my cellphone off the floor beside the tub and dialed Brooke.

"Please tell me there is not a problem. I just sat down with a glass of wine," Brooke said by way of answering. Her husband's voice murmured in the background.

"No. I don't know where we are going tomorrow," I blurted out.

"What are you talking about, Trin? Where who is going?"

"Gavin and I. He asked me out to dinner, but then he told me that I needed to dress casually, like jeans casual. I don't know where he is taking me, and I'm starting to get nervous about that."

"Did you ask him where he was taking you?" she questioned.

"No."

"Are you in the bath?" she laughed again.

"Yes, I was trying to relax, and then I started thinking about it and got all freaked out." I lifted a handful of bubbles up and studied them as if they were little crystal balls that would tell me the future.

"Stop freaking out. Gavin seems like a really nice guy. I'm sure he's taking you someplace fun."

"Yeah, well the prick I was married to was nice when I first met him, and I almost ended up dead."

"But you're not, and it's time for you to get back out there and live. If it makes you feel better, why don't you ask him where you are going? Tell him your concerns." Brooke was always so positive.

"I can't. He'll think I'm a basketcase," I pouted.

"Cut that out. You are a basketcase, and we all know it," she joked.

"Hey," I realized that just saying it all out loud showed me I was being foolish. "Okay, fine. I get it, I just need to sit back and go with the flow."

"Exactly—and start with enjoying the rest of your bath. It should be easy if you just think about how those jeans hugged his thighs." She chortled over the phone, and I joined her.

We hung up a few minutes later, and I set the phone back and did just what she suggested. While I pictured his lean strong legs, the bathwater began to feel warmer instead of cooler. For the first time in years, it seemed like my hormones were waking up. Was that good or bad?

Chapter 12 - Gavin

"Hey, Gavin, can you help me with this?"

I put my hammer down and told the kid beside me to keep working while I went to help Taylor.

I grabbed the end of the board and helped my brother-in-law carry it into the kitchen. We went back for a second one and butted it up flush to the first one. Part of a third one would be needed to cover the final area before the underlayment was placed and the vinyl tiles installed.

"You looking forward to tonight?" Taylor asked me as we adjusted the boards.

I grinned at him, "Maybe."

He snorted, "No maybe about it. You've been grinning like an idiot since you showed up this morning."

"Why is it that you are grinning?" Mike joined the conversation as he passed through to pick up some more nails.

I shrugged, not sure how he would feel about me taking Trinity out, but Taylor slapped me on the back and blasted a huge smile at Mike. "He's taking Trinity out tonight."

Mike's eyebrows arched high, mimicking the famous golden arch restaurant sign. I waited to see what he would say.

"Is this the first time you two are going out?" His shoulders rolled back, and I had a feeling that his father instinct had just kicked in.

"Yes, sir," I replied and made sure to maintain eye contact.

He tilted his head to study me for a minute. "Good." He spun around and began to walk away, calling out over his shoulder, "You hurt that woman, and I'll come after you."

One of the boys working with us asked Mike what woman we were talking about, and Mike told him I was taking Trinity out on a date. All three boys stared at me with wide eyes. The two older boys smirked at me, and one of the boys spoke quietly to Mike. Mike laughed and patted the boy on the shoulder.

"Hey, if you're going to talk about me, you can at least say it so I can hear it," I called out good-naturedly.

Mike sank to his knees before he looked back up at me, "He said that if you hurt her, he's going to help me go after you."

Everyone in the room laughed, including me. "Okay, you convinced me—not that I was scared of Mike, but, Robby, you I'm scared of."

For the next few minutes, I got some good old-fashioned ribbing from the guys. We finished our work shortly after lunch time. We would need one more full day here and then a few hours the next day to complete the unit downstairs. We had made great progress.

Taylor and I walked out to our cars when he asked, "What time?"

"I want to pick her up at six-thirty, so I hope by seven," I answered him while he climbed inside his truck.

"Okay, sounds good." He waved and pulled away.

I hopped into my Jeep and picked up my phone before I started my engine. The phone rang twice before Trinity's husky voice answered.

"Hello there, sunshine, how is your day going?" I said as I leaned back in my seat and stared out the windshield.

"Hello, Gavin," she laughed, "things are going well. How are things at the apartment?"

Her dog barked once in the background and then a thud sounded over the phone. Callie must have gone out the dog door. "Good, we just finished up for the day. That's why I'm calling you. I wanted to make sure you still wanted to go out tonight."

There was silence on the phone, and I held my breath, afraid that she would say she had changed her mind. After a few moments, she finally spoke.

"Gavin, can I ask you a question?"

I hoped to calm her with a little banter. "I think you just did. Did you want to ask another one?"

The sound of her amusement was music to my ears, and I grinned. "Okay, yes, I'd like to ask you another question." Her voice sounded stronger.

"Sure, go right ahead."

"Um…where are we going? I know you said to dress casual, but I," she hesitated, "okay, here's the thing. Ever since the trial, I have been a total control freak, and this is the first time I have gone out with a man since then, and I'm a little nervous about where we are going. Okay, I'm a whole lot nervous about the whole thing, so if you could just tell me where we are going, so I know I'll be safe, then I'll, wow…I'm rambling. Okay, I'll just shut up now."

I could imagine her cheeks flushing with color when she realized she had been going on and on. I tried not to laugh, but it was so damned cute that a small one rumbled out of my chest anyway.

"Trinity, relax. I'm not going to tell you where we are going because I want to surprise you, but I will tell you that there will be lots of people there, so we won't be alone, and you won't feel uncomfortable being with me. I promise."

"It's not that, Gavin. I do feel comfortable with you." My heart swelled at her comment. "It's just that," she paused, "I'm sorry. You're right. I will dress casually and be ready. What time?" Her voice had gained confidence, and I hoped that had something to do with how I had answered.

"Six-thirty, is that alright?"

She told me it was, and we hung up the phone. I started my car and pulled out of the lot. I had a few errands to run before I went home to get ready.

* * *

At six-twenty-five I pulled into her driveway and heard Callie begin to bark. I could see her on the other side of the fence. Once she saw me she darted toward the house, most likely through her dog door. I knew I was right when a few moments later, I heard her bark just behind the front door.

Trinity's voice reached me as she reminded Callie that I was a friend. My stomach quivered in my abdomen as my nervous energy pulsed through me. I had dreamed of this for years, and it was finally coming true.

She looked as nervous as I felt when she pulled the door back, and Callie stayed close to her side. Dogs could feel the emotions, and Callie had picked up on the apprehension. She didn't growl at me, but she did stare me down. I didn't move from my spot and glanced over at Trinity to find she had stopped chewing her bottom lip and was smiling at me.

"Hello, Gavin. Can you wait outside for a moment? I'll just get my purse and then meet you outside."

"No problem," I stepped back slowly and waited until the door closed before I turned from the doorway. I took in her front porch, the swing at the end, and could picture the two of us seated on it, relaxing.

The door opened and broke me out of the fantasy I was weaving. My heart thudded in my chest, and I wiped my damp palms on my pants.

"You all ready?" I asked her after she locked her door. She had taken my advice and worn jeans, hiking boots, and a rose-colored button-down blouse. I loved the way the color warmed her skin tone and enhanced her beauty.

"I am. Are you going to tell me where we are going now?" she questioned as we stepped off her porch.

I grinned at her, "Nope, but, like I told you on the phone, there are going to be lots and lots of people there, so you don't need to worry. We won't be alone."

She peered up at me with a nervous smile, and I pulled open the passenger door for her. She made a wide berth around me and settled into the seat. After I was in and started the car, I glanced her way, she looked so tense. "Would it make you feel any better if I told you that Taylor and my sister Greta will be there?"

"Really? I'm going to meet your sister? Are we going to their house?" Already, her features lost some of their tension.

"Yep, you get to meet my amazing and crazy sister and you also get to meet my nephew, but we aren't going to their house."

"Oh," she paused, "okay, yes, I do feel better." She hung her head for a moment then lifted it and met my watchful eyes, "Thank you."

"You bet. Tonight is about relaxing, having a good time, and just getting to know each other." I put the Jeep in reverse and we pulled out of the driveway. On the way to our destination, we talked casually about how things were going at the apartment, and I explained that we would be done within two days. By the time we were about to arrive, I realized that both of us had calmed completely. I prayed that she was going to enjoy what we were going to do and not look at me like I was crazy.

When I turned on my signal, she looked out the passenger window and laughed, "We're going to the fair?"

"Yep." I grinned at her when she turned to me. "I hope that's okay. I figured this was casual, lots of good food, some fun rides, I hope you like rides, and I was hoping to impress you with my skills at the arcade games, maybe win you a prize or two."

She threw her head back and laughed, it was the first time I had seen her so open and happy. My heart stuttered at the incredibly beautiful sight.

"This is perfect, Gavin! I love the fair, although I haven't gone in a few years, but I love it, and yes, I love the rides." She wiggled in her seat like a little girl, and I mentally patted myself on the back for taking Taylor's suggestion—well, actually Greta's suggestion.

"You aren't afraid of heights are you? Because I want to go on the Ferris wheel," she chattered on.

I parked the car and stared at her with a serious face, "I'm scared to death of heights."

Her shoulders slumped ever so slightly until I winked at her. She shook her head and laughed as we climbed out of the car.

"Actually, that is exactly where we are meeting Taylor and Greta, at the Ferris wheel." I was so tempted to slip my hand around hers, but feared she would react negatively to it, so I jammed my hands into the front pockets of my jeans.

"Can we go on that first? I haven't been on one of them in years." She concentrated for a moment, "I think it has been five years, yeah, five years since I came to a fair and got to ride one."

We were just entering the fairgrounds when I turned to her, "You can do whatever your heart desires tonight. It's all about having a good time."

My God, I wanted so badly to pull her into my arms and kiss her as her pupils dilated ever so slightly and her cheeks flushed.

She rested her hand on my bicep, "Thanks, Gavin. I'm already having a great time, just being with you." She pulled her hand away after she gave a soft squeeze. I could still feel the sensation a few minutes later when we located my family.

Taylor gave her a bright smile, while Greta's gaze was observant. She was giving Trinity the once over, and I wanted to tell her to stop, but I didn't want to make a scene.

"Hey, guys, glad you made it." Taylor held his hand out to us, and we both shook it. I placed my hand on Trinity's lower back as I introduced her to my sister.

"Trinity, this is my sister, Greta."

"Greta, it's a pleasure to meet you." She held her hand out, but my nephew grabbed it.

"I'm Peter!" he yelled while he yanked her hand down.

"Well, hello there, you must be Gavin's nephew." She crouched down so she could talk to him face to face. He stepped closer to her and let go of her hand to reach out and touch her hair.

"You have pretty hair," he exclaimed and then turned to Greta, "Mommy, why isn't your hair long like Triny's is?"

Trinity stood up, and her cheeks reddened. Greta laughed it off, "Because I like my hair short, buddy." She directed her next comment to Trinity, "Sorry, he's not shy in the slightest." She held her hand out and in that moment I knew my sister had accepted her. If her son immediately liked Trinity, then she did too. I winked at my sister when she cast a glance my way.

"And her name is not Triny, it's Trinity." She brushed his hair off his forehead.

"That's alright, a lot of kids end up calling me Triny. I'm kind of used to that."

A few moments later, Taylor and I wandered over to the ticket booth and purchased ride bracelets so we could ride as much as we wanted. When we returned to the ladies, I found Trinity squatting again, talking to my nephew. I couldn't keep the grin off my face at the picture the two of them made. She would make an incredible mother.

I put the bracelet on Trinity's wrist and, before I could say anything, she grabbed my hand and pulled me to get in line for the Ferris wheel. I went along happily, enjoying the feel of her fingers in mine. When we reached the end of the line, she looked at our hands as if she suddenly realized what she had done. I felt her fingers start to let go, and I grasped her hand just a tad more tightly. She met my gaze.

"I like it," I said softly.

The corners of her lips turned up. "Actually, I do, too." She lowered her chin, averting her eyes.

I had gotten her out on a date, and now she was holding my hand. I was ecstatic but forced myself not to whoop out loud.

When our turn came, I released her hand and followed her to the car that was ours. The carnival worker made sure the lap belt was secure and slammed down the front metal brace with a loud bang. Trinity flinched but kept the wide smile on her face.

The car started moving as Trinity giggled beside me. I put my arm on the back of the seat and rested my hand on her shoulder. She tensed for a moment and sent me a shy smile before relaxing.

And so our night began.

Chapter 13 - Trinity

I tried to focus on the normal mundane things around the house that needed to be done, but the closer it got to six-thirty, the more nervous I got. I was on the verge of calling Gavin and making an excuse when Brooke called.

"How you holding up?" she asked casually.

I sighed, "I'm a nervous wreck. I'm not sure I can do this. I don't think I'm ready to start dating. I was just thinking about calling Gavin and telling him I couldn't go."

"Don't you dare!" she all but shouted into the phone. "It has been almost ten years, Trinity. It's time to get back out there."

"But—" I started and she shut me down quick.

"No buts, period. I knew you would be second guessing your decision right now, that's why I called. I remember when I met Rick, I did the same thing you are doing, but you pushed me out of my comfort zone and made me go. Look how things turned out?"

"Yeah, but that was different," I complained.

She burst out a quick laugh, "No, it's not. Trinity, I know this is difficult, but so is speaking in front of a large group about what you went through. What is even better is that Gavin already knows this about you. You don't have to explain to him, he already gets it.

That makes this even more important that you go for it. You'll be safe with him, and it's obvious that he likes you."

I turned her words over in my head. She was right. Gavin did know me, and one of the reasons I had never reentered the dating field was because I wasn't sure I could explain my past and make someone understand my emotional insecurities.

"Well, I don't know if he likes me or not, but you are right. It does make it easier not having to explain it all." I ran my hand absently down Callie's back as she rubbed up against my leg.

"I get the whole insecurity when it comes to men, and trust me, he likes you. I could tell by the way he watched you yesterday."

"Whatever," I tossed out.

She laughed, "Not whatever—so did you find out where you are going? I know you asked him, even though I told you not to."

"No, I don't know." I had to laugh because she had caught me. "What I do know is that we are going to be around a lot of people and his sister and her family will be there."

"That made you feel better, I bet. Wow, you're meeting the family, too. I told you he likes you."

We joked for a few minutes, and when I finally hung up, I was less apprehensive than before the call. I could do this, in fact, I wanted to do this. I had told Gavin I wasn't interested in anything other than friendship, but spending the day with him last week and then seeing him and talking to him, I wanted to know more. In my heart, I wanted to feel more. Brooke was right, it was time.

* * *

I was scanning through some emails when I heard Callie bark and make a beeline for the front door. My entire body began to shake as I realized this was it. Oh God, please give me the strength to do this and let it go well.

I opened the door and just the mere sight of him began to ease my nerves. His dark denim jeans clung tightly to his hips and down his thighs. The gray polo shirt he wore stretched tightly over his chest and biceps—and those eyes, they shone in the late afternoon sun.

I grabbed my purse and met him on the porch, not sure what Callie would do since I knew she sensed my nervousness. We made small talk on the ride, and any bit of tension I had left in me fled with the twinkling lights and sounds of the fair. What a perfect first date.

Nerves tickled up my spine again when I was introduced to his sister, but little Peter helped the uncomfortable moment move right along, until Taylor and Gavin walked away to get tickets.

"I've heard a lot about you from Gavin," Greta said when they were out of earshot.

"Hopefully, it was good," I commented.

"Well, not all of it, of course. I know what happened. Gavin was torn up for a while after that. That's one of the reasons he moved home."

I didn't know what to say. I hadn't thought about Gavin telling her what had happened in my past.

She continued when I didn't say anything. "If anyone can understand what you went through, it's us. Someday I'll share my story with you," she gave me a warm smile, "but I just want to ask you to do me a favor."

I had no idea what she could want from me. "Okay," I said slowly.

She looked away and her gaze landed on the two men getting the tickets. "Gavin has had a thing for you for a very long time. Please, be careful with him. He's a good man, and he deserves to be happy."

I blushed at her words. How long had he had a thing for me? I wondered. "I know he's a good man, Greta, and I have no intention of hurting him. This is all new to me. I haven't been involved with anyone since…" I stopped not sure how to continue.

She nodded, understanding in her eyes. "It takes a long time to trust, I get that. You can trust Gavin, though. I promise."

"Triny, are you going to ride the airplanes with me?" Peter yanked on my hand to get my attention, and I bent down to look him in the eye.

"If you would like me to, I sure will."

"Yeah! Mommy, she's gonna ride the airplanes with me!" Peter turned back to me after his excited announcement and started talking about how much fun it was going to be. I told him that I would ride them right after I rode the Ferris wheel with his uncle.

Gavin slipped the bracelet on my wrist and, without thinking, I snagged his hand and pulled him straight to the line. I was so thrilled to be going on the ride that it wasn't until we were waiting that I realized I still had his hand in mine. A moment of embarrassment flashed through me, and I began to pull away, but he stopped me, and I realized I really did want to keep the connection between us. I glanced back to find his sister and family behind us. She winked at me.

We rode the Ferris wheel, and Gavin and I took turns going on some kiddie rides with Peter before we grabbed food from one of the vendors. When we were done, Taylor asked if we could watch Peter for a few minutes while they went on some of the adult rides. We meandered through the arcade area, and Gavin puffed up his chest when he declared he was going to win us both prizes.

Peter and I laughed while we watched Gavin using a water rifle to spray a target and winning a race against four other people. He won a small prize and then played again to win a second time, trading his small prize for a larger stuffed animal that he handed to Peter.

Peter wrapped his arm around the dog's neck and beamed with happiness, albeit tired happiness as he had begun to sag from all the excitement. Without a thought, I scooped him up and rested him on my hip as we walked to another game. He rested his head on my shoulder, and Gavin stopped and stared at us.

"You need one of those for yourself," he said softly.

My skin warmed at his words. Trying to play it off, I purposefully misinterpreted, "I need a stuffed puppy?"

He laughed and went along with me. "No, you need a big teddy bear, and I know exactly where to get one." He led us off to another arcade game, and Peter yelped as Gavin won game after game of free throws with a basketball. He ended up with an oversized lime green teddy bear and Peter's eyes grew in amazement.

Peter studied his small puppy dog before moving wistful eyes to lock on to the teddy bear.

"Peter, you know, I'm not sure I have room for this big guy at my house. Do you think we might be able to trade?" I asked, and his eyes grew even wider while he nodded dramatically.

Gavin laughed, "Okay, one trade it is, but why don't you keep holding the little puppy while I carry the bear until we find your parents."

A few minutes later, we met up with Greta and Taylor and joked about how the bear was going to fill up the back seat on the way home. They left us shortly after, and we went to the adult ride zone to jump on a few more before we left.

It was almost ten when Gavin pulled into my driveway, and I was sad that the night was over, but I realized it didn't have to be, not yet.

"Gavin, would you like to come in for some coffee?" I asked as he put the car in park.

Surprised by my question, he asked, "Are you sure, Trinity? I don't want to impose, but I never say no to a cup of coffee."

"You're not imposing; I'd like it if you would join me." My heart thudded in my chest, nerves and anticipation maybe.

"Actually, I would like to talk to you a little longer."

Callie barked a high-pitched yelp that meant she was excited that I was home. It was a good sign that Callie had accepted Gavin so quickly.

"Make yourself comfortable in the living room, and I'll start coffee." I wandered into the kitchen and moved around while he checked out my living room. Would he sit on the couch or a chair?

I wondered. I watched him sink down onto the couch. Okay, now where should I sit?

Oh, good Lord, what a mess I was now that he was in the house.

"How do you take your coffee?" I asked, and as he turned to me, my breath caught in my throat. He looked so amazing sitting in my family room. My heart sped.

I got our coffee ready and joined him, still not knowing where to sit. I fought to contain the groan of defeat as I sat down beside him. While the protection instinct said sit away from him, the woman in me said differently. The woman won.

"Was there something specific you wanted to talk about?" I asked him, trying to contain my nervousness.

"Actually, yes." He took a small sip and set his mug down on the coffee table. "After what happened yesterday with me not telling you where I worked, I wanted to explain a few things."

I swallowed and waited patiently for him to continue. He stared at the floor for a moment before he focused on me.

"This might seem really strange, but after the surprise of finding we both were in the same area, I figured it was best to be totally honest with you."

"Okay," I said shakily. What did he need to be honest about? Where was this going? Had it been a mistake to invite him in? My hands shook, and I squeezed my mug more tightly to control the tremors.

"Do you remember the first time we saw each other?" he asked softly and shifted to face me better.

I nodded, "The parking lot."

"Yeah, you looked so lost and scared that day." He glanced around the room, "The minute I saw the L.T. appear, I realized why you were so skittish." He clenched his jaw, and I had the urge to stroke it to release the tension. "You have no idea how many times I wanted to confront the asshole," there was anger in his voice, but I knew it wasn't directed at me, "but I didn't, because I knew it would have made it worse for you. I'm so sorry I couldn't have helped you out of that before he tried to kill you." The anger had dissipated quickly and in its place was pain.

"Oh Gavin, there was nothing you could do then. You have no idea how appreciative I was of you showing up when you did. I'd be dead if you hadn't. I never did thank you."

The smile that graced his face was sad, and he averted his eyes for a moment. "You don't need to thank me. I was doing my job." He paused, "Well, I was doing my job, but there was more." He lifted his head and met my questioning gaze head on.

"The first time I saw you in the parking lot, I developed a major crush on you." He paused and waited for me to speak. I flicked my eyes around the room, unsure of what I should say.

"Gavin, don't you think it is more likely that you were dealing with a superhero complex? You know, the thought of saving something, wanting to dash in and rescue the person in trouble?" I wasn't trying to be condescending, and I hoped my tone didn't reflect that.

He snorted, "You know, at one time, I thought maybe that was it. I wanted to save you so you wouldn't end up like my mom, but if that was it, I could have fulfilled that want with a number of people." He shook his head. "No, I know that the day I met you, I was taken with you."

I gave him a brief smile, not sure how I felt about that. Was he a stalker? My heart tripped over itself, and Callie came to sit beside me.

"Relax, Trinity. I'm not trying to confess my undying love for you. I just wanted you to know that for years I have thought about you, wondered how you were, wondered if you were happy." I stared at my mug and then lifted it to take a sip. "I watched you at the trial and you were trying to be so strong, but I know how scared you were sitting in the same room with him and telling your story—those two years of physical abuse that the attorneys were dissecting word for word. It killed me sometimes to see you fighting for control emotionally."

I thought back to that time, it had taken every ounce of courage to climb up on that stand and talk about what I had endured, but I had done it. I took another sip of my coffee as I shivered at the memory.

"When I saw you at the seminar a few weeks ago, I was stunned." He smiled, "You were so damn strong and so confident. All those years that I had wondered about you, and dreamt about you, too—there were a few of them—I never imagined you to have come so far in your recovery." He stared at me and I was glued to his gaze. "You were more beautiful than I had remembered, and I realized that standing in front of me is not a woman who needed to be rescued, but a woman who needed to be loved."

Tears filled my eyes, and my vision wavered slightly. I cleared my throat and looked at my mug. I felt him shift closer, and he put his knuckle under my chin and lifted it. A tear rolled down my cheek, but it wasn't a sad tear. I wasn't exactly sure what kind it was, except that it was created by words that were so beautiful and had never been said to me.

"Trinity, please don't cry. I'm not trying to upset you," he whispered, and his thumb brushed over my jawline.

"I'm not upset," I sniffed and wiped at another tear that had escaped. "I was just thinking about what I looked like then and now." I paused wondering if I should say the next set of words and realized that if he was opening his heart, I should try to also. "And I've never been called beautiful."

He winced and clenched his eyes closed for a moment as if he felt physical pain.

"You are a beautiful woman, and you should be told that every day, more than once a day." He slid his knuckles over my cheek and ran his fingers through my hair, lifting it from the side of my face. I trembled.

His hand moved to the back of my neck and ever so slowly he began to pull me to him. After a moment, I realized that he wasn't pulling me, but guiding me. I was moving towards him on my own.

I wanted to feel those lips that had said beautiful things to me on mine.

The first touch was so soft that I wasn't sure it counted as a kiss but more of a brush of the lips. The second time, the skin came in closer contact and little rivers of tingles raced down from every nerve ending around my mouth. I gasped at the feeling he ignited in me and he deepened the kiss, gently, slowly, lovingly.

Chapter 14 - Gavin

Her eyes shimmered with unshed tears, and my heart ached for her. Injustice had been done to her. For her to never have been told she was beautiful was a crime.

My heart thudded in my throat as I brought her face closer to mine. I could no longer hold off the urge to kiss her. I felt her gasp on my lips and took the opportunity to cradle the back of her head and enhance the kiss. Warmth traveled the length of me as she sighed against my lips, and my tongue slid in and tangled gently with hers.

I feared she would spook, so I finished the kiss and planted one more kiss on her glorious lips before resting my palm on her cheek and leaning back. Her eyes were glazed, her face flushed. I wondered if I looked the same to her.

She sat up straight, staring at me with a look of astonishment on her face.

"Do you trust me, Trinity?" I spoke softly, and she nodded once.

I took the coffee mug from her hands and placed it on the table before I scooted back into the corner of the couch. "Come here."

She hesitated for a moment.

"Relax, Trinity, I just want to hold you for a few minutes. I'm not asking for anything more."

She moved closer, and I turned her so that she faced the back of the couch and pulled her to lie over my chest. Her body was stiff at first, but as her cheek rested on my chest, I felt the muscles in her body relax one by one.

My arms wrapped around her lightly, and I trailed one hand slowly up and down her spine. Her left hand flattened on my chest and her fingers twitched.

"Are you alright?" I asked her as I laid my head back against the cushion and closed my eyes, savoring the feel of her in my arms. I felt her head nod yes against my chest.

My heart was regulating itself back to a normal rhythm and her breathing did the same. I heard Callie's chain rattle as she curled up on the floor beside my feet. Her back rested up against my shoe.

"Gavin," Trinity said softly but didn't move.

"Umm…" I responded, so relaxed in the moment, no words would come to mind.

"What would you say if I told you I was scared?" Her hand flatted against my left pectoral muscle.

"I'd say you have every right to be scared, but you don't need to fear me." I squeezed her waist once gently.

"What do you want?" she asked a few moments later.

I lifted my head and kissed the top of her head, taking a moment to inhale the fresh scent of her hair. "This…this is what I want: To hold you, care about you, and be there for you when you need me."

Her fingers wiggled on my chest and I ached inside for them to slide over the material of my shirt like my hand did against her back.

I heard and felt her deep slow intake of breath. As she exhaled, she snuggled more deeply into my chest and I wanted to whoop. For so long I had dreamed of holding her like this.

"Trinity, I promise you, I'll never lay a hand on you, not like he did. I promise my touches will only be because I care. I can't say that I'll never raise my voice because people argue, that's normal, but I will never raise my voice to threaten or scare you."

"You promise?" she asked so quietly I barely heard her.

I kissed the top of her head again, "I swear."

Her hand finally moved with movements so slow that if I hadn't been so intent on the warmth of her hand, I wouldn't have noticed. It crept up to my shoulder. Her fingertips barely grazed my neck at first. Her comfort level had risen, and I was overjoyed.

Her hand curled around the back of my neck and her fingers tickled the short hair on the back of it. I felt the soft touch in the tips of my toes.

She rolled her head back, so it was supported by my arm and I took in the features of her face. Her skin was so flawless, and her eyes so bright. Her nose had a slight bump to it on the side that only made it cuter on her perfect face, but it was her lips that held my attention. She flicked her tongue out to wet them, her gaze taking me in.

"Gavin, kiss me again."

I thought my heart would explode while we both shifted to get closer. Her hand still wrapped around my neck, she now guided me to her.

I could never have imagined a more perfect moment than when our lips met, and hers opened immediately to allow me entry. I held her tight to my chest, her hand roving over the back of my neck and head.

This wasn't a kiss of urgency but of hope of further things to come. When she ended it a few moments later, she smiled and snuggled up to my chest again.

I knew at that moment that there was no other woman I would ever want. She was my future. She was the woman with whom I wanted a family, children, to grow old with, and to hold every night.

For another twenty minutes, I cradled her on the couch and kissed the top of her head once in a while.

"I'm so relaxed right now that if I don't get up and go, I'm going to fall asleep right here."

"I was thinking right along those lines." She sighed and squeezed me before pushing herself up.

Callie jumped up off the floor with her movements, cocked her head at me, then walked away and out her dog door. Wasn't that nice of her to give us a few minutes to say goodbye? I thought happily.

Trinity stood, and I took her hand as I coerced my relaxed muscles to move. I faced her and laced my fingers in her hand, cupping my other palm against her face.

"You look even more beautiful when you are sleepy and relaxed." She averted her eyes, but I saw the brief smile she tried to hide.

"Thank you."

I hugged her to me for a moment and then laced our fingers again as I walked to the front door.

I brought her to me and wrapped my arms around her waist. Her hands rested on my biceps. "Thank you for a wonderful night."

"It was my pleasure, Trinity." I kissed her one more time slowly before letting her go. She opened the door, and I winked before I walked out. "I'll call you tomorrow."

I felt like skipping down the driveway. Instead, I kept my composure and climbed into my Jeep. It wasn't until I had pulled out of her driveway and turned the corner that the largest grin I had ever had spread across my face, and I finally released that whoop.

So excited to know that I finally had a chance, I never looked in my rearview mirror.

* * *

I showed up at the work site the next day with a spring in my step and a smile plastered to my face. I knew I was in for a world of ribbing from the guys today, but I didn't care.

Taylor was just unpacking his tools when I walked into the unit. He laughed when he glanced my way.

"I can see your night continued to go well. What did you guys do after we left?" he asked as he went back to unpacking.

"It was an amazing night, Taylor. We rode a few more rides, shared a funnel cake, and then went back to her house for a cup of coffee." I dropped my tool belt to the floor.

"By the grin on your face, I'd say the cup of coffee was more than just some ordinary java." He turned back to me. "Did you kiss her goodnight?"

"Yes, I did," I wandered over to some equipment then cast him a glance over my shoulder, "and it was the most amazing kiss I have ever had."

"That better be all you did." Taylor and I both spun to find Mike standing at the door.

"Yes sir, I swear, I only kissed her. Trust me, Mike, I would never force her to do anything." He studied me for a few seconds before he grunted.

"Fine, you better not. Sounds like you all had a good night. She enjoyed the fair?" He walked in and went about setting up the coffee. We were using the coffeemaker that came with the unit.

"She loved it," I beamed at the two men.

Taylor laughed, "I'll tell you someone who loved something: Peter. He talked about her nonstop from the moment we left you guys. Even fell asleep mid-sentence on the way home talking about how awesome it was that she didn't have room in her house for the bear. By the way, where the hell am I supposed to put that thing?"

I burst out laughing, "Sorry, that was supposed to be for Trinity, but she gave it to him."

He rolled his eyes, "So I heard."

"What did Greta have to say about her?" I asked as I wrapped my tool belt around my waist.

"She really liked her, but she's worried about you."

I shrugged, "Tell her I'm a big boy and to stop worrying."

Mike chimed in, "Well, I'm more worried about Trinity. This is the first time she has been on a date since her husband tried to kill her. You know that, right?"

"Yes sir, I do. Are you aware that I am the one who found her and arrested her husband?"

Shock crossed his features. "What? Are you serious?"

"Yes, I used to work with her husband. I got the 911 call and broke the door down when I saw him sitting on her chest through the living room window. My partner and I rushed in, and I tackled him off of her. We cuffed him and then I carried Trinity out of the house to the ambulance. If we had been a few minutes longer, she wouldn't have made it."

Mike eyed me suspiciously. "Did you follow her up here?"

"No, I never knew she moved away. I moved home to be near my family. I had no idea she lived here until I saw her at a seminar."

The coffeepot gurgled to announce that the coffee was ready, and Mike walked to the pot and poured out three cups. He turned to hand me one, "If anyone deserves to be happy, it's Trinity, I thank you for what you did. I know you won't try to hurt her, so I'll ask you to continue to protect her and love her with all your heart."

I accepted the cup as emotions filled my chest. "I will, and I already do." He slapped me on the back and turned away. I heard a sniff from him and knew I wasn't the only one who was feeling teary-eyed.

The three boys were in school today, so the unit was quieter than it had been over the weekend, but with us not having to stop and explain things, we got the work that we needed done more quickly.

By late afternoon, the unit was ready to be occupied, and we planned on working on the downstairs unit tomorrow. Taylor and Mike would finish up the work on Wednesday, but I had to head back to my shift work, my time off was over.

I hadn't spoken with Trinity all day, although I did shoot her a quick text early in the morning. *Hello beautiful, have a wonderful day.*

She had answered a moment later, *Thank you, Gavin, you too!*

I looked forward to a hot shower before I called her to see how her day was. I craved the sight of her, but I would have to settle for a phone conversation. I wasn't kidding when I told Taylor I wasn't rushing anything.

It had been almost ten years, and I could handle taking things slowly over the next few months. I refused to lose her now that I had found her again.

Chapter 15 - Trinity

There were moments the next morning when I felt giddy, and then my mind would churn the events of the night before over and over, and something close to panic would begin to set in.

The thought that Gavin had harbored feelings for me for ten years was a heady thought. I wasn't sure how I felt about that. I guessed if I was honest, I was humbled by that knowledge, but I was also scared that he would want more than I could give him. While he was kind and gentle when he held me, there was a time in my life when my ex-husband had been also.

Brenden had charmed his way into my life while I was in college. I was in awe that an older man of such importance would be interested in someone like me, a student studying business. I came from a happy and healthy home, and when Brenden had begun to demand my time and that I be with him, I had found it, at first, cute.

It wasn't until years went by that I realized the possessiveness he had displayed was only the beginning of an abusive relationship. Over the last few months of college, my friends had drifted away as I made repeated excuses not to meet up with them because he had coerced me into feeling like he was the only one that mattered. My life soon centered around him.

The choices I made about where I would go and what I would do were set around his schedule. Every minute of any of his days off was spent with him. If he was working, I sat at home alone waiting for him to call—it wouldn't do to be out when he called. Of course, that was before everyone had a cellphone. His excuse of knowing the dangers of the public and his wanting to know I was safe were good enough reasons for a young naive woman to put her life on hold or mindlessly fall into the trap.

He had proposed to me on my graduation day, and with all the excitement around me, I had said yes. Even my parents were thrilled that my future looked bright and secure. To them, he was the perfect catch. I thought so, too, but eventually I learned that the ring around my finger was in all actuality a noose around my neck.

Brooke broke into my heavy thoughts as she barreled through my office door. Her briefcase still hung over her shoulder, and her to-go cup of coffee steamed in her hand.

"So? How did it go?" She dropped her briefcase to the floor and plopped down on the chair.

"Wait!" I heard Marcy yell from the other room. "Don't you dare start without me." She raced into the room, her eyes so excited that I laughed. "Go ahead, you can start now," she sank down on another chair.

I cleared my throat as I ping-ponged between them for a moment. "It was nice." I shuffled a few things around on my desk. They looked at each other with perplexed expressions.

"What does nice mean?" Brooke asked. "Where did he take you? What did you do?"

I kissed him, and what a mind-melting kiss it was. That's what I wanted to say, but I refrained. "He took me to the fair. We had fun."

"The fair?" Marcy sat back in her seat with a look of surprise on her face.

"Yes, the fair," I said. My phone pinged, and I picked it up to see Gavin's message. If you could swoon over typed words on a screen, then I was swooning.

"Okay, you put that phone down and spill!" Brooke sat on the edge of her chair. "We want every single detail!" She slapped her hand down on my desk and I laughed. I realized that no work would be done until I confessed every detail of our date. Brooke and Marcy were important to me, and I had been with them side by side through their ups and down, the least I could do was let them get on for my first roller coaster ride.

I leaned back in my chair as I set my phone down after answering Gavin's message.

"He picked me up right on time, and we went to the fair. We met up with his sister and brother-in-law, and he has the cutest nephew who is, I think, four. Anyway, we rode all the rides, ate junk food, watched little Peter so Greta and Taylor could go have some time to ride, and played some games." I recounted the events nonchalantly like it was an everyday occurrence.

"And?" they both said at the same time in high-pitched voices.

Nervous laughter burst from my chest, "Okay, he won me this huge teddy bear, but I traded it for a smaller puppy he had won for Peter." Brooke raised her eyebrow at me. "And when he dropped me off at home, I invited him in for coffee."

"Finally we are getting to the good stuff!" Marcy announced. "Continue."

"And I made coffee and we talked." They both stared at me expectantly. I flicked my eyes back and forth between them. "Okay," I threw my hands up in the air, "he kissed me." The moment the words were out of my mouth, I felt refreshed and excited.

They grinned at me like high school adolescents.

"He kissed me and it melted my toes, and then we snuggled on the couch, and kissed a few more times." They waited for more. "That's it, that's all that happened, I swear." I held my palm out to them.

Brooke leaned closer, "It melted your toes?"

"Yes, and made my knees weak and scared the hell out of me, too."

Brooke laughed, and Marcy smirked, "Yeah, well I'm sure it did. How are you feeling today?"

I blew out a breath, "Confused, nervous, excited, giddy. I am running a huge gamut of emotions right now."

"That's to be expected. Remember, you need to take it one day at a time, don't go jumping in head first," Brooke counseled before she took a sip of her coffee.

"I know." I hesitated, not sure if I should talk about this or not, but I decided I needed their help. "He admitted to me that he has had feelings for me since he met me."

"What, a whole month?" Marcy tossed out laughing.

Brooke turned to her, "No, Marcy. Gavin has known Trinity since she was married. He's the one who arrested her husband."

Marcy's eyes flashed wide, "What? How did I not know that?"

"Yes, he is the one that answered the call, and the one who arrested Brenden."

"Wow, that's a little strange." She turned to Brooke, "Is that strange to you?"

"I don't think he is stalking her or anything. I think it's cute."

A burst of laughter left my lips, "Cute?" I shook my head. "We actually talked about the whole stalking factor, because at first I was thinking along the same lines as you, Marcy, but he has valid reasons for being here. Our meeting again was just a chance happening."

"I think it's more like fate," Brooke declared.

"Fate? I don't know about that." I rocked my chair back and forth a few times thinking it over, "Maybe."

"Maybe, nothing," Marcy called out. "This gorgeous man rescues you, falls in love at first sight, almost loses you to an abuser, and then finds you again ten years later when you are at the prime of your life! This is fate, and you better grab it!" She stood up, "If you don't, can I have him?"

"Marcy!" Brooke yelled as she laughed. Just then the phone rang on Marcy's desk, and she bolted out the door to answer it.

"She is right, though, you should grab this," Brooke said.

"I want to, but I'm afraid. I told him that last night."

"Of course you are. What did he say to that?" she asked after she had sipped her coffee.

I shrugged, "He said he wouldn't rush me."

"Did you believe him?"

"Yeah, I do. I like him, Brooke. I'm just afraid that he'll pull the wool over my eyes like Brenden did."

She stood up and threw me a grin, "No chance of that, not now, not with what you know. Just take it slow. I felt the same way, and I couldn't be happier."

Marcy yelled from the other room, "Trinity, Mary's on the phone. She needs to talk to you."

"Okay, send it through." We didn't need fancy intercoms here. We all knew how to raise our voices loudly enough to get someone's attention.

Brooke walked out of my office towards her own, and the phone on my desk rang. I lifted the receiver and tucked it into the crook of my neck so I could log onto my computer.

"Morning, Mary, what can I do for you?"

"Trinity, we had another attempted break-in last night," she stated quickly.

"Same apartment?" I sat back in my seat, feeling suddenly very tense.

"Yes, same apartment, and I did call the police last night, as much as I didn't want to," she continued.

"I'm glad you did. What did they have to say?"

"I gave them the name of the client's ex-boyfriend, and they said they would look into it. I doubt they will do much more."

I sat up and tapped a pen on my desk, thinking. "Was the client home?"

"No, she was at work. I'm wondering if the guy is trying to get in and hide before she comes home."

"He could be."

"Trinity, I know we talked in the past about adding alarms to the lower floor. Has anything come of that?"

"Actually, Brooke has a meeting with a group of potential benefactors for just that sort of thing. Hopefully, they will be willing to make some decent donations. If we do get the money, you'll be the first to get it."

"And if we don't get the money, is there anything we can do?" she asked solemnly.

I sighed heavily, "We'll find the money, even if we have to cut something else."

* * *

The day flew by, and at five o'clock I was grateful to be going home. I clicked my key fob as I walked into the parking lot. Unlike when I was younger, I didn't stroll along and daydream. I paid attention to my surroundings. I listened to the sounds and to my inner voice. Normally, my voice stayed quiet, but today, there was something niggling at the back of my mind as I approached my car.

My step quickened, and I scanned the parking lot and nearby street. I didn't see anything out of the ordinary, but I felt like I was being watched. I panned the parking lot again before I opened my door, but I could see no one paying attention to me.

I tried to brush off the feeling, but it remained with me all the way home. It wasn't until I locked my front door and punched in the code for my alarm that I felt the tension ease. It had been a long time since I had felt this kind of impending doom and wondered if it had anything to do with Gavin.

Chapter 16 - Gavin

I groaned when my alarm went off at four-thirty A.M. My few days off were over, and it was time to get back to my rotating schedule. I still had two more day shifts before I would have a three-day weekend and then flip to night shift for two weeks.

I thought about Trinity as I got ready for work. We had spoken Monday and Tuesday night for about thirty minutes each time. While we were on the phone, we played five questions. I would ask her five, and then she would ask me five. They always started out easy like favorite color, and got progressively harder and a bit more personal.

My last question to her last night was, Do you miss me? Her answer had been somewhat breathy as she replied, "Yes." My heart had sped and the rest of my body had responded in a very manly way to the sound of her voice. We had made plans to get together Friday night after she got off from work.

This time I asked her what she'd like to do, and she offered to cook me dinner. The thought of relaxing at her house again for an evening thrilled me like nothing else ever had.

I sat in the squad room waiting for roll call to begin. Our squad had ten officers and two sergeants. Coven and I shared the supervisor positions and split the patrol area in half. When a major incident transpired, we shared the responsibility.

Coven and I had been on the same squad since I had been promoted two years ago. We worked well together and respected one another. He sank down into a seat beside me, a Styrofoam cup of coffee in his hand.

"You do know that the coffee they brew in the administrative office will put hair on your body in places you don't want hair, right?" I teased.

Coven scoffed, "Funny, very funny." He blew on the top of the hot liquid. "Hey, I ran into your friend Trinity the other day at the hospital."

"Did you go over and take Tabitha's statement?" I had forgotten to ask her who had responded.

"Yeah, I did, but only after Derek was dispatched and she kicked him out of the room." He laughed.

"Trinity kicked him out of the room?" I sat up straighter.

"Yeah, not only that, but she filed a complaint on him. I just saw it in my mailbox. I dropped it on the chief's desk before I came in here."

"Whoa, what is this, his fourth or fifth complaint?" I asked as I heard someone walk into the room—the devil himself.

"Fourth, this might put him on suspension. He's going to be pissed," he whispered to me after he watched Derek plop down into a chair and take a bite out of a muffin. Crumbs fell on his uniform, but he either didn't care or didn't notice.

When everyone was situated, Coven got up and talked about the latest goings-on in the area. He finished up by stating that a warrant had been issued for Wayne. *I'd love to be the one to pick him up on it*, I thought to myself.

Coven was just finishing up announcements when Chief Randall walked into the squad room. "Sergeant Coven, I'd like to see you in my office, along with Officer Wilson. Sergeant Brooksfield, you might as well join us." He did an about face and left the room.

All the patrol guys glanced between the three of us before Coven got their attention, "Okay, go relieve the guys from night shift. We will be on the street in a few minutes. Wright, let the guy Derek's to relieve know he can go, just do me a favor and cover his area until we are done."

Or maybe the rest of the day, I thought to myself. If he got suspended we would be shifting the units around.

Derek was spouting off to all the guys that he had no idea what this was about, but when his eyes landed on mine, I saw the daggers in them. He knew what this was about. I followed Coven out of the squad room and to the chief's office.

Coven sat in front of the desk, and I stood off to the side. Derek would take the other chair next to Coven when he finally felt the need to appear.

The chief was reading a document as he sat at his desk, and I assumed he was rereading the complaint that Trinity had filed against Derek.

The chief raised his eyes when Derek finally meandered in and sat down with a huff.

"Sergeant Brooksfield, please close the door." He sat up to his desk and set the paper down, drumming his fingers on the desk as he looked Derek over.

I closed the door and went back to where I had been standing. Derek shot me a quick look. Coven stared at the chief.

"Derek, we got another complaint against you. This makes four in less than a year."

"I didn't do anything. I don't know what that woman told you." He shifted in his seat.

"How do you know it was a woman?" he asked him point blank.

Derek shifted again under the chief's scrutiny. "Because I had a run in with that Morris woman this weekend. She didn't think I was being sensitive to the victim's needs."

"Were you?" he questioned.

"Was I what?" he threw the question back.

The chief actually rolled his eyes, "Were you being insensitive to the victim?"

"No." He said nothing else and the chief glanced at Coven.

"Sergeant Coven, can you please tell me what you know about this." He sat back in his seat and rested his chin in his hand.

"Derek was dispatched to the hospital to take Tabitha Stream's statement. Shortly after he cleared, I received a message that Ms. Morris wanted to speak to a supervisor. I called her and found out that Derek had given both her and the victim an attitude. Ms. Morris had told him to leave." He glanced at Derek, "I ended up taking the statement and filed the charges. I have the warrant punched for the suspect."

"Okay, thank you, Sergeant Coven." He looked at Derek hard, "Derek, you are being placed on a five-day suspension, and you will need to attend sensitivity training."

Derek shook his head and mumbled something.

"Excuse me? What did you just say?" the chief asked him while he raised an eyebrow.

"I said I already took that training."

"Well, maybe after taking it a second time, you might actually learn something." Derek and the chief stared each other down for a moment, "Five days, no pay, starting today. You are dismissed."

"Whatever," Derek huffed and strode to the door, ripping it open and slamming it closed.

The chief sighed, "I don't see him being part of this department much longer." He picked up a pen and tapped it on his hand for a moment. "Gavin, what do you know about this situation?"

"Not much, sir. I had spoken to Trinity this weekend before she went to see Tabitha in the hospital, but Trinity didn't tell me she filed a complaint against Derek." I moved over to stand closer to Coven.

"How well do you know Trinity Morris?" he asked me.

"Umm…" How did I explain it to him? "We're friends."

He raised his eyebrow at me, "Friends?"

"Well, how about I say I took her out on a date the other night, and I am taking her out again this Friday night." I wasn't sure where this was going.

He gave a brief snort, "You know about her past, right?"

"Yes sir, I know all about her past. I was there."

He thought about that for a moment. I could see the wheels spinning in his head.

"That's right. I remember reading your commendation from that in your file when we hired you. Huh, small world." He tossed the pen on the desk, "Okay, gentlemen, thank you. Let me know if there is any more trouble with him. He's being put on a very short leash for a while."

Coven and I left the office, and we weren't five feet down the hallway when he grinned at me, "You're dating Morris?"

"Yeah, I guess you could say that."

He slapped me on the back, "Good for you. I hope it works out for you both."

I thanked him and then went to hit the bathroom before I went on patrol. I was washing my hands when Derek walked up behind me and sneered at me in the mirror reflection.

"You better tell that bitch to watch herself," he seethed.

I flicked the excess water off my hands and turned slowly. "You go near her, and you will answer to me, Derek. You got that?" My hand fisted at my sides, moisture dripping to the tile floor.

"You're doing that piece of ass, aren't you?" He threw his head back and laughed, "What, you can't get a real woman? You have to settle for a weak, broken one instead?"

I didn't think before I moved, and I don't think he realized I could move as fast as I did. Before either of us knew it, I had him against the wall, my forearm against his throat.

"You say one more word about her, and I will knock your teeth down your throat. You got that, Derek? Not one single word." My teeth were clenched as I spoke, and my body shook with unvented anger.

"Gav, let him go, he's not worth it," Coven's voice reached me from the door.

I shoved one last time against Derek and spun around to get away from him as fast as I could. If he had said one more thing, I would have knocked him out.

I wasn't a violent man, but hurt someone that I cared about, and watch out.

Chapter 17 - Trinity

"What are you and Rick doing tonight?" I asked Brooke as she sat reading something at her desk. She looked up at me in surprise.

"Nothing planned, why?"

"Would you two want to join me for dinner tonight, well Gavin and me, that is?" I slipped into the cream-colored chair in front of her desk.

"You're having dinner with Gavin and you want us to join you? Why?" She dropped the papers and gave me her full attention.

"Well, I kind of invited him over for dinner tonight, but I thought it might be more fun if you all joined us," I said straight-faced.

"You're scared to be alone with him, aren't you?" she grinned.

"Fine, yes. You know me too well. Yes, I thought it was a good idea when I first thought about it, but the more I consider it, the more it freaks me out." I chewed my lip, "Is that stupid?"

She laughed and waved a hand at me, "No, that's not stupid, that's natural. Sure, let me just make sure Rick has no other plans. I'm sure he doesn't, so what time should we be there?"

"Six work for you?" I stood up, "And thank you."

She winked and reached for her phone, "No thanks needed. You did the same for me."

The afternoon flew by, and Brooke popped her head into my office on her way out, "See you at six, I'm heading over to pick up Rick. His car is in the shop, so we might be a little late. He wants to go home and change out of his suit. Will you be alright alone for a little while?"

"Yes, Brooke, I'll be fine. Thank you, and I'll see you later." I grinned at her. She was such a good friend. I had been so lucky to find her when I had.

After Brenden's final attack, I had been in the hospital staring at the ceiling, trying to figure out how I was alive, and if I even wanted to be after everything that Brenden had done to me, when Brooke and another woman walked into my room.

My mother had been sitting watch in a chair in the corner of my room reading. She stood up, and by the look on her face, I knew she had been expecting the visitors. I had watched them warily as my mother thanked them for coming and shook their hands.

"Hi, Trinity." A woman of about forty walked closer to my bedside. "My name is April, and this is Brooke." She pointed to the woman who stepped to the other side of the bed. My heart beat faster as I took in their faces.

Who were these women, and what did they want with me? I desperately wanted to flee even though I was connected to machines and couldn't have gone anywhere if I had tried.

Brooke reached out and touched the back of my hand, "Relax, Trinity, we know you are scared right now, but we are here to help you. We're from the local domestic violence center."

Tears had filled my eyes and spilled over, and Brooke had taken my hand, "You're not alone, not anymore." It was in that moment, as she held my hand, that I knew I had a life ahead of me and that I would do everything I could to make life better for victims of abuse.

I glanced at my watch. I had just enough time to stop by the bakery and pick up a loaf of fresh bread before I got home to get dinner ready. I grabbed my shoulder bag and made a hasty trek to the parking lot.

"Are you kidding me!" I groaned as I approached my car. "This can't be happening, not again. Dammit!" I dug my cellphone out of my pocket and called the same company I had called yesterday to repair my tire.

They said they had someone right down the street, and I thanked them profusely. I thought for a moment and then dialed Gavin.

"Hello, beautiful," he answered, and the sound of his voice made my frustration slip down a notch.

"Hi," I took a deep breath, "I need a favor."

"Sure, what can I do for you?" His calming voice wrapped around me and soothed me like a hot bath after a long day.

"I have another flat. I'm waiting for the tow company to come, and I was wondering if you might be able to stop by the store and pick up a loaf of French bread for tonight. Would you mind?" I bit my bottom lip, not sure if asking a man to do such a thing was wrong.

"Sure, that's not a problem. Do you need me to come by and pick you up? Wait, what do you mean another?"

I waved at the towtruck driver as he pulled into the lot. He really must have been down the street.

"Would you believe I had one yesterday, too, a nail in my tire. They were able to plug it up for me." The tow driver was the same one from yesterday. "Hold on a second, Gavin."

"Did the plug come out?" the driver asked as he swung down from the cab of his rig.

"No, it's a different tire." I pointed to the rear driver's side tire.

"Better keep an eye out for where you are driving. You keep this up, and you'll be buying four new tires." He gave me a friendly smile and told me it would only take a few minutes.

I returned my attention to Gavin, "Sorry. Thank you. I'm sorry to ask you to do this, but I made lasagna and you can't have that without fresh garlic bread."

Gavin's deep rumble of laughter carried over the phone line and straight to my heart. "It's not a problem. Do you need anything else? Want me to pick up a bottle of wine?"

"Actually, that's not a bad idea. Oh, and I forgot to tell you something." I bit my lip again worried he would be upset that Brooke and Rick were going to be there.

"What's that?"

"I invited Brooke and her husband Rick to join us tonight. I hope you don't mind." I held my breath and released it when I heard him chuckle again.

"If that is what you want, a double date, I'm all for it. I'd love to get to know Brooke and her husband. You said his name was Rick?"

Whew…wow…how did I get so lucky to find a man like Gavin? "Yes, Rick. Thank you."

"Thank you for what?" His voice was light and friendly, no hint of disappointment.

"For being so accepting," I said, genuinely thankful for him.

"Trinity, if it makes you feel more comfortable to have others around us for a while, I don't have a problem with that. I think that's a good idea."

My God, I fell a little bit in love with him with those words.

We talked for a few more minutes before saying goodbye. The mechanic finished up quickly and blew up my tire with the air compressor he had on his truck. I was on my way home twenty minutes after I hung up.

I rushed into the door and turned on the oven. I set the lasagna on the counter to get it ready to go in and started pulling out vegetables and stacking them on the counter for the salad.

Callie wiggled all around me, attempting to get my attention, and I gave her a few loving pets before washing my hands.

I glanced at the clock; it was already ten minutes till six, damn. I was hoping to have a chance to change out of work clothes. I settled for kicking off my shoes while I pulled the ingredients out of containers and started to wash them off.

Callie yelped and took off for the door. "Darn it, he's early." As I said the words, excitement flourished through my body. I hadn't seen him since we went to the fair, although I had talked to him every night. Callie barked from the hallway, and I wiped my hands on a dish towel and dropped it on the counter to go open the door.

Would he kiss me again tonight? Of course he would, right? I couldn't believe I was having this conversation with myself, or that I wanted him so badly to kiss me again.

Gavin knocked as I turned the handle. Callie slid out and rubbed up against his pants the moment I had the door open enough.

Our eyes locked, and he took my breath away. He was even more gorgeous than I remembered. I pulled the door open wider so he could step inside. I took a slow calming breath as I closed the door and turned to face him.

Gavin was staring at the dog, "Callie, get your nose out of there." He pulled the two bags out of Callie's reach.

I laughed, "Here, let me take those. Thank you so much. You have no idea how much I appreciate it."

Gavin handed me the bag with the fresh bread in it and carried the other one which I assumed contained wine.

"No need to thank me. I'm glad I could help." I set the bread down and shifted some things around on the counter. The oven beeped that it was ready, and I slipped the lasagna pan into the oven.

When I stood up and turned, Gavin was right behind me. I jumped a little.

He reached for my elbow, "Sorry, I didn't mean to scare you."

"You didn't. I just didn't expect you right behind me."

"There's something I need to do," he said and stared deeply into my eyes. My heart skipped a beat.

"What's that?" I swallowed.

He moved closer. "Break the ice," he whispered as his mouth moved towards mine.

I sighed as I leaned toward him and allowed him to wrap me in his embrace for a gentle kiss. When he pulled back, I rested my hands on his shoulders. "Nice ice breaker," I stated.

"Umm…I think I need one more." I met him halfway and enjoyed another toe-tingling smooch.

"I don't think the ice broke, I think it melted, along with my knees," I said when we pulled apart. He laughed and stepped away from me.

"That, I agree with. Now what can I do to help with dinner? If I keep you in my arms, I'm not sure it will be ready anytime soon." He winked and I felt my skin warm with his meaning.

Oh man, I wasn't ready for that. Maybe some good old fashioned making out, but definitely not sex—not yet, maybe someday soon, but not yet.

"Brooke and Rick might be a little late. She had to take him home to get changed and showered." I glanced down at myself, "Speaking of which, I didn't have time to go change. Do you mind starting on the salad while I get out of my work clothes?"

"Not at all, what do you want me to put it in?"

I pulled out a large glass bowl, along with a cutting board and a large knife. When I set the knife down, I stared at it. I must really trust him to be putting something like that into his hands.

I stepped back from the counter quickly and spun around to go change, but Gavin blocked my escape. "I told you I wouldn't do anything to hurt you, Trinity. Trust me, okay?"

"I do trust you. That's why I gave you the knife." I stood on my tiptoes and pressed my lips to his for a split second before scooting around him and to my bedroom to change.

Did I really just initiate that kiss? I asked myself as I slipped into jeans and a short-sleeved blouse. Wow, talk about stepping out of my comfort zone.

I heard the doorbell ring and Callie barking. I glanced at the bedside clock. How long did Gavin and I stand around breaking the ice? It was twenty after six. I didn't rush as I heard Gavin's voice in the foyer talking to Brooke and Rick. He actually answered the door. Why that gave me a warm fuzzy feeling, I didn't know, but it did. My lips were still slightly swollen from the mind-melting kisses to which Gavin had subjected me. I laughed, like I wasn't a willing participant in that.

When I entered the kitchen, Gavin was opening a bottle of wine, and four glasses sat on the counter. I froze in place. Just like the night he came in for coffee, I thought about how wonderful he looked standing in my house. Would he one day become a fixture? Would my dream of filling this place I had bought with a lovely family finally happen?

Gavin winked at me as he popped the cork, and I moved into the kitchen to stand by his side.

Chapter 18 - Gavin

When I saw Trinity's name on my phone, I immediately thought she was going to cancel. In the back of my mind, I knew she was wondering if her decision was a good one. The fact that she invited another couple over not only confirmed it, but also let me know that she was interested in me. Why else would she want her best friend and her best friend's spouse to join us for dinner?

I stopped by a large shopping center that not only had a bakery but a package store for wine. I grabbed two bottles of wine first then hit the bakery. The loaf of bread was still warm from the oven. The yeasty smell filled my car, and my stomach growled.

The anticipation of seeing Trinity again after almost a week had me tapping my thumb against the steering wheel as I sat in traffic. I knew she would be nervous, but was she looking forward to seeing me as much as I was her?

She pulled the front door open, and my heart skipped a beat. Her pink silk blouse gave her skin a rosy tone, and the gray slacks she wore showed off the curves of her waist and hips. The compulsion to wrap my hands around her tiny waist and pull her to me was foremost in my mind—that is, until Callie tried to get her nose into the fresh bread.

I could feel the anxiety wafting off of her as I followed her swaying hips to the kitchen. It was time to confront her and break down the barrier between us so we could relax and enjoy the evening.

I watched her pants smooth out over her backside as she bent to put the lasagna into the oven. My hormones surged. If I wasn't careful, I'd be sticking my head into the freezer to cool the hell off.

The squeak that crossed her lips when she turned did nothing to cool the slow burn I felt, and I wondered what sounds she would make when we made love. There was no doubt in my mind as I dipped my head to take her lips that one day we would do just that.

I couldn't get enough of her touch, her taste. Her natural fresh scent invaded my senses and drove me wild. Yeah, we melted the ice alright, but could I get past her defenses to allow her to open her heart and let me in?

I took a moment to inhale a few cleansing breaths when she went to change. I barely had my hormones in control when Callie barked and the doorbell rang. Would Trinity be upset if I answered it? Probably not, especially since she was expecting Brooke and Rick.

Callie stood at the door and barked again as I walked to the door. "Callie, sit." I didn't expect the dog to respond to me, but she did and turned to look at me with excitement in her eyes. "Huh, would you look at that? Good girl." I rubbed the top of her head and opened the door.

Brooke looked startled when I opened the door, "Hi, Brooke, Trinity got home a little late, she's changing clothes." I stood back and allowed them to enter. Callie sniffed Brooke quickly then stepped back to my side. "You must be Rick. I'm Gavin."

"Gavin, pleasure to meet you." Rick had the firm grip of a businessman. He had the look, too—not the intense I'm-watching-every-move-you-make look of a cop, but a look of intelligence and confidence. He gave me the once over, and if I had been in his shoes, I would have done the same.

"Gavin, it's good to see you again." Brooke shook my hand after I let go of her husband's.

"Come on in. I was finishing up the salad and getting ready to open up a bottle of wine." Brooke and Rick walked in front of me, and Brooke made a beeline for the counter.

"I'll finish up the salad, you open the wine. That's the important job. Glasses are up there." She pointed to a cabinet to the left of the sink.

"Brooke told me you and your brother-in-law helped out at the shelter," Rick filled the silence as I pulled the glasses down.

"Yeah, it worked out well. Taylor finished up the job on Wednesday. Everything is as good as new."

Trinity entered the kitchen, and I pulled the cork out as I winked at her.

This all seemed so normal: Opening a bottle of wine, getting ready to have dinner and spend a quiet evening with friends. Other than hanging out at my sister's house, I hadn't had many of these normal kinds of things in my life—and I loved it.

Trinity put her hand on my back in passing, but it was long enough for me to know she was glad I was there. The shy smile she tipped in my direction spoke volumes, and a real lump actually caught in my throat. I cleared it as she stepped around me and hugged Brooke.

"Nobody drink that wine yet, I have some news," Brooke called out as she tossed some tomato pieces into the salad.

"What news?" Trinity asked as she opened the oven to check the lasagna. She grabbed a pot holder and pulled it out, along with the warmed up garlic bread I'd brought over as I finished pouring the wine.

Brooke wiped her hands on a towel and picked up two glasses, handing one to Trinity as she set the pot holder down.

Rick and I picked up our glasses and I glanced at his face. He had a knowing smile on it.

"I got a call this afternoon just after I left the office." Brooke stated the words like they would explain what the news was.

"Okay," Trinity said encouragingly, "and what phone call was that?"

"We got the money, Trinity." Brooke grinned larger than life.

"What?" Trinity squeaked.

Brooke grabbed her arm, "Trinity, we got the money!"

Trinity's eyes were huge, and she stared at her for a long moment. "Are you serious?" she asked in disbelief.

Brooke nodded dramatically, "Yes!"

"Oh my god, oh my god! Brooke! We got the money!" Trinity squealed and threw her arm around her friend as the two of them bounced up and down. Rick's grin was almost as wide as his wife's.

"So here's to a brand new, major private contributor to our organization!" Brooke held her glass up, and we all toasted the good news.

Trinity turned to me, her eyes glistening with tears, I reached out and touched her cheek, wiping away one of the drops that had escaped.

"I can only assume with the squealing, hugging, toasting, and tears that this is a great thing," I said looking between Brooke and Trinity.

"Yes," Trinity nodded emphatically and took a sip of her wine. "We have a lot of corporate donations that we get, and lots of grants, big and small that we need to fight for. It's hard to get big personal contributors, and this one is the largest we have ever had."

"Can I ask how much?" I wasn't sure if that was my business, but Trinity didn't seem to think it was a big deal.

"Three hundred." She grinned, and I thought three hundred didn't seem like that much. I could donate more than three hundred.

"Thousand," Rick added, and I snapped my head towards him.

"Three hundred thousand?" I asked. All three heads were bobbing up and down, and instantly I felt like part of the excitement. "Are you serious? That's a lot of money."

"We know!" Brooke squealed. "We were shocked when they came to us and told us they wanted to donate such a large sum."

She turned to Trinity, "The money will be transferred to our account on Tuesday."

That started a conversation about all the things that they had to get quoted, such as alarm systems and new equipment. It evolved into how they could get more contributors involved and how many more people they could approach for grants. Brooke and Trinity even talked about hiring another person for the office.

Over dinner, the conversation bounced around the table, mostly between Trinity and Brooke. Rick threw in his opinions on some of the business ideas, and I was the one who asked all the questions.

We were sitting back in our chairs, stuffed from the excellent meal when I asked a question that I had been wondering for a while. "Where did you all come up with the name of the organization?"

Rick smiled momentarily, and the energy in the room dipped slightly. Trinity and Brooke shared a knowing smile, and Trinity turned to me.

"Two days after you saved my life, Brooke walked into my hospital room. I had no idea who she was or why she and another woman were there." Trinity closed her eyes, and the emotions rolled off of her. I didn't realize that my question would take her back to that awful time in her life and I wanted to kick myself for it.

When she focused on me, she reached for my hand as it lay on the table. "Brooke came to me and squeezed my hand," she showed me as she did it to mine, "and she told me, 'You're not alone.' I cried. For the first time in years, I cried."

Trinity hadn't let go of my hand, and I reversed it so I now had my hand lying over hers, protecting her anyway that I could.

"I'll never forget the moment she said that because I knew that I wasn't alone anymore. Even though I didn't have my husband, and I had no friends, I wasn't alone. Brooke and I became best friends from that moment forward, and when we started talking about creating the organization, those words said it all."

"Yes, they do," I said quietly and squeezed her hand again. I wanted so much to tell her she would never be alone again, that I would be there for her through everything. The look in her eyes held me captive, and I wondered what she was thinking. Could she be hoping for the same?

Brooke cleared her throat a moment later, pulling Trinity and me out of our moment. I let go of her hand, and we all helped to clear the table. Trinity suggested making coffee, but Rick and Brooke shared a look and said they needed to get home.

Rick made a general comment about having to get up early the next day and being tired. I wondered if they were leaving early to give us time together.

We said goodbye to Brooke and Rick, and I helped Trinity do the dishes and put away the extra food. She showed me how to use her fancy, super-quick coffeemaker, and I brewed us each a cup.

We moved into the living room, and as I sank onto the couch, I remembered sharing our first kiss in this exact spot. The memory ignited the need to feel her up close and personal again, but I somehow managed to ignore it.

Trinity sat on her curled feet a few inches from me. She had no idea how much it meant to me that she trusted me the way she did.

She leaned her head back against the cushion and closed her eyes, a look of pure satisfaction and delight on her face, and I moaned internally. God, if only I could put that kind of look on her face. I set my coffee cup down and reached for hers. She opened her eyes, surprised for a moment, and watched me set it down. My palms grew damp, and I wiped my hands down the front of my jeans before turning back to her.

I didn't need to say a word. She shifted towards me, and I drew her into my arms and pulled her into a heart-stopping kiss. She opened up to me immediately and allowed her hands to travel over my shoulders, head, and neck. I traced a line of kisses along her jawline and down the column of her throat, stopping to nibble on the sensitive point just under her ear.

The sound that left her mouth on a sigh went straight to my heart, and I felt the blood in my veins pounding in every inch of my body. I drew in a steadying breath and pulled back to see her eyes glazed with desire. I almost lost the last part of my control. I shifted her so there was some distance between us.

"If you keep kissing me that way, beautiful woman, I'm going to come undone, and I'm not sure you're ready to take it to that level yet."

Trinity swallowed deeply. "Gavin, can I ask you a question?" she asked in a shy voice.

"Of course, you can ask me anything." I ran my hand down the side of her head, memorizing the silky feel of her brown hair.

She tensed, and I tried to stay calm. "Do you want to make love to me?"

I stared at her, trying to figure out where the hell that question had come from. Couldn't she tell how badly I wanted her?

"Trinity, of course I do." I ran my thumb over her bottom lip. She quivered. "I want to make love to you so much that I am fighting to control myself. Why would you ask me that question? Can't you tell how much I want you?"

She looked away, and I pulled her chin back to face me. "Don't shy away from me. Tell me what's going through your mind, please."

She tried to shift away from me, and I held her tight, "Oh, no you don't. You stay right where you are."

"I want to talk to you about this, but I'm not sure I can look you in the eye while I do." She bit her bottom lip.

"Fine," I shifted a little bit. "Lay your head on my chest, that way you're still with me, but you won't have to look into my face."

She snuggled up in my lap again like she had last week and sighed.

"Is that better?" I asked as I made circles on her back, I felt her nod against my chest. The feeling of her nuzzling my chest did nothing to diminish my raging need for her. There was no way with her on my lap that she could miss it either.

"Now, why did you ask me that?" I kissed the top of her head.

"Okay, yeah," she inhaled deeply and released it, "I can tell you are physically attracted to me, but what if I'm not any good," she hesitated, "and you are disappointed?"

I sputtered, "What? How could you possibly think I would be disappointed?"

She tensed against me. "Brenden said that I was horrible in bed."

Every muscle in my body stilled including my heart for just a moment. That prick! If he weren't already locked up, I'd hunt his ass down and kick it into the next century.

Chapter 19 - Trinity

What an amazing night it had been. Granted, the evening had started off a little shakily with my flat tire and racing around at the last minute, but it turned out to be incredible—that is, until my insecurities came rushing to the surface in Gavin's arms.

What a moron I was to ruin the moment, but the need to tell him how I felt was too strong. Gavin had awakened feelings in me that had lain dormant for years. I could not remember the last time I had craved the touch of a man and not shied away from it. When was the last time my body responded to a mere look and warmed in places I had forgotten existed?

The muscles in Gavin's body grew rock hard, and his arms tightened around my back and waist.

"Don't you dare believe a word that man said to you," he paused and took a calming breath. "Trinity, I can feel the passion in your kisses, I can see the desire in your eyes when I gaze into them. The only person who was ever bad in bed was him."

I listened to what he said, I knew he was right, but having been criticized so many times in my prior relationship, I had come to believe it, even if I logically knew it to be wrong.

"Can I ask you a question?" he continued.

"Yes," I whispered against his chest.

"Did he ever try to please you? Or was sex just about him getting off?" His voice was rough, almost as if he were in pain.

I shrugged, afraid to tell him the truth.

"Trinity," he urged.

"Do you mean did he ever give me an orgasm?" I asked into his shirt, embarrassed to admit the answer.

His hands stilled on my back. "Yes, that's exactly what I meant."

"No, I don't think it's possible for me. Maybe, I'm just one of those women who can't."

He put his hands on my shoulders and lifted me off his chest. "Excuse me?"

"I probably can't." My cheeks reddened as he scrutinized my face.

He closed his eyes and dropped his chin for a moment. "I want to kill that man," he muttered. He lifted his face and while he had just talked about hurting a man, the look in his eyes was far from aggressive. His eyes smoldered as they bore down on mine.

"Honey, I'm going to prove that wrong, over and over again. I'm going to show you what it really means to make love to someone," he ran his thumb over my bottom lip, "how wonderful being with someone that cares about you is, and how much you can share of yourself."

My eyes filled with moisture as his loving words rolled over me.

"Then I'm going to show it to you again, and again," he leaned forward and kissed me gently one time, "but not until you are ready to make that commitment." He touched his lips to mine again. "Not tonight, not now, and that has nothing to do with me not wanting you. That has everything to do with the fact that when I do make love to you, he will not be anywhere in your thoughts."

"Thank you, Gavin." I cleared my emotionally-clogged throat. "Thank you."

"Please don't thank me." He closed his eyes. "Do me a favor and forget every negative thing that man ever said about you because every single one of them was a lie."

I snuggled back onto his chest, wrapping one arm around his neck and the other around his back. His grasp on me was solid, strong, and in his arms I felt loved and protected, for the first time in my adult life.

"You know I used to think about you," I stated.

"Huh?" he responded.

"After I saw you in the parking lot, I used to wonder about you."

"You did, really?" His voice had relaxed, and I closed my eyes to allow it to wash over me.

"I did. I lost an earring that day. My parents had gotten them for me when I had graduated from college. They were these little gold studs in a teardrop shape with a diamond. I guess when I dropped my purse, one popped out."

"It did, huh?" he said softly and rubbed my back.

"Every time I would come across that earring, I wondered if you might have found it. I used to dream that you did and that you brought it back to me."

"What did you do when I brought it back to you?" he whispered in my ear and kissed my head again.

"I threw my arms around you and kissed you."

His hands stilled for a moment and then he laughed. "You did not," he said when his laughter died down.

I sat up and looked at him, "I did." I smiled at him. "I used to fantasize that you were in love with me. You were my knight in shining armor, and you rescued me."

The smile died on his face, and the desire that had dissipated in his eyes flashed back with such intensity that I felt it deep in my core.

"I guess your fantasy came true," he murmured as he pulled me against him in a rush. There was no hiding the need in his kiss—or the feelings that rushed through me. I wrapped my arms around his shoulders and kissed him with everything that was in me, with the passion I had dreamed of showing years ago.

His hands roamed over my back and along my side, brushing the edge of my breast. I ached to feel his touch. He nipped at my lip, and I whimpered against his mouth. He shifted under me and his erection pushed against my hip. A need I had never felt whipped through me, and I pulled away.

My chest heaved with pent-up emotions, and I stared into his eyes feeling bolder than I ever had. I sat up and moved to straddle him. He groaned and dropped his head back to the couch cushion, putting his hands on my hips and pushing up against me.

Oh god, I wanted this man. I wanted to touch him and lose myself in his touch. I wanted to feel those things that he had promised me I would feel.

I held his face and brought it to mine. His arms held me snuggled against him as I spread kisses over his lips and jaw. I rolled my hips against him and felt him shudder. "Trinity, you have to stop."

"I don't want to," I whispered in his ear. "I want you, Gavin. I need you, please," I begged.

His hand wrapped around the back of my neck, and he tilted his head so his mouth could ravish my throat. Our hips moved against one another, and I thought I would combust with heat.

I heard Callie growl behind me, and I was about to suggest we move into the other room. I thought maybe she didn't like us being this close, but she barked and raced off to the front door.

Gavin and I broke apart with the urgent sound of her barking. A crashing sound reached our ears, and Gavin picked me up and dropped me on the couch in one move. He reached for his ankle, and I sucked in a breath when I saw his gun. He stood and glanced at me, "Stay here."

Callie continued to bark and growl, the kind of bark that meant business. I heard Gavin reach the door and tell Callie to stay.

I raced to the hallway to give her a command, knowing she wouldn't listen to Gavin. He opened the door and Callie rushed right past him, her ears up, her teeth bared. She was upset about something, and my adrenaline surged.

Gavin went out behind the dog, and I heard Callie barking down the roadway. Tires from a car squealed and sped off away from the house. I ran to the door, worried that Callie would chase the car and get hit.

"Callie!" I yelled as I hit the doorway.

Gavin stood staring at my car. "Oh, no!"

I ran down the steps and stopped at my car, thoughts of my dog on hold as I stared at the shattered window.

Gavin bent down and holstered his gun and stood back up. "Callie!" he shouted.

I stared at the broken windshield of my car. "Who did this?"

Gavin put his arm around me. "I have a feeling I know."

"What? Who?" I stared up at him and saw Callie trot over to us. Gavin reached down and rubbed her head.

"Good girl, Callie. You almost got him, yes you did."

"You saw who it was?" I reached down and patted Callie's head as she rubbed against my pants.

"Not really. When I got to the steps, I saw Callie tearing down the street. Damn, she's fast! Anyway, I saw a guy jump into the passenger seat of a car and it raced away. They were in a Dodge, not sure what make it was, there are a few with the new taillight design, but Callie almost got him right before he closed the door."

"Who was it?" I turned to look at my damaged car.

Gavin sighed, "Let's go inside, I need to call this in."

I stomped my foot. "Gavin, who the hell did this?" I demanded, crossing my arms over my chest.

"I think it was the same guy who probably put nails in your tires," he paused, "Derek."

"What?" I dropped my arms. "Why?"

"Let's go inside and let me call the station, and then I will explain what happened the other day."

Gavin ushered Callie and me inside and made a phone call to get someone over to take the report. I paced back and forth in the kitchen until he hung up.

"Explain." I spun on him.

He sighed and put his hands into the front pockets of his jeans and leaned back against the counter. "Derek got suspended on Wednesday."

She considered what I said. "Because of the complaint I filed?"

I nodded, "But yours was not the first. This was his fourth complaint in six months. He got a few days' suspension."

"Obviously, he needs more than that!" I barked out.

"I figured it has to be him. He was pissed at me that day, too. Probably why he threw a rock through my window, too."

I stared at him. "They broke your window? I didn't even notice." I shook my head. "Wait, why was he angry with you?"

I had hoped I wouldn't have to tell her this, but I figured it would probably get back to her if I didn't. It would be best coming from me.

"The day he got suspended, he mouthed off to me about you. I got pissed and slammed him up against the wall in the bathroom. I told him to stay away from you."

I wasn't sure how I felt about him getting physical with another guy over me, but in a way I was flattered. On the other hand, the thought of Gavin threatening someone gave me flashbacks of Brenden, and an uneasy feeling slipped into my gut.

"I'm sorry, Trinity." He pulled me to stand in front of him, his hands on my hips. "I can see it in your eyes. I would never hurt you that way. I was pissed that he was saying things about you. I would never lay a hand on you like that."

I knew that, and I felt guilty for the few moments the thought took shelter in my mind. I stepped into his arms and laid my head against his chest. "I know you wouldn't."

Police officers showed up a few minutes later and took the report. Gavin's passenger window had been smashed instead of his windshield which he said was better, because he could still drive it home that night. I wasn't able to see though my spider-webbed glass.

After the police left, Gavin pulled me into his arms. "I should probably go. You need to get some sleep."

"You don't have to," I said as I snuggled up to his wide chest.

"Yes, I do," he chuckled. "If I don't, we are going to wind up back where we were on the couch, or in your room."

"Hmm…" I thought for a moment and realized he was right. "Okay, you better go." I walked him to the door.

"Thank you for tonight," he said as he kissed my forehead. "I had a great time."

"Until someone busted our windows," I added and he laughed darkly.

"Yeah, until then. What are you doing tomorrow?"

I shrugged, "Probably nothing since I won't have a car to drive until I get the glass fixed. Why?"

"Would you like to spend the day with me?" he asked, and my heart danced in my chest.

"I'd like that."

"Me, too. I'll call you in the morning." He planted a firm kiss on my lips. "Lock the door and put your alarm on."

"Yes sir," I gave him a mock salute. "I'll talk to you tomorrow. Drive safely."

He started to step out the door but spun and wrapped his arm around my waist, hauling me against him. He kissed me with enough passion to weaken my knees and give pause to my heart—again.

He pulled away, "I miss you, already." He closed his eyes for a brief moment, kissed me on the forehead, and walked out the door, leaving me to droop against the wall as my body continued to hunger for his.

Chapter 20 - Gavin

I took a minute to dust the fragments of glass from my seat and swore I'd get that bastard for breaking our windows. It had to be that prick, Derek. I growled as I climbed in my car and backed out of the driveway.

At least the anger I felt had calmed my raging hormones. I could still smell Trinity on me. The fact that I didn't have a passenger window whipped her scent off my skin and around my head, almost dizzying me.

I thought back to the incredible time we'd had tonight. I loved kicking back with her friends and enjoying a nice relaxing dinner. I was happy that they'd obtained the new funds because as I listened to the two women go on and on about their plans, I realized they were going to need a lot of money to finance it all.

I finished my drive reliving the quiet moments as I had held Trinity in my arms. A frown passed over my face momentarily at the memory of her saying she couldn't be pleased in bed. What a freaking jerk her husband was for never trying to help her enjoy sex.

I snorted: his loss, my gain. When the time was right, I couldn't wait to make her scream my name and finally know what making love was all about—with me.

I entered the foyer of my townhouse and made a beeline for my bedroom, taking the stairs two at a time. There on the top of my bargain basement dresser was a wooden box. I slid my finger over the top of the scarred wood where a dove was painted, faded and worn. It was one of the few things I had kept of my mothers. The top gave the faintest squeak as I lifted it. Inside were a few trinkets, my dress watch that I hardly ever wore, and a little green felt bag. I grasped the bag and lifted it as if it were the most precious thing in the world. The strings at the top were pulled tight, and I loosened them and shook out the single object from inside. It was finally time to return it to its rightful owner.

I fell asleep that night with her on my mind and woke up with a start. My heart blasted against my ribcage as I sat straight up in bed. My God! I had to stop dreaming like this!

Unlike last time, I wasn't in Trinity's old house, this time it was the house in which she lived now, and I hadn't shown up in a patrol car, I had ridden in on horseback.

I had rushed inside to find Trinity on the floor, a man on top of her choking her, but as I gasped at the sight, the man turned and it wasn't Brenden, it was Derek.

Obviously, I was worried about her and what Derek might do next. I glanced at the clock, four-fifteen. I sighed and rolled over, hoping I could drift off for a few more minutes. I tried to recall happier memories of Trinity and forced thoughts of the dream away.

I was remembering the look on her face while we were riding the Ferris wheel when my phone started to ring. For a brief moment, I wondered if it was her and she was awake thinking of me.

Reality crashed back down when I saw it was work. "Yeah," I said in the way of a hello.

"Sorry to wake you, Brooksfield," I recognized the voice of Tony Ridder, one of the sergeants from the other shift.

"No worries, I was awake. What do you need?" I sat up, wiping my eyes with the fingers of one hand.

"Any way you could cover a shift today? Tom is out of town on vacation and Vickery just called in sick, sounds like he got the flu from his kid." His portable police radio chattered in the background.

I thought about how I had planned on spending the day with Trinity, but I hated to leave the squad in a lurch. "Yeah, I can do it." As much as I wanted to be with her, duty came first.

We hung up a few minutes later, and I stumbled into the shower. I was disappointed that I wouldn't be able to see Trinity, but I knew she would understand.

Later that morning, I got in touch with the company which repaired our police car windows and asked if they had any windshield in stock for Trinity's car, and they did. I passed along the address and asked them to stop there before they came over to fix my passenger window.

I dialed Trinity's cellphone, and she answered it on the third ring. "Good morning," her voice was so husky it gave me chills while totally turning me on.

"Good morning, beautiful, did I wake you?" I shifted in my seat.

"No, not really. I woke up a little while ago. I just didn't feel like climbing out of bed yet. I was lying here thinking." I heard her yawn and could just imagine her snuggled under her covers.

"What were you thinking about?" Did I really ask that? Did I really want to know?

"You," she whispered.

Yeah, I really wanted to know. Damn! Why had I taken this shift? I wanted to smack myself.

"I hope those are good thoughts." Like really good thoughts, maybe she was having another fantasy. That thought gave me a chill, but not for a good reason as it reminded me of my dream.

"Of course they were good. What are you doing now? Is that the police radio I hear?" I glanced at the radio in my car and turned the volume down.

"Yeah, that's why I was calling you. Unfortunately, I got called in to cover a shift. I won't be able to spend the day with you."

"That's okay, I understand. Work comes first, I get that." She paused for a moment, "Do you want to come over for dinner tonight?"

Boy, would I love to have a repeat of last night, but I wasn't sure my hormones could take it. "I'm not sure. It would have to be an early night. I have to get up and meet Taylor. We have to go pick something up for a job he's doing, and it's a six-hour drive, one way."

"I could warm you up some leftover lasagna. You don't have to stay late, just come by and have a warm dinner."

"Seriously?" Other than my sister, no one had ever invited me over for a quick hot meal after work. I thought for a moment what dessert could be, but put a stop on those thoughts quickly.

She laughed, "Yes, seriously."

"Okay, if it's not too much trouble. I should be off around seven. I could be over there by seven-thirty."

"Great, no problem. I'll have it ready, feed you, and then send you off to bed."

This woman was going to be the death of me. "Okay, oh and by the way, you should probably get dressed. Someone is coming by your house in a few minutes to fix your windshield."

"What? Really? How did you get that done so quickly?"

She thanked me after I explained.

"Can you do me a favor, Trinity?" I tensed, wondering how she would take being asked to be extra careful until we got a chance to talk to Derek.

"Sure, Gavin, what is it?" The sound of drawers opening reminded me that she was probably getting ready to change, and my thoughts took a nose dive, again.

"Uh," I started to answer her when the dispatcher on the radio called out to me, "hold on, Trinity."

The dispatcher was sending me to a holdup alarm at a bank. "Trinity, I gotta go, I'll call you back later."

I took off to backup the other two officers responding to the call. It turned out to be an actual bank robbery, and the subject got away. Every available officer in our jurisdiction and surrounding areas flooded the area and searched, but we didn't find anything.

The FBI showed up, and I went from being the supervising officer to standing around waiting for them to give us directions.

My stomach growled, and I glanced at my watch. It was already three o'clock. Damn…I wasn't going to get out of here until late. I sighed, I was going to have to call Trinity and cancel again.

We finally cleared the call a little before five when I climbed into my car and pulled out my phone. My battery was about to die, I plugged it into my charger and dialed her number.

"Hey, you, busy day?" she asked when she answered.

"Yeah, long day. I've been on a bank robbery since I hung up with you this morning." I was exhausted and starved.

"I guess you are calling to cancel, huh?" She sounded disappointed and my heart tripped over itself. I loved hearing those little things in her voice. It showed me that she cared.

"Yeah, unfortunately, I'll be late getting all these reports taken care of and approved. Sorry." I started the patrol car and drove out of the parking lot while I talked.

"Don't apologize. Have you eaten anything today?" Her coffeemaker made startup sounds in the background. I could so use some coffee.

"No, didn't have time. I'll get something quick when I get off."

"Absolutely not, I'll bring you dinner. You can eat while you work. Are you on the way back to the station now?"

"Yeah, I am, but you don't need to do that." The woman was offering to bring me dinner? At work? Where did I find this woman?

"You're right, I don't need to do that, but I'm going to."

"Have I told you lately that—" I stopped myself. I almost said I love you. I rushed to finish, "—you're the best." Talk about putting my foot in my mouth, I just tried to stick both in, with my work boots on, damn! I rolled my eyes.

Trinity laughed, she knew exactly what I'd been about to say. "I'll see you in a little while." Before I could say anything else, she hung up.

What a fool I was. Okay, maybe not a fool because it was true, I did love her. I had fallen in love with her ten years ago, and over these last two weeks, I'd gone head over heels. No wonder I was sticking my feet in my mouth.

I parked at the station and put the conversation behind me as I ended up in the chief's office filling him in on what had happened since we'd last spoken.

One of the patrol officers knocked on the door a little while later, "Sarge, there's a woman out front for you. Looks like she has food for you." He raised an eyebrow and grinned.

The chief excused me, and I hustled to the reception area. Trinity stiffened when she saw me; her eyes flowed from my head to my feet.

This was the first time she had seen me in uniform in ten years. I could only imagine what went through her mind. She seemed to shake herself and meet my eyes.

"Are you alright?" I asked in a subdued voice so the guys behind us wouldn't hear me.

"Yes, sorry, I knew you were at work, but I forgot you wear the uniform. It was stupid of me not to think about it."

"It's okay, don't apologize. I'm sure seeing me in the uniform is difficult." I rubbed her arm.

"It brings back memories." Her eyes saddened for a moment.

I leaned in and kissed her forehead, "I'm sure it does." Before I could say anything else, she stepped a half step back and handed me an insulated lunch box. "You really didn't need to do this."

Her real smile came back. "I wanted to."

"Thank you, I'm starving." We both laughed when my stomach growled in agreement.

"Go eat," she shooed me away with her hands, but I grabbed one before she could turn away.

"Thank you, beautiful." I leaned in and kissed her one time.

"You're welcome, Gavin. Have a good night." I held the door open for her as she exited and kept an eye on her until she got to her car.

As the door closed behind me, the ribbing started. "Sarge finally has a girlfriend!" one of them called out.

Another one laughed and threw out, "She's hot, man. Can't believe you took a shift to work with us when you had that at home. Damn!"

"Awwww, how sweet, she brings you dinner! Man, where can I get one of those? My old lady doesn't do that." They all laughed good-naturedly, and we went into the squad room to start on the paperwork from the very long day shift.

They all stopped giving me a hard time when the smell of the heated lasagna filled the room. "Damn, she could have brought more with her."

"Sorry, guys, leftovers from last night's dinner. Wouldn't have been enough for everyone," I talked around the food in my mouth. Manners weren't the same in here as they were every place else. No one complained if you talked with food in your mouth or burped after you drank a soda.

The food hit the spot, and I was able to focus on my paperwork. It was almost nine-thirty when I finished reviewing the last report and signed off on it. I was bone tired and weary as hell.

I sent Trinity a message, *Thank you for the food. You know the way to a man's heart.*

A few minutes later she responded, *Lol, glad you enjoyed it.*

Three times I typed, *I missed you today*, and three times I erased it. Finally, I typed it one more time and hit the send button.

I waited for a response with bated breath. Was that too forward?

My phone pinged at me right after my screen went to sleep. I woke it up and read her reply.

I missed you, too, more than you know. Sweet dreams, Gavin.

Sweet dreams, beautiful.

Chapter 21 - Trinity

I was disappointed that I wouldn't see Gavin during the day but excited to have him over for dinner at least. I'd decided last night while I lay staring at the ceiling that I was ready to give it a real go. It had been way too long for me not to get out there and live a life with someone. I trusted him, and I daresay that I was falling in love with him. Was that even possible?

I knew I could fall in love, I'd done it once, but that hadn't been real. The man I'd fallen in love with, pledged my life to, had been an imposter. It had all been an act. Would the same thing happen again? It took a long time for me to realize that Gavin was nothing like Brenden. I knew Gavin was honest and would do anything to protect me. I knew in my soul that he would never do anything to hurt me on purpose.

Maybe that was why I'd told him about my crazy dream. It had been a young woman's wish to be happy and free in a time when I wasn't. How ironic that so many years later, that same man walked back into my life and started bringing that dream to life.

Instead of spending time with Gavin, I spent my normal morning with Brooke over coffee. I shared with her my feelings of how I was ready to move forward, and she praised me on it, while still cautioning me to move slowly.

Ha, she had no idea how slowly I didn't want to go. Gavin had promised to show me all that I had missed while being married to Brenden, and I was ready and willing to find out everything—and I meant everything—that I'd missed.

I spent the afternoon cleaning and thinking through a new presentation that I would give later this week at another seminar. This one wasn't for law enforcement but for a corporation. We were branching out to educate as many people as we could. This was going to be the first one, and I was nervous about it.

I had a good plan of what I was going to say, and like normal, I rehearsed it a few times in my mind. I wasn't one to write things down. I felt more comfortable moving around and keeping my eyes on the audience. If I forgot to mention something, there was always next time.

When Gavin called in the late afternoon, I was on the couch reading a book. It was a rare moment when I allowed myself the time to sit back and really relax.

I picked up on his little slip, and while I laughed it off, it both scared and excited me to know that he might feel that strongly towards me. It reminded me of my thoughts earlier that morning.

It had been a long day for him, I could hear it in his voice, and I had no trouble offering to bring him dinner. It gave me a purpose, and I rushed to dish out a large serving and cut some bread. I even made him a large travel cup of coffee. I could still remember Brenden complaining about the coffee at the station.

I smiled as I walked out to my car. The windshield was fixed, and I had thoroughly cleaned the car.

As I drove to the station, I never once thought about the fact that he would be in uniform. I had not seen him in one since the night Brenden was arrested. When he stepped out into the reception area, my heart stilled.

Visions of Brenden in his uniform flowed through my head like a raging river. Like Gavin, he had looked amazing in it, but Brenden should never have been allowed to stand behind the badge—not the monster he was. A tiny sliver of fear filled me as I wondered if the badge on Gavin's chest hid anything that would hurt me in the future.

Gavin picked up on my insecurity immediately. I was amazed that he could see it in my eyes and knew me well enough to not only see my fear but to understand it.

I waved to him as he stood at the door watching me get safely to my car. How I wished he had been able to come by my house for dinner, but I understood the demands of his time.

I had always been thankful for the few times Brenden had called and told me he would be late. Most nights he came and went when he felt like it, and I never knew when the front door would open.

He is not Brenden, I reminded myself, Thank God! That time in my life was over. Brenden was tucked nicely into a metal cell down south for another twenty years, at least.

I remembered the day they read the verdict. I'd sat beside my parents in the back of the courtroom, holding their hands. When the juror chairman read the ruling for the one count of attempted homicide, I stopped breathing until the final words left his mouth: Guilty. My world had spun. I had dropped my head into my hands and balled.

Total chaos had broken out in the courtroom, and the judge had slammed his gavel. I had jumped and looked up. Gavin had been turned in his chair, watching me. The smile that slid over his lips had been bittersweet.

That had been the last time I stared a hole into Brenden's back. His head hung down and his shoulders sagged. It had been fitting to see that, especially after all the times he had made me do the same.

I went home and watched television, pushing the thoughts of Brenden far into the recesses of my mind. I would never see him again, and that was fine with me.

* * *

Sunday slipped by in a blur of things to get done for the organization. Brooke and I sent emails back and forth discussing details of the money we were to receive. Yes, we could have talked, but sometimes when you got on the phone, you went off on a tangent. Shooting emails back and forth kept us on task. We did it all the time in the office, even though our offices were side by side.

On Monday morning, we shared the news with Marcy and then with the property managers at the sites. Everyone was ecstatic, and they all asked what changes they would be seeing. Tuesday morning, Brooke and I waited with bated breath for the money transfer confirmation email to arrive. The moment Brooke got the email, she squealed, and Marcy and I ran into her office. She pulled up our account online as we rushed around her desk. When the account popped up and showed the money sitting in our account, we screamed and jumped up and down, hugging each other.

"This calls for a celebration! Why don't we go out for lunch? We always order in or bring our own stuff. Let's go have... I don't know, let's go have Mexican and toast this with a margarita," Marcy exclaimed in a rush.

Brooke looked at her watch, "But it's only ten-thirty."

"So? By the time we get our desks cleaned off and are ready to leave, it will be after eleven. We can walk to that place down the street. That will take what, a good twenty minutes. I think they open at eleven anyway, so no big deal," Marcy begged.

"You know what?" I looked at both of them. "I think that is a great idea—my treat."

"Okay, boss!" Marcy giggled and went back to her desk to finish what she was doing.

"Trinity, I can't believe we got this contributor. This is so major!" Brooke sank down in her chair and stared at the computer screen.

"I know, it's huge!" My face already hurt from smiling so hard. "I know you were keeping all the information quiet so no one knew the details, but who is the guy who made the donation? You never told me."

"To be honest, I don't know," she said.

"What do you mean, you don't know?" I sat next to her.

She shrugged her shoulders, "I met with the solicitor. I never met with the actual benefactor."

"How can you not meet with the benefactor? I thought you had three meetings with the man." I couldn't fathom that someone who had never met us would give us three hundred thousand dollars. Did they have more money than they knew what to do with?

"I was told that someone in the man's family had been abused, and he wanted to help others, but wished to remain anonymous." She shrugged again. "There is nothing wrong with that."

I thought about it, she was right; there was nothing wrong with that. It wasn't like we didn't have contributors who wanted to remain in the background, but this was a lot of money. "I guess not."

"Go finish up what you were working on, I'm ready for a margarita and some enchiladas." She shooed me out of her office, and I returned to mine.

I knew I should have been bouncing off the walls with glee, but I felt uncomfortable with this revelation. I had reservations about using the money without really knowing the source.

At eleven-fifteen, we locked up the office and took the twenty-minute walk down the road. Brooke and Marcy chatted almost nonstop the whole way, still caught up in the excitement. I listened to them and wished that I could reclaim the jubilance that I had felt earlier, instead threads of impending doom feathered around my mind, and I kept swatting at them.

We were about to enter the restaurant when my phone rang, Gavin was calling. I told the ladies I would meet them in a minute and answered my phone.

"You have no idea how much I needed to hear your voice right now." The moment I saw his name, I knew that he would be able to calm the strange fears invading my mind.

"Hey, beautiful, what's going on? Are you having a rough day?"

As he spoke, it suddenly all felt so inconsequential. "Strangely enough, no. I'm not having a bad day. In fact, Brooke, Marcy, and I are about to have lunch to celebrate."

He paused for a moment. "Okay, what's going on, Trin? Your voice sounds tense."

"What are you doing tonight?" I blurted out.

"I work until seven; I don't have plans after that. Do you need me to do something for you?" His radio crackled in the background.

"No, yes." I felt like a teenager. "I need you to come see me."

Gavin laughed cautiously. "What's going on Trinity?"

"I don't know. There's something bothering me about the donation that we received. I was hoping we could talk, and you could ease my unusual fears," I bit my lip, "and I'd like to see you."

"Did the donation not go through?" he asked quickly.

"No, it did, that's why we are out celebrating with lunch and margaritas."

"Oh, okay. Well, if I get out on time, I can be there around seven-thirty. Would that work?"

We spoke for a few more moments, and I told him I would have something to eat for him when he got there. Yes, the way to a man's heart was through his stomach. I felt better knowing I would see him later.

I walked into the restaurant and found our table, feeling better than I had since learning about the anonymous donor. If anyone could make me feel better about this, it was Gavin.

I marveled at how easy it was to trust him, and how important his opinion had become to me. I'd come a long way in a very short time.

"Who was that?" Brooke asked as I sat down. "Never mind. With that dreamy look on your face, obviously, it was Gavin."

Marcy and I laughed, and my telltale blush made its appearance. "That obvious, is it?"

Marcy laughed harder, "Um…yeah!"

I hid myself behind the menu for a few moments and listened to them chatter about a new shoe store Marcy loved.

The waitress took our orders and left, and then both pairs of eyes came to me. I looked between them, "What?"

"So…" Marcy said expectantly.

"So what?" I knew where this was going and my stomach fluttered. I took a sip of the margarita in front of me. If I had more than one, I'd have no trouble talking about this.

"Come on," Marcy spouted out, "tell me about him. Brooke was lucky enough to have dinner with you two, but I don't know any more than that he is a walking billboard for sex."

I choked on my drink. "Marcy!"

"Don't 'Marcy' me! Is he as good as he looks like he'd be?"

Brooke laughed, enjoying my thorough discomfort.

"You're not helping," I stared pointedly at her.

She waved her hands in front of her face, "No way. Don't you remember how much you busted on me when I started dating Rick?"

She was right, I had busted on her, worse than they were doing to me.

I sighed dramatically. "No, I have not slept with him." I focused on Marcy, "but I have plans to do that very soon, maybe tonight."

Marcy whooped and Brooke patted me on the shoulder, "About time. Welcome back to the world."

I cringed, "But what if I'm not any good."

Marcy snorted, "No way. Leave Brenden out of this. Don't bring all the clutter from that relationship into this one."

"Easier said than done," I twisted my napkin in my lap. "I did tell Gavin that same thing. You, Brooke, know exactly what I'm talking about. Your ex used to say you sucked in bed. At least Brenden never said the words. He just got off and was done."

Brooke winced for a moment, "Yeah, but my ex was wrong, and so was Brenden. What did Gavin say?"

My cheeks decided to speak for me, and I reached for my drink.

"She needs some liquid courage, this has to be good." Marcy winked at me, and I almost spat my drink over the table.

"He said he was going to show me just how incredible sex was, and show me what I was missing," I blurted out quickly.

Brooke and Marcy glanced at each other, and then we were all giggling. I was transported back to college, pre-Brenden, where I would sit around with my girlfriends, gossiping about who was doing whom and how small their junk was supposed to be.

Lunch arrived and so did another tray of drinks. Good thing we were walking because I knew I wouldn't be in any shape to drive after two.

I had just taken a bite of my food when Marcy turned to me again, "So you plan on riding the baloney pony tonight, huh?"

I literally choked on my food, as did Brooke, and ended up spitting into a napkin, tears running down my face as I laughed so hard I thought I would throw up.

"Baloney pony?" Brooke sputtered in between cackles. I noticed other diners watching us; some looked annoyed, some smiled, taking a small part in the fun we were having."Oh…my…god. I have never heard it put that way," I sputtered between laughs.

Marcy snorted again, a very bad habit of hers, and we continued our hysterics for a few more moments before getting ourselves under control.

"Well? Are you?" she asked once we were able to breathe again.

"Why is it such a concern for you?" I asked.

"I just want to make sure you're ready." She lifted one shoulder.

"I'm almost thirty-five, Marcy. I think I'm ready." It wasn't like I was a virgin. This was about taking back my life in one final step, about giving myself to someone I could trust-someone who would love me back in return, in a healthy way.

"That's not what I'm talking about. Do you have the right lingerie?"

"What does underwear have to do with anything?" I stared at her, but it was Brooke who answered.

"Oh, child, you are far from ready! It has everything to do with it." She took a bite of her food while I stared at her. After she swallowed, she decided, "That's it, we are going shopping right after lunch. Isn't there a lingerie shop on the way back to the office?"

"Sure is!" Marcy exclaimed.

I hadn't thought of underwear. My only thought was getting naked. I guess I wasn't ready, yet, after all.

Chapter 22 - Gavin

"I just heard from the chief that Derek put in to be transferred from our squad," Coven stated as he sat down in the chair next to me in the squad room.

I laughed, "Really? Did he say why?"

"Yeah, he said he had a hard time working for us, said you had it out for him," Coven smirked.

I leaned back in my chair. "He's got that right. What did the chief say?"

Coven chuckled, "The chief told him to suck it up until the squads change later this year."

"Good, the guy's a schmuck. If we are lucky, by the time the squads change, he won't be working here anymore."

Coven stood. "You want to grab a beer after work? These last two shifts have been hell."

I glanced at my watch. "I would, but Trinity invited me over for dinner after work."

Coven slapped me on the back and said jovially, "Damn, now that you have a woman, you dump all us guys! I see how it is."

"Damn right!"

"How are things going with her? You guys getting serious?" he asked as he shifted through some paperwork on his section of the desk.

"Things are good. As far as serious, well, I'm leaving that up to her. As far as I'm concerned, I'm off the market for the rest of my life," I grinned up at him.

"Good for you, Brooksfield. I'm glad to hear that." Just as he finished, two of our patrol guys wandered in with questions, and we busied ourselves for the rest of our shift.

I ended my shift right on time and sped back to my apartment to take a quick shower and grab something for Trinity.

Callie barked at the door as I knocked at seven-forty, and when Trinity opened the door, she took my breath away. She wore old jeans and a soft baby blue t-shirt, but to me she had never looked more beautiful.

"I'm sorry I'm late, I ran home to shower and change." I stepped inside and pet Callie for a moment.

"No problem, dinner is ready. I just need to take it out of the oven when you are ready to eat." She closed the door and leaned her back against it.

"It can wait a few minutes." I approached her and curled my hands around her hips. "There is another kind of sustenance that I could use just now."

She tilted her head in a sexy way, her long auburn hair falling away from her cheek. I cupped it with my hand and ran my thumb over her cheekbone.

She tipped her chin up as I wet my lips and leaned in to her. If I could possibly live off her kisses, I would choose them over food any day.

She wrapped her arms around my neck and deepened the kiss. I pressed her back against the door, our bodies in full contact from chest to thigh.

Callie yelped beside us and nuzzled us with her wet nose. We broke apart laughing. "Guess someone is jealous," Trinity said as she rubbed Callie's head.

"Yeah, well she better get used to it," I said as I dropped my arms from around her.

"Come on, let's go feed you before the quiche gets dried out." She walked into the kitchen.

"As long as you promise that I can pick that back up where we left off." I loved seeing her cheeks begin to color.

"I don't think you will have to twist my arm," she said flirtatiously while her emerald eyes twinkled.

Okay, how long would it take to eat because if she looked at me like that, or spoke in that soft husky voice any longer, food be damned!

She asked me to pour some wine, and I did while she served up some spinach salad and plates of quiche. It smelled great, and my stomach commanded me to stop the hanky-panky for a little while.

We chatted over dinner about some of the things we had done at work. I marveled over how comfortable and normal it all felt. Being here with Trinity, sitting in her home, talking about our days, and eating were what most people took for granted. I wanted that. I wanted her—forever.

While I finished up the last few bites on my second helping, Trinity sat and watched me.

"A penny for your thoughts," I offered after I wiped my mouth and pushed my plate back.

She shook her head playfully. "Sorry, my thoughts are worth more than that."

"I have no doubt." I rested my elbows on the table. "So what's on your mind?"

She shrugged and stood up, picking up our plates to take them to the sink. I grabbed our salad bowls and followed her.

"What's going on in that head of yours, sweetheart?" I persisted as I set the bowls on the counter.

"You'll think it's silly," she said as she glanced my way, but didn't quite meet my gaze.

"What I think is silly," I took the plate out of her hand and set it down, turning her in my arms so I could look her in the face, "is that you won't tell me what you're thinking about."

She hesitated, and a light pink started to rise on her cheeks. "Fine, I was thinking that I really like being able to sit down and talk to you after a long day. I like having you here for dinner. I like having you here in my house." She shrugged, "I just like having you here."

Had she been reading my mind? "Trinity, ironically, I was thinking the same thing while we ate. There is nothing silly about it." I kissed her forehead. "You know how I feel about you."

"Yes, I do." She leaned up and kissed me once.

I took her by the hand. "Come on, let's go sit down. I have something for you."

"You have something for me?" she echoed as she followed. I stopped at the table to grab our wineglasses and then led her into the family room.

Before I sat down, I reached into my front pocket and pulled out the little felt bag and palmed it so she couldn't see what it was.

"Yes, I have something for you." I sat down at an angle so I could better see her. "Well, actually I am returning something to you."

She asked, confused, "What are you returning? Did you borrow something that I don't know about?"

I shook my head, "No, you lost something, and I found it." I opened my hand and held out the small green bag. "It's time to give it back to you."

She stared at the bag for a few seconds before her eyes flashed to mine. "What is it, Gavin?" Her voice was huskier than normal, and I knew she already had an idea of what was inside the bag.

"Open it." I held my hand closer and saw her fingers shaking as she reached for the bag. She upended it, and the earring she had lost in the parking lot the first time we met fell into her palm.

"Oh, my god! Gavin! You found it? You've had it this whole time?" Tears spilled over as her words left her lips.

"Yeah, I've had it since the day you dropped your purse. I held onto it with the hopes that someday I would see you again and could return it. I wasn't sure if it meant anything to you or not. I thought maybe Brenden had given it to you and you wouldn't want it back, but when you mentioned that your parents gave you the earrings, I figured it was time to bring it home."

Trinity threw her arms around me, "Gavin, thank you. Thank you." She sniffed, "You have no idea how much this means to me."

She pulled away from me and slipped it into her ear. "Hold on, I need to go get the other one." She jumped up and raced from the room.

Good job, Gavin! I gave myself a mental pat on the back.

She skipped into the room a few minutes later, her hair pulled behind her ears so she could show off the matching pair. "You know, I kept them in my purse because Brenden had gotten rid of all my jewelry. I was wearing these the day he took it all. If they had been in my jewelry box, he would have gotten rid of them, too."

"Why did he do that?" The guy made good money, so he wasn't pawning the stuff for cash.

"I was cleaning the house, and I had a necklace on that he gave me. I broke it by accident, and he said that since I couldn't take care of anything, he was getting rid of it all," she spoke without emotion.

"Are you kidding me?" I was stunned and a little pissed off. Accidents happened, why would he punish someone for something like that? Oh wait, because he was a controlling prick who would do anything to abuse his wife, mentally and physically.

"Nope, dead serious," she shook her head, "but I don't want to talk about that, or Brenden." She moved towards me, "I want to thank you properly."

"Oh, really? And how are you going to do that?" I asked as she pushed me back against the cushion and climbed onto my lap. My body responded immediately to the look in her eyes.

Those beautiful green eyes were no longer shy but seductive as she ran her hands up my chest and around my neck. "Like this."

She leaned in and kissed my lips slowly, running her tongue along my bottom lip before I opened up to take part in the loving touch.

Her kisses and hands were bold, much bolder than the last time we were in this position, and she ground her hips against mine. This woman was trying to kill me.

I took her face in mine, "Slow down, Trinity."

"No." She pushed forward to kiss me again.

If I didn't stop her soon, I wouldn't be able to stop. "Trinity, honey. You don't have to do this."

She kissed my jaw and nibbled on my neck. I was so about to be a goner.

"I want to," she whispered in my ear, and I almost exploded in my pants.

"Trinity, if you don't stop, I'm not going to be able to," I murmured as she bit my ear lobe.

"Good," she giggled in my ear.

Did she really just giggle? How much wine did she have tonight?

"Trinity, we have to stop." I pushed on her shoulder to put some space between us and hoped that she realized what she was saying.

She met my heated gaze, her own eyes glazed with desire that quickly began to fade as she looked at me. Her cheeks began to color. "I get it, you're not interested. Oh god, I'm so sorry." She began to climb off my lap, and I planted my hands firmly on her hips to hold her still.

"Are you kidding?" Her cheeks grew brighter, and she stared at my chest. "Trinity, you have no idea how much I want this, want you, and I'm well aware that we are consenting adults." I swallowed, "I don't have any protection with me. I never expected this to happen, and unlike most single guys, I don't carry one in my wallet."

She continued staring at my chest for a long time. I lifted her chin with my thumb. Emotions flickered through her eyes and over her features until she finally seemed to grab one and hold it tight. "So you really do want to make love to me?" she questioned softly.

"Are you kidding? Trinity, honey, I have dreamed of holding you and making love to you for years. This," I pointed to her chest and then mine, "this is something I could only pray would someday happen." I cupped her face, "You have no idea how much I want you, how beautiful I think you are."

The color began to recede from her face and I placed a soft kiss on her nose. "Can I ask you a question?" Trinity stared at a spot over my shoulder as she spoke.

"Of course, you can ask me anything." I kept hold of her face so she couldn't hide from me.

"Have you been with a lot of women?" She could barely look at me.

"I've been with my fair share, Trinity. I'm thirty-four, I was engaged at one time, and I lived with another woman for a while. Are you worried about me having a disease? Is that why you are asking?"

She shook her head, "No, I'm sure you get tested. I'm…" she clenched her eyes closed, and inhaled deeply, "I'm just afraid that I won't be what you are expecting, and then what we have will disappear. I don't have very much experience."

"Honey, I told you before, that when the time was right, I was going to show you what it was like to be loved. There is a huge difference between having sex and making love with someone, and I'm going to show you that—and I hold no expectations on how it will be because I know that when I make love to you, it is going to be the most incredible experience of both of our lives." A lopsided smile began on her face. "Trinity, I don't think you quite understand how much I care about you. All those years ago, knowing what was going on behind closed doors and knowing I couldn't do anything, especially that night." I looked away for a moment and rubbed her arms. "That night, I felt useless. I had to take Brenden back to the station, so we could process him and I could get the charges filed, and the whole time all I could think about was if you were okay. I called the hospital five or six times to check on you, and they would only tell me you were alive.

"Did you know that after I finally had Brenden arraigned, I sat at the hospital until the next morning so I would be close to you?" A wry laugh escaped my lips. "A doctor finally felt sorry for me and told me you were going to be alright physically, after a long recovery, and that you were going to live."

She cocked her head to the side. "I didn't know that."

"It's true. Then when we were going through the trial, I wanted so badly to talk to you, to check on you, but you were always surrounded by family and friends and I was afraid to."

"I wish you had." She traced a finger down the side of my face.

"I wish I had, too. I wish that we hadn't lost touch, maybe we would have been able to start a relationship back then."

She looked thoughtful for a moment. "Maybe, but I think I needed this time to find myself, to find the strength to try again, the courage to try to love someone again."

She finally met my gaze head on. She'd said the courage to love again. Did that mean she was falling in love with me? Dare I ask?

"Trinity, can you answer a question for me now?" She nodded once. "Have you finally found the courage to love someone again?"

She chewed on her bottom lip as she gave a very small nod.

"Can I be bold enough to think that it might be me that you are finding the courage to fall in love with?" I held my breath, afraid that if I moved she would bolt.

She surprised me by leaning in and staring at my lips as she grew closer. Her nose touched mine gently, and her gaze flashed up to mine. "You may be so bold," she said softly right before she closed the final inch and kissed me.

I allowed her to control the kiss.

I swallowed and couldn't tear my gaze from hers as she continued. "I care about you, Gavin. I'm falling in love with you, fast." She stopped and bit her lip, but I waited because I could see in her eyes that she wasn't done. "I'm scared, scared of trusting another man, of loving someone so much that they could destroy me, but I can't stop the way I feel around you. I crave the sight of you and the sound of your voice. When I'm happy, I want to tell you. When I'm angry, I want it to be you that I vent to. I want a future with you. I want you."

Tears came to her eyes, and I felt as if I had lost my own voice. To hear those words roll off her tongue after so long of dreaming of them, I was speechless.

"I can understand if you don't want that, especially with someone like me, but—" she rushed the words out when I didn't respond, but I never let her finish her sentence.

"Stop." I pushed her hips down over my groin. "Does that feel like a man who doesn't want you? Trinity, I told you before, I want you, I want this. My concern right now is that I don't have any protection. I don't want you to get pregnant."

"Would it be so bad if I did get pregnant?"

"What?" the word flew out of my mouth so suddenly I couldn't have stopped it if I had tried. She jumped and then froze, staring at me with wide eyes. Did she even know what she just said?

"Trinity, what are you saying? Do you want a child? With me?"

Chapter 23 - Trinity

Holy crap. Did those words really come out of my mouth? I'm not sure if I was more surprised by asking if getting pregnant was such a bad thing or the harshness of his voice when "What?" flew from his lips.

All I knew was that at that particular moment, my life flashed in front of my eyes. While Gavin and I had eaten dinner, I pictured us five years from now doing the same thing. I could see him as a permanent fixture in my life. I also knew that when I had bought this house, I'd had every intention of someday having a family. At that very moment, as those words flowed off my tongue, I wanted all of that with Gavin.

How that was possible after only getting to know him for two weeks? All I knew, from the depths of my being, was that it was possible.

I tensed while I took in Gavin's surprised features and couldn't figure out if he was angry or ready to have a heart attack.

What a fool I was to think I could have it all: a family, someone who would treat me as an equal while loving me and protecting me.

"Whoa…whoa…whoa…come back here." Gavin grasped my hips to keep me from moving off his lap. I was mortified as I watched my dreams begin to fade like smoke in a breeze.

He held my face in his hands and forced me to look at him. I realized that as I stared into his eyes, he wasn't angry, he looked anxious, like my answer was more important than anything else that he had ever asked. Did I want a child, or was it having a child with him that was the most important?

Of course I wanted a child, most women wanted children, not all, but most. Dinner flashed back into my mind, and the moments I had caught him watching me, and laughing with me. Our dinner with Brooke and Rick, the day he kept me from falling through the floor and, most importantly, the day he saved my life. All those moments crossed my mind, and I knew that when he had handed me back my earring, I had stepped off the cliff edge and fallen in love with him.

What man would keep a trinket like that for over ten years? What man would wait to see if it was a good memory or a bad memory before he did return it? Gavin. Gavin would, and he did.

I met his eyes and felt strength rise in me that I had not felt in years. "I'm falling in love with you, Gavin. I know what I want. I want you. I want a future with you."

I cursed my emotions as my eyes welled with moisture. I didn't want to cry, but he hadn't said anything, and I had just bared my soul. Maybe I had been wrong about how he felt.

When he yanked me to him and blazed a kiss over my lips hot enough to boil water on the frozen tundra, I had my answer, and my heart stuttered.

"Where is your bedroom?" His voice was so low and husky that I shivered.

"Upstairs," I muttered as I devoured his neck. "Wait, put me down." I wiggled in his arms after he had taken a few a steps.

I slid down his body, but kept my arms wrapped around his neck. I hesitated for a moment before I kissed him one more time and took his hand. "I need to be in control of this."

He grinned, "Be in control all you want." He followed me up the stairs, running his thumb over the back of my hand as we walked.

When I reached my bedroom, I turned to him and fought the shyness that threatened. I took a slow cleansing breath and stared up at him.

His arms wrapped around me, and he reeled me in slowly. The kiss he placed on my lips was a tender seduction, and my knees grew weak as I inclined towards him.

Gavin kissed my jawline and nibbled on the top of my ear. "It's not too late to stop," he whispered as his nose ran along the rim of my ear.

I pulled his face back. "Do you want to stop, Gavin? If this isn't what you want, then tell me."

Gavin ran his hand down the back of my head, "Trinity, I have wanted you from the day I saw you in the parking lot. The only way I am going to stop is if you tell me to."

My heart melted into a puddle in my chest. I knew that if we were in the middle of sex, and I told him to stop, he would. That knowledge helped push me over the edge, and I pulled him tighter to me. "Make love to me, Gavin," I whispered before our lips met.

Gavin scooped me up and carried me into my room. On the bed, he stopped and pulled my sneakers off slowly, keeping eye contact the entire time. He set my shoes on the floor and toed off his own before he ran his hands up the tops of my legs. When he crawled onto the bed, I pushed myself into the center, and he inched his way over the length of me, stopping with his hands beside my hips.

His gaze finally left my face and journeyed down the column of my neck and over my chest. I sucked in a ragged breath and swore I could feel his eyes on my body like a gentle caress. Gavin hadn't touched me yet, and already he had made me feel more than anything Brenden ever had.

"Are you sure, Trinity?" he whispered just loudly enough for me to hear over my pounding heart. I nodded, afraid my voice would squeak if I attempted to speak. I heard his soft, husky chuckle as he leaned in to kiss me.

The moment his lips touched mine, all nervousness fled, and I embraced the moment in ways I had never thought possible. I opened my heart and allowed the feelings I held inside to fly free.

I cupped his face in my hands and met him halfway. Gavin's lips were addictive, and for the first time in my life, I knew what it was to crave the next hit. I pulled him back, bringing his body in contact with mine as I lowered myself to the bed. My foot ran up the length of his leg and wrapped around the back of his thigh, while his hand stroked softly along my hip and curled to lift it in perfect contact with his.

A whimper rushed from my throat as I felt his longing, and I grasped a handful of his t-shirt and pulled it out of his waistband. I needed to feel the skin on his back, needed to feel every inch of this man. My fingers flexed and grasped at the tight muscles under my hand. I fought not to dig my nails into his back, but the moment his palm slid under my t-shirt and touched my sensitive waist, I involuntarily shivered, and claws scraped over his back. He hissed in my ear as he continued to assault the column of my neck with tender kisses.

Shirts were yanked off, his fast, mine a centimeter at a time. It was almost to the point that I wanted to scream, Take it off already. He was so careful, so sensitive, and my body ached for him.

He moved off the bed to slide my jeans from my legs and dropped his to the ground. The absence of his body against mine brought the anxiety back to the surface, and I clenched the comforter under my hands to still the shaking.

His eyes said the words before his mouth did, "You're beautiful, Trinity."

He ran his hand over my hip, taking a moment to finger the satin of the lavender panties that Brooke and Marcy had talked me into buying.

"So soft," he rasped as he placed kisses just under my collar bone, "so beautiful."

Moisture pooled in my eyes, and he kissed my lids. "You deserve to be loved, Trinity, totally and completely, every single day of the rest of your life." He kissed down my cheek again, pausing to nibble on my jawline. "I want to be the one to do that."

"Love me, Gavin, please," I whispered, and I wrapped my hands around his head to bring his mouth back to mine. "Love me."

"I do, Trinity, I love you." His voice held so much conviction that I knew he would do as he said, he would love me totally and completely, as long as I lived.

"I love you, Gavin."

He stared into my face, and his eyes glistened with emotion a second before he began to show me in earnest just how to love and be loved.

* * *

I woke before my alarm and almost jolted upright when I realized there was an arm slung over my hips. It took only a moment for me to remember it was Gavin who lay spooned around me. His hand lay flat on my belly, his breath floated slowly and gently over the back of my head.

My heart expanded in my chest to the point I thought it would explode. For hours last night, Gavin had touched, tasted, and loved every inch of my body. He had shown me what pleasure was all about and that I wasn't one of those women who couldn't be pleased.

In those hours that we held and touched each other, my heart completely thawed, and I gave him access to every piece of me. He filled me, made me grow, and for the first time in my life, I felt like a complete woman.

Gavin's hand twitched briefly and sent a tingle through my midriff. I laced my fingers through his and felt his body stiffen. Like me, he was probably momentarily confused about his whereabouts. His body relaxed, and he pulled me more tightly to him. He nuzzled my neck; the light scruff on his face made my skin sizzle and sent a shiver down my spine.

"I didn't dream it," his husky voice whispered against my sensitive skin.

"I thought the same thing when I woke up." I rolled over and stroked the side of his face, loving the way the rough stubble felt on my fingertips.

"Can we stay here all day? I don't want to get up." He kissed my forehead.

I sighed, "I wish I could, but I have a seminar today. Speaking of which, I need to get up and get ready."

"Where is your seminar?" His hand trailed up and down my lower back, I was on the verge of purring.

"About thirty minutes away, not too far. I'm talking to a corporate office today, not law enforcement." I leaned forward and kissed his collar bone, a gruff noise rolled out of his mouth.

"Don't do that unless you have extra time."

"Oh, I wish I did, but I need to get up. Can we take up where we left off later?" I asked as I leaned away.

Gavin rolled over so his chest rested on mine, his hand brushed the hair off my face. "I'd like nothing more than to take up where we left off, over and over again."

He placed a fiercely-tender kiss on my lips that ignited the flames. The annoying buzz of my alarm blared out from the nightstand, and I absently hit the top of my digital clock without breaking the kiss. Maybe I could spare a few minutes.

Chapter 24 - Gavin

Waking up with Trinity in my arms was the highlight of my life. Never had I felt as full and satisfied as I did at that moment.

I had spent hours showing her how it felt to be loved, making sure to give her pleasure over and over again. I forced myself to take a back seat and basked in the heady emotions that rolled off of her.

Not only was she the most beautiful woman I had ever met, but she was the most passionate one, too. The sounds she made and the way she moved brought a whole new level to making love.

I rolled onto her to kiss her good morning and laughed against her lips as she turned her alarm off and wrapped her arm around my neck pulling me closer.

"I thought you had to get up," I said as I pulled an inch back.

"I do, but I want you first." She kissed my neck, "I can skip breakfast."

I laughed, "I think after the workout we had last night, you need to eat." I kissed her one more time and rolled away. "Go take a shower; I'll make you some breakfast."

For a moment, I saw her insecurities appear in her eyes, and I leaned back over her and put my palm on her cheek. "Trinity, I love you. I spent all night loving you, and tonight I'm going to love you again." I kissed her. "Right now, you need to get dressed for work, and I need to go fix us something to eat."

She examined me. "Do you still feel that way, after what we did last night?"

I knew my eyes grew wide, "Are you kidding me? I love you even more deeply. You are such a beautiful woman," I stroked the side of her face, "a passionate woman, and I don't ever want you to think that you aren't."

"Thank you," she said simply and lifted her head from the pillow to kiss me.

"You're welcome. Now go get dressed and stop tempting me."

She swatted me gently on the arm as she rolled out of bed and grabbed her robe off a hook by the closet.

I waited until she went into the bathroom and closed the door. If Trinity saw how turned on I was, I knew she would feel guilty that she didn't help relieve it.

I rested back against the pillow and stared at the ceiling. I thought back to the night before, the look in her face when she'd said she loved me. I was living in a dream—except, in my dreams, she had never said anything about wanting a baby. Jesus! What was I thinking?

We couldn't have a baby! Not now. How screwed up would that be if she got pregnant the first time we made love? What if she changed her mind and decided that's not what she wanted or I wasn't what she wanted. That thought alone killed any last traces of lust in my body, and I threw the covers back and picked up my boxers, pulling them on in haste.

I heard the shower turn on, and for just the briefest of seconds, I thought about stripping down and joining her. No, I hung my head for a moment, I felt like I had taken complete advantage of her.

I wanted nothing more than a life with her. For years, I had dreamed of her, had fantasized of making love to her, of holding her every night for the rest of my life. I'd only been in her life for, what, six weeks? I snagged my t-shirt off the floor and snapped it angrily against my leg to shake it out.

I wouldn't be surprised if by the time she got out of the shower, she was regretting her decision.

I snatched my shoes off the floor and went down to the kitchen to make her something to eat. What if she regretted it? What if she did get pregnant and then said she didn't really want to be with me? What if she only wanted to get pregnant to have a child, not to be with me?

That thought had me tripping over my bare feet. I sank down in a chair next to the table and put my head into my hands. What was I thinking? Shit. I wasn't thinking—not of her—I mean I was. I was thinking about nothing but her, of what I had dreamed of for years, but I hadn't been thinking about what was best for her. What an ass I was.

After I put my socks and shoes on, I made a cup of coffee and got the coffeemaker ready to start a cup for her when she came down. I sifted through her fridge and found ingredients for omelets and started preparing them so all I would have to do was cook them up after she was dressed.

I was just searching for a skillet when the tap of heels on the hardwood floor of the foyer approached. My stomach knotted, and I stood up slowly and put the pan on the stove. Her steps slowed as she got closer.

"I'm making omelets, hope that's okay," I said over my shoulder.

"That sounds good." I clenched my eyes. Her voice sounded different, more reserved, and I realized I had been right, she was second guessing what had happened.

I heard the coffeemaker turn on and went about heating up the pan and getting the eggs ready to pour in. My hands shook as I poured them into the pan.

"What are you doing today?" she asked as she moved to the table. I glanced over my shoulder and saw her putting some papers into a briefcase.

"I have to help Taylor with a job today," I responded and turned my attention back to the eggs.

"Oh, that sounds good." Did it? I glanced at her and saw that she was reading something. The paper wobbled in her hands. Was she nervous? Was she trying to figure out how to say last night was a mistake?

I needed to say something, but what? Thoughts were spinning and my stomach rolled in the opposite direction. I poured the eggs into the pan and almost dropped the bowl on the floor.

"Trinity," I started to say.

"Gavin," she said at the same time. We both laughed nervously, and she bridged the distance between us, keeping eye contact as she did. She paused before she entered my personal space.

I took the two steps to reach her and ran my hands from her shoulders to her elbows. "Are you okay?"

She nodded, "Yes, I'm okay. I was going to ask you the same thing." She averted her eyes for a moment, "Actually, I'm just wondering if last night was—" I put my fingers over her lips before she could finish. I refused to think of last night as a mistake.

"It was not a mistake, not to me. It was intense and beautiful, and I loved every minute of it. I love you, Trinity, in the light of day, I feel no different toward you than I did last night." I ran my thumb over her bottom lip as I held eye contact with her. "In fact, I love you even more now." I paused.

"Do you feel like you made a mistake?"

If she said yes, my heart would shatter, but I could deal with it. I would prove to her that we were right for each other, that these feelings we had were real. I could barely stand it as I waited for her reply.

"Oh, Gavin, are you sure that is how you feel?" she asked plaintively, some unknown emotion staring back at me in her eyes.

"I'm absolutely positive. You are the most beautiful, strong, loving, passionate woman I have ever met, and I love you and want to love you for years to come." I wrapped her in my arms for a moment, "I want this, Trinity. I want you," I kissed the side of her head and pulled back, "but if this is not what you want, you tell me, and I'll step back. I'll give you space. I won't pressure you."

She grabbed my forearms and blurted out quickly, "No!" The rush of that simple word shocked me. No, what? No, she didn't want this, or no, she didn't want me to step back?

"Gavin, I don't regret what we did. How could I when you treated me like I was the most precious thing in this world?" She cupped the side of my face and ran her thumb over the stubble on my jaw. "I wanted to make sure that this is what you want. For years, I thought I would never get involved with another man, not after Brenden. I didn't think I could ever trust another man. Then, a few years later, when I saw Brooke fall in love with a wonderful man I began to wonder if that could happen to me. Part of me wanted that so badly, while the other part of it scared me to death." She smiled and leaned forward to place a kiss on my lips.

"I bought this house with the hopes that one day I would have a family, and I could raise my children in a safe, loving environment. Over the last few years, I began to doubt that I would ever find someone I could trust and love. Then you walk into my life again, and I found myself on that very first day we spent together thinking things I had not thought about in years. I started thinking about my future, but not just mine. I started thinking about a future with someone else, with you.

"I don't regret a moment of last night. I was ready. I was ready to put the past behind me and move forward. I want to move forward with you, wherever it takes us."

I blinked back the moisture that was beginning to form in my eyes and pulled her into my arms. "Then we move forward. No more looking behind us. Let's get to know each other better, and move forward." With my hand behind her head, I tipped it so I could access her lips and showed her how much she meant to me in that one kiss.

And that's when the smoke detector went off. We were so wrapped up in ourselves that neither one of us smelled the smoke coming from the pan behind us. I grabbed the pan and tossed it into the sink while Trinity ran to the back door and swung it open. Callie came running into the house barking at the ceiling and trying to push Trinity out the back door.

I climbed up on a chair and waved smoke away from the detector with a kitchen towel while Trinity ran to the alarm panel and started punching buttons. Once the alarm turned off, we looked at each other and burst into laughter.

"Talk about a smoking kiss," she joked, and I tugged on her arm to bring her back into the circle of my arms.

"No, that wasn't just smoking, that was a five-alarm fire." I kissed her once slowly before I stepped back and cleared my throat. "I guess I better start that over so you won't be late."

"Don't worry about it, Gavin. I don't normally eat before I do a seminar. My stomach is usually tied in knots." She scrapped the burnt eggs into the sink and pushed them down the garbage disposal.

Chapter 25 - Trinity

All the way to my seminar I sang to the radio. I was on top of the world. My life had taken a drastic turn, and it was all for the better.

It felt so good to be free of demons that held me back from loving. Why hadn't I tried to do this sooner?

I gasped and grinned as the answer bubbled up inside of me. I didn't find it sooner because I had been waiting for Gavin to find me.

My cellphone rang as I pulled into the corporate center. "Morning," I answered when I saw it was Brooke.

"Oh, I can tell by your voice that you had a wonderful night! Please tell me you had a wonderful night!" she begged playfully into the phone.

"I did. I had an incredible night. Brooke," I paused, embarrassed to admit this, even to my closest friend, "I didn't know sex could be that amazing." I almost whispered the words even though I was alone inside my car.

She laughed so loudly that I pulled the phone away a little bit, "Oh no, did we create a monster?"

"No, you didn't, but I can't say that about Gavin." I joined her in more laughter. "Did you need something, or were you checking up on me?"

"I was making sure you were on your way to the seminar, and I wanted to make sure you were alright."

We chatted for a little longer and agreed to catch up on everything at our next Saturday morning coffee chat. For now, I had to get inside and get ready for this seminar.

* * *

"I asked ahead of time to have a volunteer for this exercise that I am going to do with you all. Lisa was nice enough to find me someone, and I want to welcome Donna up here."

A woman in her late twenties joined me at the front of the large conference room. The room was large enough for about a hundred people, roughly half men and half women.

I applauded companies that made sure that their employees knew this was a safe place for them to work and that they would not try to hide abuse or pretend it wasn't happening. A safe employee was a happy employee, and a happy employee didn't cost you as much money in sick days and not being productive because of stress from home.

When I had set this seminar up with Lisa, I had asked her to find me someone who was not claustrophobic or had not been a victim of domestic violence. I stressed that the volunteer had to say no to both of those.

When Donna joined me up front, I leaned closer to her and covered my microphone to ask her once again if she wanted to volunteer.

"Yes," she replied firmly, "my sister was a victim of domestic violence, and once she got away from him, I vowed I would do everything I could to help others."

I thanked her and asked her to have a seat.

"Donna is not the only volunteer that I need, but she has a tough job ahead of her. I need to ask for twelve other volunteers." I had more than enough people raise their hands and come forward to join us. I had everyone stand in a semi-circle around Donna so the audience could see what was happening from their seats.

Once everyone was in place, I handed out large pieces of fabric that had a small scrap of paper pinned to one corner. "For now, just hold these in front of you, you can read them to yourself, but don't read them out loud."

I finished handing them out and turned back to the audience. "This exercise is called Layers. It was designed by one of our employees to show what victims will endure over time. It is very rare for an abuser to begin domestic violence at an intense violent level. It is much more common for them to start out slowly as they gain the victim's trust. It comes in as layers."

I had everyone's attention. "What we are going to do is read you examples of domestic violence, and after each person reads his card, he or she is going to lay it over the top of Donna and cover her up. Each piece of fabric is relevant to the example that is given." I glanced back at the volunteers and noticed them all looking closely at the pattern on their material.

"You are going to notice several things as we go along, and I want each of you to listen to what is being said." I stepped closer to Donna, "If at any time this becomes too much for you, you let me know and we can stop."

"No, I'm ready," she beamed at me and sat up straight and tall, ready to be a good volunteer.

"Alright," I pointed to a woman who appeared to be around forty years old, "I think you have number one, is that correct?"

"Yes, I do." She moved to join me.

"Stand right here," I pointed to right behind Donna, "and open your fabric up and then read your note. After you do that, lay the material over her head to cover her."

She nodded and unfolded a piece of fabric that was about three feet by five feet in size and had sunrises on it, "Okay, so I'm sorry. You'll get over this and forgive me. Let's go to bed, and everything will be better tomorrow, you'll see I'm right." She placed the fabric over Donna and turned to me.

"Thank you, okay who has number two?"

A younger woman in her mid-twenties stepped forward.

"I do." She stood next to me and unfolded a piece of denim material the same size as the previous piece. "You just want the attention of those guys. Don't you ever wear those jeans again, you hear me!" She cringed and then giggled nervously while she put the material over Donna.

A man of about thirty, wearing a suit, stepped forward for number three, "You're Mine now! And don't you forget it!" The fabric he placed over her head had cowboy lassos on it. He had used a direct voice and spoken clearly, and Donna's knee flinched just a tad. He shook his head as he turned and went back to the line.

Number four was another older woman, maybe in her late forties. She unfolded the fabric that was colorful and had what could be raindrops or teardrops on it and then read the card, "That was just a little punch. It didn't hurt you all that much. Stop crying. Can't you take a little teasing? Geez." She mumbled how horrible that was as she placed the fabric over Donna's head and then patted what she thought was her shoulder.

I glanced around the room. Some people sat back, watching casually. Some sat back, but they were anything but relaxed, a few had their hands clenched together and I could only guess they knew something first-hand about domestic violence.

Another man came up to start number five, and his material was white lace. "Remember at our wedding you said, 'For Better or worse.' Well, things are pretty bad for me, too, you know. I don't care that you have that little nothing job. I never have clean socks, the children's toys are everywhere. Stop that crying! I can't stand your crying!" He forced the last words out and his voice cracked with emotion as he dropped the fabric on Donna and spun away. He was a haunted man.

Number six joined me behind Donna, and she unfolded a piece of fabric that was black and blue plaid. "I'm sorry, I didn't mean to hurt you. I promise I will never hit you again."

Before the man with the number seven came up, I leaned down to Donna and asked her quietly if she was alright. She had already started to lean forward. The material was getting warmer, and it would become more difficult for her to breathe, plus the weight on top of her would be starting to catch up. She assured me that she was fine.

"You can leave, but don't even think about taking the children. You can't even take care of yourself, much less the kids. Besides, you know how much I love you and our children. I took you to Disney World, didn't I?" The man stared at the Mickey fabric for a moment longer before he gently placed it over Donna. He gave me a brusque nod before he returned to his place.

A woman I had met earlier stepped forward and swiped at a tear on her cheek. She had been a victim, and I knew how hard this was for her. Even with all the times I had done this exercise, I always became extremely tense as it progressed.

She opened the eighth piece of fabric and held the card in shaking hands, "Not everyone needs to know what happens in My House. Stop calling…that mom of yours and those sisters…" she read the paper haltingly, "I don't like the way they treat me, you know that. I provide all that you and the kids need. What we do in here, in My House, is no one else's business. Do you understand that? We have our secrets! Everyone has secrets!" I rubbed her back once while she placed the material that had large lips all over it on top of the others. She wiped her cheeks again as she turned away.

Number nine was another younger woman, and she moved with purpose as she approached Donna, her fabric had large sunglasses and bright shining suns on it. "I really didn't hurt you all that much. So if I didn't, why did you even go to the hospital? You are so full of drama. Just wear sunglasses, or you will have to tell you girlfriends how pitiful you are. By the way, I have your keys, so you aren't going anywhere anyway. Understand?"

That particular one always hit close to home for me, and I clenched my jaw and stared at a blank spot on the floor while she covered Donna.

We were almost done, and I waited patiently for the tenth person to come forward. When she did, she rushed through her card and put the police car fabric over Donna as quickly as she could, "Go ahead, call 911, you want to see me in jail? Do you want the kids to see me in handcuffs and behind bars? Really? Get a grip. You're not calling the police."

Donna was now bending forward more, and I knew that the material was starting to get really heavy. She probably felt that it was getting harder to breathe, like she was starting to suffocate, although she wasn't.

The man who held number eleven joined me and stared at the dark red rose fabric for a moment before reading, "You love roses. You see how much I love you? Nobody has ever loved you as much as I do." He set the fabric down and walked away with his head hanging.

A woman stepped forward to put the next one on, "You know what? You always start the fights and then get a little upset when things get rough. Well, now I'm going to show you what rough really is!" She took the blood-red fabric and put it on over the other eleven pieces stepping backwards without turning away.

I reached behind to a table and lifted up the last piece of fabric. I let the black fabric drop down to the floor as I read, "You just won't listen. You think you know it all. You think you're so smart. Well, actually you're Crazy! Real Crazy! That's why I need to take control here. I'm the boss. Understand?!" I used an angry, almost-yelling voice for the last lines, "You are making me so mad that I could kill you and me—and I could take the kids out with us! Do you understand me?!" My body shook like it always does at the way those words vibrated through my soul and brought back haunting memories.

I set the fabric over Donna and stepped back while I surveyed the people in the room. Almost everyone was staring at Donna and her body as it bent over to allow air under the fabric.

"Okay, do you all see how things progress?" I saw a lot of heads nod and heard a few people speak. "We aren't done yet, though."

All eyes flashed to me, "Now we need to fix the damage. Every one of you," I turned to my volunteers, "need to come up with something that could help this victim: a word of advice, or something that we might tell her when she calls for help, maybe something that might help build her self-esteem."

I stepped forward and lifted the fabric, "You're not alone, we can help. It only takes a phone call." I dropped the fabric on the table next to me and stepped out of the way. "It doesn't matter what order you go. When you think of something, step forward."

This process also moved much faster, and Donna would soon be free. "You are a beautiful woman, you deserve so much better," one woman said.

"Your kids are awesome, and that's because you're a great mom," the last man said as he pulled off the material and handed it to me.

"I love your smile, and you work so hard at your job," another man said and gave me half a smile when he handed over the material.

The woman who had been crying stepped forward, her chin up, "Don't you dare believe a word he said. You are better than he could ever be. Believe in that and believe in yourself."

I swallowed back the emotion as she hugged me and left the material in my arms.

"There are people who can help you," was another response along with, "there are a lot of people who love you, and someday you will find someone who loves you more than life."

One of the men stepped forward and pulled the fabric free, "You can be anything you want to be, and you make your own decisions."

"There are plenty of people who can help you get out of this," a woman said.

The next one was right behind her, "Your children need you to be strong and start a new life. You can do it, I have faith in you."

Donna was now sitting up straight again, the weight being lifted from her quickly. "You are not to blame for this, it is his fault," said the man who seemed very tense earlier.

"He deserves to be arrested. I'll put the cuffs on him myself," said the second to last woman with a smile. I smiled back as she handed me the denim material.

The last piece was removed when a woman came forward and said quietly, "There are people who want to hear your secrets and help you heal. Just take baby steps."

When the material came off of Donna's head, I saw her reach up and wipe her face. I wasn't sure if she had been crying or if she was wiping sweat away. When she glanced my way, I could see the tears.

"Are you alright, Donna?"

She stood and stretched her back, glancing around the room and at the people behind her. "Yes, I'm alright, but that was an incredible experience. Now I know what my sister was going through. It was like I was getting buried a little at a time until it was hard to breathe. It was so heavy my neck was starting to hurt."

I thanked everyone, gave Donna a hug, and sent them back to their seats.

"What Donna explained, that it feels like you are getting buried a little bit at a time, well, that is exactly what it feels like. As time goes by, the layers get thicker and thicker, separating you from everything that makes sense, from your family and friends." I paused and scanned the crowd, "Abusers alienate you from everyone and everything. They control you, possess you, and they are not afraid to let you know that they own you." I took a few steps, "But they don't. You don't have to let them. You can have your freedom, your life back. There is hope. You're not alone, you're really not."

Chapter 26 - Gavin

A week later, I was still floating on cloud nine. Trinity and I had spent every moment we could this last week together. Since I was on day shift, I stopped by after work and had dinner with her. Afterwards, we would lie on the couch and talk.

Some nights, that was all that we did. Those nights were just as special as the ones where we fell into each other's arms and explored the passion between us. Well, maybe they were more incredible because the bond that we had grew with every single word that slipped from our lips. I knew after a few days that if something were to ever happen to her, my world would shatter like a mirror under a sledge hammer.

We talked about what we had done over the last ten years, and how she and Brooke had started the organization and why they chose this area to start it in. I was so glad to hear that Brooke's parents lived in the area.

We even ventured to talk about the dark past. I filled her in on how my father had been an alcoholic and how from the earliest age, I had heard him yelling and my mother crying. It had been like a television rerun that we could never turn off. I even spoke a little about my sister and how my mother found out what was happening but felt powerless to do anything. By that time in our lives, she was mentally beaten to a pulp and holding onto life with a heart string. It was our mother's suicide that ultimately saved my sister. I was seventeen then, my sister only fourteen. That was when it all came out. The suicide note that she left spelled it all out to the police, and an investigation began immediately.

Through the death of our mother, Greta and I had finally found life. Luckily my mom's sister was local and took us in. We were safe, loved, and finished our schooling. After I graduated from college, I took off to get away. Russia wouldn't have been far enough for me, but I'd interviewed for a department in Tennessee and been hired right away.

Trinity shared how Brenden had charmed her right off the bat. She had been flattered and whisked off her feet by the older man who was a hero in the eyes of many people. She explained that during the first several months, he groomed her to see only him, and once he had her affections, the abuses started. She talked about how at first he had cut her off from her friends, not allowing her to go out and making her feel guilty if she did. Of course she didn't realize what was happening then. She told me that soon after, the little spiked comments began, like, your opinion doesn't matter. He used to do that all the time when she would chime into a conversation he was having with other people. Trinity told me that she learned quickly to keep her mouth shut because it was one of those comments that had initiated the physical abuse.

She told me about that night in detail. We'd been cuddled up on the couch, and she had been holding one of my hands between her two, tracing the lines on my fingers with her own. It would have tickled if I hadn't been horror struck by what she recounted.

"His friends had just gone home. Do you remember Randall Dovers and Patrick Alton?"

"Yeah, I worked under Sergeant Alton," I'd replied.

"Those were his two best friends," she continued. "They knew what he did to me, but they never tried to help me."

My anger had begun to rise that someone had known she was being abused and had done nothing. These guys had been cops! There had to be a reason they didn't say anything.

"How do you know they knew?"

Her pointer finger travelled up and down each of my fingers.

"They were all sitting in the living room talking one night, and I had joined the conversation," she sighed. "I knew better than to do that, but I did it anyway. Brenden told me to shut up and go get them more beers. I did."

"That's all they saw?"

"Oh, no, they saw more. When I came back with the beers, he tripped me on purpose, he said I was just uncoordinated, but I saw him put his foot out. I fell and dropped all three beers. One of the bottles shattered when my forearm hit it. I needed six stitches."

She had pulled her sleeve back, and I ran my finger down the length of the faded scar before pulling it to my lips.

"It wasn't just that he tripped me. When I hit the floor he screamed at me about the mess, and then he kicked me."

"He what?"

"He kicked me in the stomach, only it was higher and he ended up breaking a rib."

"Didn't you tell the hospital when he took you in?"

I felt her shake her head against my chest. "No, he never left me alone with the doctor or nurse, and I never told them about the rib. I let them sew me up with the explanation that I had been clumsy, and my big powerful husband had rescued me and brought me in to be cared for. I never even told Brenden that he broke my rib. I figured it was better to stay quiet."

I had pulled her closer to me and held her as tightly as I dared.

That was last night, and tonight I was working night shift and couldn't be with her. I missed her more than I could possibly imagine. We had texted earlier, but it was now almost midnight, and I knew she was probably sound asleep.

I drove the dark streets and wished that I was holding her in my arms. I wondered if she felt as off kilter as I did since we weren't together. It was amazing how far we had come in seven weeks. She was my whole world, and I was already toying with the idea of looking for an engagement ring.

Was it too early to think like that?

Hell, no! I had been in love with this woman for over ten years, and the more I found out about her, the more I loved her. I wanted her in my life full time. I wanted to be the one to protect her and be there for her when she was down or afraid or excited over some news. I wanted to lie in her bed every night and know that she was mine forever.

Now, she might not be ready to say yes, but I sure was ready to put that ring on her finger and start planning our life together.

I turned the corner onto a dark street in our lower-income area. The row homes on this side of town were run down and in need of some major renovation. Even one of the street lights needed repair as the large phosphorescent light was dim. People sat out on their porches even this late at night. I learned a long time ago that poverty never sleeps, and neither do many of the people who lived in this area.

They eyed my patrol car warily. This particular street was one of our top crime areas. Drugs were prevalent, and armed robberies happened at least once a week to someone walking down the street at the wrong time.

There was one person I was searching for, and I was bound and determined to find him. There had been a warrant out for him for over a week, and no one had caught up to him yet. That was my goal tonight, to find Wayne Drummond. If I didn't lock his ass up tonight, I would start knocking on doors and trying to pry information from people tomorrow night. I wanted this guy off the street, not just to arrest him, but for peace of mind for Tabitha and Trinity, too.

It was a little after two in the morning, and I idled stationary, having coffee in my car while I sat beside one of the other officers on our squad when I looked up to see Wayne come strolling around a corner. We were blacked out and parked away from street lights so we had an advantage on him.

"Tom, dock your coffee, Drummond is over there, and he's going to run." I picked up the radio microphone in my car and switched over to our side channel to let a few more guys know to head this way, just in case.

Tom and I used a tactical approach since it was so late at night, and there was no traffic on the roadway. Neither of us turned our lights on as we slowly moved from the parking in his direction. We both tried to keep our feet off the brakes so the red lights wouldn't reflect on the walls around us either. We managed to get about ten feet from him when he glanced toward the road and saw us.

The moment he realized two cop cars were coming down on him, he froze for two seconds, long enough for me to slam on my brakes and start to open the door. Tom called out on the radio as I did a Dukes of Hazzard move over the corner section of my car to cut out a few feet and took off on foot after him.

He beat feet the moment my door started to open and had a little bit of a head start, but even with twenty pounds of gear on me and being in my thirties, I was catching up to him fast.

Another three seconds, and I dove onto his back and took him to the dirty asphalt as a siren blared behind me in the alley and the headlights illuminated us. Wayne struggled to get out from under me, attempting to buck me off and swinging his arm to strike out. Tom caught up as the other officer got out of his car, and between the three of us, we got him into custody.

My mission was complete! I couldn't wait to tell Trinity I had found him.

Three hours later, I finished up the papers on a second set of criminal charges against Wayne Drummond—for resisting arrest and assaulting an officer. This time, Wayne wasn't going to get off so easily. The judge would set his bail higher than normal now that he had tried to flee and fight with us.

I sent a text message off to Trinity around five asking her to call me when she got up. I wasn't expecting to have my phone ring thirty seconds later.

"Did my text message wake you?" I asked when I answered. "I'm so sorry if it did."

"No," her voice was so husky that I shivered at the intensity of it. "I wasn't sleeping. Funny thing, I have slept in this bed for almost ten years, and until last night, it had never felt empty."

Her words warmed my heart, "So you missed me. That's nice to know."

"I'm not sure if it was you, or just your body heat," she teased.

"Oh, so you are only using me as a body warmer, okay I see how it is." The grin on my face was hurting my cheeks.

She laughed harder, "You know you are more than that, and yes, I missed you last night. It was hard to sleep. I'm amazed at how quickly I got used to having you beside me. I guess I'm going to have to get used to you not being here every night."

Oh, man, this woman knew what to say to make me feel good. "Think you can do that? Get used to me being there and not being there some nights?"

She was quiet for a moment, "Yes, as long as the only reason you aren't here with me is because you are working."

"God, I wish I was there with you right now." I glanced up and saw Coven grinning. Man was he going to bust my balls when I got off the phone.

"I wish you were, too, but you are working and that is important. Speaking of which, how was your night?"

"Very productive, actually. I picked up Wayne Drummond early this morning. He took off on foot, and we caught him. He has another set of charges now, too, so I doubt he will make bail. Our judge doesn't like to give bail when someone tries to assault one of us."

"Assault one of you? Did you get hurt?" Concern radiated from her words.

"Don't worry, we are all fine. I will probably have a bruise on my knee from hitting the pavement when I took him down, but otherwise I'm fine."

"Well, that's good then. When will we know when the hearing will be?" Her alarm went off in the background, and she rustled the sheets while rolling to silence it. I waited to answer until it was quiet on her side again.

"The preliminary will probably be next week, but I'll let you know for sure, and make sure that a subpoena is issued to Tabitha. Do you want me to give that to you so you can make sure she gets it?"

"That sounds good. Bring me a copy of the subpoena, and I'll make sure either Brooke or I bring her to the hearing."

Trinity and I spoke for a few more minutes as she told me about a meeting she'd had with a security company that was going to outfit all the shelters with new alarms and cameras, thanks to the large donation she had received. She had been telling me over the last week of all the things she and Brooke had planned, and this one was at the top of the list, along with some new appliances and a few makeovers for the community rooms.

"I hope you sleep better today than I did last night," she said as we got ready to get off the phone.

"I doubt that. You won't be in my arms. I'm not sure I will be able to sleep without you in them."

"You sound tired enough that you will probably fall fast asleep the minute your head hits the pillow."

"Maybe, but until it hits that pillow, I will wish you were right there with me. I missed you last night."

"I missed you, too. Go finish up your paperwork and get some sleep. Call me this afternoon after you get some rest."

"I will. I love you, Trinity."

"I love you, too, Gavin. Sleep well."

I hung up the phone and stared at it for a moment. My thoughts were rudely interrupted by Coven asking, "Whoa, you guys are already at the 'I love you' stage?"

I nodded and knew I had a big-ass grin plastered on my face.

He slapped me on the shoulder, "Good, I'm damn glad to hear that. Does she have a sister or maybe a good friend? I need to find me a good woman."

Trinity's administrative assistant flashed into my mind. "No sister, but she might have a friend." I'd have to ask Trinity later if Marcy was seeing anyone.

Chapter 27 - Trinity

I didn't lie to Gavin when I told him I hadn't slept well. I had tossed and turned all night and found myself hugging the pillow he'd used close to my chest. The fact that I missed him so much almost put me into a panic. That was the real reason I was wide awake at five in the morning.

When I heard his tired voice, it helped to ease the tension and paranoid feelings creeping into my head. I had fallen so hard for Gavin, and so quickly. Could this be real? Could I really love him the way I thought I did? Even more importantly, could he love me as much as he said he did? Was he hiding something behind those beautiful eyes and handsome face?

I had to take that into consideration. Many people who grew up in a family with abuse ended up being abusers themselves. Could Gavin be anything like his father? How could I ever assure myself that he wasn't?

I threw the covers back after we got off the phone. I needed to bring this up with Brooke and see if she could help me find a resolution. I knew deep in my heart that he was a good man and that he would never hurt me, not intentionally anyway.

God! Get a grip, Trin! He would never do anything to hurt me period. With that resolve I got ready for work.

I was at my desk when Brooke arrived at the office. I gave her a few minutes to get settled before I invaded her space with my head games.

Marcy was on the phone when I slipped into Brooke's office and shut the door. "You have a minute?"

"Yeah, of course." She pushed aside the paper in front of her, "Oh boy, I know that look. You look freaked out about something."

"Stop it," I said as I sank down into her other chair.

"What's on your mind? Something happen with Gavin?"

"Nothing bad," I said as I twisted my fingers together. "It's all good, like, it's too good to be true."

"Aw," Brooke laughed, "so you are afraid that this is fate's way of playing a joke on you, right?"

"Yes, well no." I dwelled on what exactly I was worried about. "Brooke, how do I know he won't abuse me later?"

Brooke got serious and leaned up to her desk, "You don't know that, you have to trust him."

"I trusted Brenden, too, and he tried to kill me."

"Yes, and Brenden showed classic signs of an abuser a few weeks after you started dating him. Has Gavin done something to make you think he might be hiding it?"

I shook my head, "No, that's the thing. What if he is hiding it and grooming me to gain my trust? What if he is just better at controlling it?"

Brooke considered my questions for a long moment. "Do you really think that is possible, Trinity? You know Gavin a lot better than I do. Has he ever done or said anything that made you think he would be less than a gentleman to you?"

"No."

"So this is all just your insecurities coming forward?"

"Yes," I sighed.

Brooke stood up and moved her chair so it was beside mine. She took my hands into hers. "Trinity, how do you feel about Gavin?"

I swallowed, "I love him."

"Do you trust him? Do you, in your heart, think that Gavin would do anything to hurt you?"

I reached inside of myself and tried to find one thing that Gavin had done that could have caused these feelings to surface, but there was nothing. He was an absolutely perfect gentleman. He could be silly and playful, or protective and serious, and when he was passionate, he was a whole other person. Not once had he done something that should cause me alarm, yet I still felt uneasy, as if the happiness I was experiencing was temporary.

"No, he hasn't. I know this is silly, and it's my own issues causing this problem." I squeezed her hand and tried to smile. "The problem is that I feel like I don't deserve to be happy, like I'm going to get the happiness and love that I always secretly dreamed of and it is all going to blow up in my face."

"And you could be hit by a bus on your way home."

I jerked my eyes to her face, "Where the hell did that come from?"

Brooke let go of my hand and sat back in her seat, crossing her legs. "You can't keep thinking that something bad is going to happen right around every corner. Trinity, what do we try to teach people here? Don't we teach them that life is worth living and that they can be happy and have a loving relationship in a safe environment? Do you not listen to your own words?"

I rolled my eyes. Nice. "Oh, go ahead and use my own words against me."

"Try using them. I did and look how happy Rick and I are."

I flicked a hand at her in dismissal. "You guys are different."

She guffawed. "We are not. Do you not remember when I went through this same stage with him? You said these exact things to me when I came to you with these very same concerns."

I thought back to when they were dating and, oh, crap, she was right. This conversation was almost word for word, except in reverse.

"So I'm being stupid," I stated as I shook my head at myself.

"No, you are being careful. There is nothing stupid about that. What would be stupid is if you let Gavin get away and didn't take advantage of this relationship to its fullest."

"Thanks, Brooke." I stood up and waited for her to do the same so I could give her a hug. "I'm not sure what I would do without you."

"You will never have to find out. So how are things with Gavin?"

I stepped away and moved to the door, "Moving quickly. I think that is what kind of freaked me out a little bit. He has stayed at my house every night this last week, except last night when he had to work. It gave me a lot of time to think—and freak myself out."

She squeezed my arm and then pushed her chair back behind her desk, "You're going to be fine. You might think this is going fast, but true love always does. You can't control it, it controls you, but unlike abusive people, that kind of control is the good kind." She winked at me.

I was so lucky to have a friend like Brooke. I needed to call my mother and thank her for the hundredth time for calling the domestic violence hotline when she had. If it hadn't been for her, I would never have made that call. It is always the hardest thing for a victim to do.

* * *

The day went by quickly, and I pulled into the driveway later than normal. I'd attended a late afternoon meeting that ran an hour longer than expected. It was close to eight and almost dark when I climbed out of my car and looked up at my house.

It was depressing knowing that I was going to be alone. How had I lived so many years without someone in my life? It was a shame that Gavin had to work tonight, amazing how quickly I had gotten used to him. Disappointment flowed through me, but almost as quickly vanished when I considered taking him some leftovers and dropping them off for later tonight—or maybe I could just bring him some coffee.

With a spring in my step, I grabbed the mail and went inside. The house was dark, and I flipped on a few lights as I kicked off my shoes and dropped my shoulder bag in the hallway. I tossed the mail on the entrance table as I called out for Callie.

"Callie, where are you?" Did she get locked outside? Maybe her dog door battery died. It had happened before and she couldn't get back in the house. "Callie!"

I yelled again and expected to hear her barking outside, but there was no sound. I stepped from the hallway into the kitchen area, and her door sprang open, causing me to jump and squeal.

She trotted over to me, her tail wagging wildly and her paws dirty. "Were you digging in the garden again? You're a mess, Callie."

I yanked a towel out of the hall closet to wipe her paws and noticed as I leaned down that she had blood around her mouth. She had a habit of catching small animals and burying them in the backyard. "Gross, you were hunting again."

I got her cleaned up and went over to turn off her dog door so she couldn't go back outside and dig anymore until I could figure out what she had caught.

"You are staying inside for the rest of the night, young lady." I mixed up her dinner, not sure if she would even eat it after having a snack and set about pulling leftovers out for Gavin.

Once I got them ready, I packed a small insulated lunch bag with the leftover meatloaf and potatoes and made him two cups of coffee, putting them into a large thermos. This would keep him going for a little while at least.

I hustled back to my car while Callie whined at me for leaving her so soon after I had returned. For several years, Callie had had my undivided attention. She was going to have to learn to share me with Gavin.

I grinned as I pulled out of the driveway and headed toward his station. I didn't even bother to call or text him that I was coming. If he wasn't at the station, I would leave it there to surprise him when he did come back.

My talk earlier today with Brooke had made me feel so much better. When I realized that our conversations had been almost word for word years apart and that I wasn't crazy for asking these questions, I calmed down. I knew that Gavin loved me, and I knew that he would never hurt me.

I also knew that I was a different person, and I would never allow a man to control or abuse me again. If Gavin began to display signs of abusive control, then I knew where the door was and how to walk out.

I was no longer a victim. I was a survivor, and it was time for me to live my life, time to have the family I had dreamed of and be everything I could be like I told so many other survivors to do.

I was at a red light, stunned for a moment. Had I not been living my life? I had been going through the daily motions, but I hadn't been enjoying it, living it to the fullest.

By damn, I was going to do that now.

With renewed purpose, I pulled into the parking lot of the police station and headed in to surprise Gavin with not only dinner, but a nice big juicy kiss if he was here. I wasn't going to deny what I wanted anymore. I had done that long enough.

It was my turn to live, and I was starting right this second.

Chapter 28 - Gavin

"I need you to fill out this statement form," I told the forty-two-year-old yuppie man who had come in and complained about his neighbor's dog chasing after his toy poodle.

The things we had to take reports for, I sighed inwardly.

"What happens after I do this? Are you going to arrest them?" I didn't know that men could get that uppity sound in their voices, the kind in which they look down at you because you are a public servant.

"We will pass your statement and our report over to the SPCA, and they will touch base with the dog owners and warn them," I replied. I looked over his shoulder to the front door as it opened—Trinity.

One look at her, and she had just made my night.

"That's it? That's all you are going to do? You're the police. You should go arrest that woman and have her dog put down for what it did."

"Sir," one glance at Trinity and my patience was magically restored, "I promise that the SPCA will look into this. We don't handle animal calls. We take the reports and pass them along to them to take care of. I know they will contact you first thing tomorrow."

He grunted and mumbled under his breath as he went back to writing his statement. I winked at Trinity and pointed to a door off to the side.

I allowed her to come into the administration office. At night, we only had one person in here to answer phones and speak to people who came in off the street. Kim was on a break right now, hence the reason I was dealing with this nut ball.

"What are you doing here?" I wanted so badly to pull her into my arms and kiss her, but that probably would not go over well with the guy grinding his teeth as he finished up his statement about the emotional damage the neighbor's overexcited lab had done to him and his poodle, sorry, toy poodle.

"I missed you." She cut a look at the guy at the counter. "I brought you some dinner. I wasn't sure if you had brought anything, and I still had some meatloaf leftover from the other night."

The man cleared his throat, and I winked at Trinity, "Give me a minute." I turned to the man, "You all done, sir?"

"Yes." He eyed Trinity briefly while I took the statement from him.

"Okay, I just need you to sign the bottom, and you are all set." I set the statement down for him again, and he signed with a dramatic flourish. "Very good. You will hear from them tomorrow. Have a good night, sir. Drive safely."

The guy gave me curt nod and stalked out of the lobby.

"What did he have his panties in a bunch for?" Trinity asked as I tossed the statement onto one of the desks.

"He said his, quote, toy poodle, unquote, was being harassed by his neighbor."

Trinity started to laugh and the sound echoed through every ounce of my being. I pulled her out of view of the front lobby and into my arms. "How did you know I didn't bring any dinner with me?"

"I was hoping," she said as she stretched her arms around my neck and pulled my lips down to reach hers.

The kiss about blew my tactical boots right off my feet. "Damn, girl," I sucked in a deep breath as I rested my forehead against hers. "You are going to kill me if you kiss me like that again."

"Oh, really," she said coyly.

"Yes, really, and getting all hot and bothered in uniform is not very comfortable."

She unlatched her hands, "Ah, true." She had set the food down on the desk next to us, and ran her empty hand over the front of my uniform. I watched her face carefully to see if any demons would come out, but what I saw almost choked me up. I saw pride in her eyes, as she ran her finger gingerly over my badge and name plate. She smiled up at me and in that moment I knew there was no more waiting. I was going to make her mine as soon as possible.

"I should go," she said wistfully.

"I wish I was going with you," I whispered as I pulled her in for a hug.

"Me, too. You are off tomorrow, right?"

"Yes, and I have every intention of being right by your side the moment you get off work. How about I cook dinner for you tomorrow night?"

"What, at your place?" She looked surprised.

"No, I could pick up some things and bring them over. We could cook together. My place is hardly furnished; your place is much more comfortable."

"It's a deal." She kissed me one more time, dialing back the passion to a four on the heat index, thankfully.

"I love you. Send me a text when you get home to let me know you arrived safely."

She stepped up on her toes and gave me a delicate kiss, "And I love you, too, more than you know."

I kept an eye out for her as she walked back out to her car, then I glanced over at the food she had brought me. I had expected to pick up something greasy from the all-night diner, but it looked like I wasn't going to have to do that.

Kim came back from break a few minutes later, and I went into the squad room to do the report for the dog issue after I popped the food into the kitchen fridge.

Thirty minutes and two phone interruptions later, I had finished the coffee and the report and printed it out. I glanced at the clock, it was almost nine-thirty. I pulled the report off the printer and turned around to use the fax machine. There were several faxes on it, and I put them off to the side as I punched in the numbers to the SPCA.

I glanced at the clock again and then over to my desk. What time did Trinity leave? I should have gotten a text from her. I shot a quick text asking if she got home alright and went back to the fax machine. I was tapping my fingers, waiting for the confirmation page to print when I looked down at the pages I had taken off of the machine. At the top of the page under the top sheet were the words, "CRITCAL – PLEASE CONTACT IMMEDIATELY". I pushed the cover sheet away, and my knees almost buckled.

There on the page under those words were: "SECOND REQUEST". There, right in front of me in black and white, Trinity's ex-husband stared back at me. I snatched up the paper, reading it over as quickly as I could.

I grabbed my phone and found her contact information, punching the button to call her.

My hand shook as I stared at the paper in front of me. He had been released on an appeal technicality, and he had failed to report to his parole officer. The message was to notify the victim immediately and put her into protective custody.

The phone rang four times and went to voicemail. Jesus! "Trinity, answer the damn phone!" I redialed and stared at the paper again, zeroing in on the "SECOND REQUEST". The scene with Derek laughing and muttering something yesterday as he took a paper off the fax machine played through my mind, and I took off running for the back door.

Trinity's phone had gone to voicemail again, and I dialed one more time, putting it on speaker this time as I ran out the back door and almost plowed into Derek and Coven who were just coming into the station.

"You son of a bitch!" I slammed Derek in the face with my fist, knocking him almost to the ground as Coven grabbed a hold of me.

"What the hell are you doing?" Coven yelled.

"I'm gonna kill him if something happens to Trinity!" I shouted and tried to get out of Coven's hold.

"What the hell are you talking about? Calm down." Trinity's voice caught our attention, and we all looked down at the floor where my cellphone lay on the ground. It was her voicemail again.

"I gotta get to her." I thrust the paper I had balled up in my hand at Coven. After I snatched my phone off the ground I yelled over my shoulder, "And arrest that asshole next to you for obstructing justice. He shredded the first one we got last night."

Coven stared at the paper then at Derek for a moment as if he were replaying the same scene over in his head. One of the other officers in our department pulled up, and Derek started yelling that I had no idea what I was talking about.

"Go check on Trinity. I'll take care of this," Coven yelled as I jumped into my car and put it into drive before I even had the door latched.

"Car twenty-six-one," I called out on the radio after I flipped on my lights and siren.

"Car twenty-six-one, proceed," the dispatcher called out.

"Put me en-route to a suspicious condition at six fifteen Perry Drive and have a few more units head my way." They confirmed, and I heard a few of our guys key up and state they were on their way.

I pushed my driving abilities and those of my car as I rushed to her house. "Please, God," I prayed, "let her have forgotten her phone in the car. Let her be safe."

As I was trained, I turned my lights and siren off a mile from the house so I could make a silent approach. Of course, anyone looking outside would have seen my patrol car streaking through the dark neighborhood at unsafe speeds, but I was willing to risk getting chastised by my chief if it meant I got to Trinity in time.

"Car twenty-six-one, I'm on location." I never heard her reply as I stopped out front of Trinity's house, so focused on getting to her. It was a bad tactical move, I knew that, but there was no way I was wasting one second. I jumped from my patrol car and ran towards the house, not even bothering to shut my door. Her car sat in the driveway, the windows in the house dark. Even her bedroom window was dark. It was too early for her to be asleep.

I drew my gun as I cleared the four steps and zeroed in on the fact that the door was not completely shut. A sick feeling pervaded my gut, and I fought to control the anguish.

Memories of a time over ten years ago crashed down on me: a door not closed tightly; a man on his knees over a woman's prone body, his hands clenching her throat; and pallor to the woman's face that was not natural.

I pushed the door open enough that I could see the entranceway and checked it with my gun outstretched in front of me. No one was there, but two grocery bags were lying on their sides, contents scattered over the hardwood floor. I heard a crash in the back of the house and took off. Every aspect of my body tore in two as I thought about the fact that I should wait for backup but also that Trinity's life was in danger.

I rounded the corner into the kitchen and aimed my gun toward the family room. Two shadows were struggling in the dark. There was no way I could take a shot, not without risking Trinity's life; and that was not going to happen.

I holstered my gun as I ran toward them and went for the bigger of the two, knowing exactly who it would be. How he didn't hear me coming, I will never know, but I was able to get him in a choke hold and yank him back. I heard Trinity scream as she fell to the ground. A loud thump accompanied her fall, then silence.

Oh shit! What did she hit when she fell? She will be fine, I told myself as I struggled with Brenden.

He was thinner and stronger than he had been ten years ago. All that idle time in jail had given him time to work out, but I still had an upper hand. He wanted revenge, but I wanted Trinity. Love would win out.

We wrestled and tripped over Trinity's body, both of us falling to the ground. Fists flew as we both fought for the upper hand, I nailed him in the face and he returned one right to my left eye. I saw stars, but there was nothing that was going to stop me from keeping this man away from Trinity. It was only a matter of time before one of my guys got here, and then we would have him in custody—except things turned bad real quick when he went for my gun. In the turmoil to get to Trinity, I had made one critical mistake. I had shoved my gun into my holster but forgot to put the safety strap on.

It was now a struggle of life or death as we struggled over control of every cop's worst nightmare: being killed with your own gun.

My radio was crackling on my chest and the dispatcher was calling out for me, but I couldn't respond, not when I was fighting with every ounce of my strength to stop this man from turning the gun on me. Sweat dripped down my face, and my hands were slick.

Somehow he managed to get over the top of me and sweat dripped from his face down onto mine. No matter how much I fought, he seemed to have just a little bit more strength. Did knowing that as soon as another officer arrived, he was going to be going back to jail contribute to that?

A light turned on in the kitchen. Brenden's face was still in dark shadows as he faced away from the light, but I saw the details. An intense evil glinted in his eye as he pointed the gun at my face, and I stared down the barrel. "If I can't have her, nobody will." His voice chilled my skin even though I was sweating profusely. Those were the words of a man who was prepared to die, and take someone else with him.

A siren in the distance—or was that over my radio?—reached me, and I wondered if they would make it in time.

The dark metal barrel drew my attention away from the sounds around me. Never had I felt the fear that I did at that moment. My life seemed to flash in front of my eyes, the good and bad all twisted together in a single moment as a deafening gun-powdered explosion filled the room.

Chapter 29 - Trinity

I floated on air. I had never felt as good as I did at that moment. I had a future to look forward to and a past that could remain there, buried.

I pulled up to the house and climbed out, staring up at the stars that shone above my head. The air was crisp, refreshing; fall was on its way. I inhaled deeply and savored the rich scents of the night.

I had stopped at the grocery store on the way home to pick up some ingredients for a dessert I wanted to make for Gavin tomorrow night. He said he was going to cook dinner, so I thought I could offer up the dessert.

I was bummed that Gavin had to work, but I knew I had to get used to that. I couldn't have him with me every night. His job was important, and people relied on him. I could learn to do it. I wanted to do it.

I hummed to myself as I climbed the steps and unlocked the door. I kicked my shoes off again as I entered the hallway and closed the door behind me, flipping the dead bolt. When I turned, I froze as every vein in my body filled with icy dread.

I thought I had left the lights on in the foyer. Something felt wrong. "Callie?" I said quietly, but got no response.

Oh, god! Something was wrong, I could sense it. Callie should have been at the door waiting for me. I remembered locking her inside. Where the hell was she?

I stepped backwards slowly, feeling for the door while I scanned over the shadows of the house. I had stepped further into the foyer than I thought as I shuffled back and finally made contact with the heavy wooden door.

My heartbeat thudded inside my chest; it was the only thing I could hear. I struggled to hear any sounds that weren't caused by me as I took one more look around the area and then felt for the lock. If I could just get the lock undone I could get out of the house. I wouldn't be trapped, I could get help. I could scream, someone would hear me, windows would be open tonight.

"Hello, Trinity." My knees gave out under me, and I caught myself before I could fall to the ground. The voice from my nightmares filled my ears and echoed through my mind: Brenden. "Did you miss me?" His voice grew closer, and I stood frozen in fear.

Run, Trinity, run! I screamed inside my head.

I jumped as my cellphone began to ring. It was in my purse on the floor at my feet, and I knew without a doubt that it was Gavin calling to check on me.

I wanted to scream! I wanted to cry! How could life be so unfair? How could I finally find love, a man that I could love and be loved by and have it ripped right out of my hands. There was no doubt that along with all that, my life would be ripped out, too.

No! No! Brenden had taken enough of my life! He was not going to take the rest of it! I was not going down without a fight, and if I went, I was going to take him, too.

I grabbed the deadbolt and flipped it while I turned the doorknob and began to open the door. I didn't get the door open more than an inch before my head was yanked back by the hair, and I screamed. My hands flew up to automatically protect myself, trying to pull his hands away while trying to keep my hair attached to my head. My foot bumped against my purse, and I realized my phone was still ringing.

Would Gavin come check to make sure I was alright? Maybe he would. Maybe I could hold Brenden off long enough, and I could get to my phone and alert Gavin. During the struggle with Brenden, I managed to stick my foot through the strap of my purse and pull it with me as he dragged me back toward the kitchen.

"Did you really think you were going to live a life while I was wasting away behind bars?"

"How did you get out of jail?" I asked, hoping that if he talked, Gavin would have time to show up and check on me.

"I have a good lawyer, one that will get me out of this, too." He yanked my head again and pulled me up against his chest, inhaling loudly as he sniffed my hair. "You smell better than I remember."

"Brenden, please don't do this. Please, just leave and I won't tell anyone you were here, please," I begged. I wasn't above that.

"What, and leave you alone to play house with that asshole kid who managed to lock me up. Stupid prick! How dare he lock up one of his own!" he growled out as he wrapped a tight arm around my waist and began to grope my body.

"Brenden, please!" I fought against him, while also trying to hold down the bile that threatened to come up with his unwanted touches. He spun me around and slammed me up against the wall in the kitchen. My head bounced off the drywall and my vision darkened.

"What did you think of my gift?" He leaned close enough that I finally got a look at him. There were lines around his eyes that I didn't remember from ten years ago. He had a mustache now, and his hair was longer, almost to his shoulders.

"What gift?" I managed to ask.

"Your anonymous benefactor."

"What?" I stuttered out. "That's not you."

His grin was evil. "It wasn't? You sure about that? Because I do believe I donated the money my mother left me when she died to help fund your stupid little business. I thought it was rather ironic, don't you?"

"You're sick," I ground out.

"No, I'm not. I'm pissed." He shoved his body up against mine and forced my head back as his lips slammed against mine. I clenched my mouth as hard as I could. His hand came up to my face and he pressed his thumb and fingers against my cheekbones until they felt like they were going to crush. I gasped and he took advantage of it by shoving his tongue into my mouth.

I gagged and fought with everything I had, trying to knee him in the groin.

He pulled his head back and laughed, "You have gotten feisty in your old age, but I can get rid of that, like I did before." He pulled his arm back and I saw it coming, saw the arc of his arm as his hand came toward my face. I was powerless to stop it as it cracked against my cheek and turned my face to the side with incredible force. I tasted blood on my tongue and opened my eyes to see Callie lying motionless on the ground. The sight brought a sob to my chest.

Brenden grabbed me by the throat and yanked me off the wall. The feel of his hand around my throat brought back the haunted memories I had fought so hard to bury. I knew what he was going to do to me now. He was going to rape me and then strangle me. Within the hour, I would be dead, or so damaged that I wished I was dead.

By the time he got done with me, Gavin would want no parts of me. No one would.

He put me in a head lock and shuffled me forward into the living room. I knew that he was going to push me over the arm of the couch. That was what he used to do when he was punishing me. He'd push me over the couch, pull my pants down and spank me, then he'd either masturbate all over my back or he'd rape me.

Another sob tore through me, and I began to fight with him. I was not going to allow him to do that to me. I would rather be dead than tortured by that man any further.

One second I was fighting with him, the next I was shoved away and falling. There were noises behind me, but I didn't know what they were. A crackling sound was just reaching my ear when my head came in contact with something and bounced off, knocking me out.

The darkness was peaceful, and for a few moments I wondered if I was dead. It was too dark in here. I didn't want to be here anymore. I fought to get out, but my body was so heavy. I pushed against the dark veil and slowly started to feel like I was coming up through molasses. Noises reached my ears and throbbed inside my head.

My hand went to my temple where it touched something sticky and warm. I cringed in pain as I tried to remember what had happened. I heard more noises and the static sound that I thought I had heard earlier…more voices, a grunt, a siren and voices…a siren…

Gavin! Gavin was coming. I had to wake up. I had to protect myself long enough for him to get here. I forced myself to open my eyes slowly, and saw two people fighting over to the side. I knew without a doubt that one of them was Gavin.

I had to get to my purse. Where was my purse? I pushed myself up, trying to stay out of their way. Waves of dizziness washed over me, threatening to bring me back down. I heard someone calling out for a car number over and over again, were they calling for Gavin? Sirens seemed to be getting louder. Where the hell had my purse gone?

I got to my knees and started to feel around. The sounds of the fighting continued, the siren grew louder.

My hand fanned out over the ground. Damn it! Where is my purse? I need light! I crawled to the wall and kneed something on my way. My purse! I grabbed it and flipped it upside down to drop the contents on the ground.

I found what I needed and stood up, reaching for the light switch. As my hand flipped the switch up, I spun around and extended my arms, pointing the gun towards the two men. The sight in front of me scared me more than anything else I had ever witnessed.

Brenden held a gun pointed just inches from Gavin's head, and they struggled intensely.

I did the only thing I could do. I would protect what I loved. I pulled the trigger.

* * *

Three hours later, I was lying in a bed at the hospital. I had a concussion and a few lacerations, but all in all, I was in good shape. Brooke sat by my side, holding my hand. "They want to keep you here overnight for observation."

"Yeah, they told me."

"I'd ask you if you were alright, but I know you're not." She swiped some hair off my forehead. "I'm so sorry." Tears spilled down her face.

I fought not to cry. So far, I had not done so, and I refused to do so. I would cry later, when I was alone. Right now I needed to be strong.

"Do you know where Gavin is?" I asked and realized my throat was still sore. At least he hadn't crushed my windpipe like the last time. I could deal with some bruising.

"I think he is at the station. They wouldn't let him come here or stay at the scene. He told me that there was a lot that needed to be done, and he had to be interviewed."

"Okay," I said, wishing he was here with me. After I had pulled the trigger, things had happened so fast that I wasn't sure what had really happened.

"His sister and brother-in-law are out in the waiting room. They have been here as long as I have. Gavin asked Taylor to stay here until he could get here. He didn't want you to be alone or interviewed yet."

"That was sweet of him." I winced as I smiled. My cheek was swollen.

"He is sweet. If I wasn't married to an incredible man, I think I might have fought you for him." She laughed, "Although, I'm pretty sure that man only has eyes for you."

"You think?" I asked her.

"Oh, I know, and soon you will, too."

Chapter 30 - Gavin

Police Incident #30PJ140013968

LOCATION: 615 PERRY DRIVE, EAGLESVILLE

REPORTING OFFICER: SGT. GAVIN BROOKSFIELD

THE REPORTING OFFICER IS A SERGEANT WITH EAGLESVILLE POLICE DEPARTMENT AND WAS SO EMPLOYED AND ON DUTY, IN FULL UNIFORM, OPERATING A MARKED PATROL VEHICLE ON SEPTEMBER 15, 2014 AT APPROXIMATELY 2125 HOURS.

AT APPROXIMATELY THAT TIME, I WAS ON STATION COMPLETING PAPERWORK FOR ANOTHER INCIDENT AND FOUND SEVERAL PAGES ON THE FAX MACHINE. ONE OF THOSE PAGES WAS A NOTIFICATION FROM ANDERSON COUNTY, TENNESSEE. THIS NOTIFICATION REPORTED THAT BRENDEN MARKS HAD BEEN RELEASED FROM PRISON ON A TECHNICALITY BROUGHT UP AT AN APPEAL. THE NOTIFICATION FURTHER STATED THAT THEY HAD ATTEMPTED TO MAKE CONTACT WITH THE VICTIM, HIS EX-WIFE, TRINITY MORRIS, WHO CURRENTLY RESIDES AT 615 PERRY DRIVE IN OUR JURISDICTION. THE NOTIFICATION ALSO STATED THAT THIS WAS A 'SECOND REQUEST' AND HAD THE DATE OF SEPTEMBER 14, 2014 BESIDE IT.

I DID RECALL HAVING SEEN OFC. DEREK WILSON PICKING UP A PIECE OF PAPER OFF THE FAX MACHINE THE DAY BEFORE AND

MAKING A COMMENT UNDER HIS BREATH. I DO NOT RECALL THE COMMENT MADE. HE THEN PROCEEDED TO LAUGH AND SHRED THE PAPER WITHOUT DIVULGING ANYTHING FURTHER.

I AM PERSONALLY AWARE OF WHO TRINITY MORRIS IS, AND IN FACT I AM THE ONE WHO ARRESTED HER HUSBAND OVER TEN YEARS AGO FOR ATTEMPTING TO KILL HER THEN.

I ATTEMPTED TO MAKE CONTACT WITH MS. MORRIS VIA CELLPHONE, BUT RECEIVED HER VOICEMAIL SEVERAL TIMES. AT THAT TIME, I EXITED THE REAR OF THE STATION AND FOUND SGT. COVEN SPEAKING WITH OFC. DEREK WILSON AS THEY APPROACHED THE BUILDING.

I ADVISED SGT. COVEN OF WHAT WAS HAPPENING AND HAD HEATED WORDS WITH DEREK WILSON BEFORE I LEFT TO RESPOND TO MS. MORRIS'S RESIDENCE.

AT APPROXIMATELY 2133 HOURS, I ARRIVED ON LOCATION. UPON APPROACH OF THE RESIDENCE, I FOUND THE FRONT DOOR PARTIALLY AJAR. THERE WERE NO LIGHTS ON INSIDE THE RESIDENCE. I REMOVED MY SERVICE WEAPON FROM MY HOLSTER AND OPENED THE DOOR. THERE WERE SOUNDS, CONSISTENT WITH A STRUGGLE, COMING FROM THE REAR OF THE HOUSE. I DID NOT ANNOUNCE MY APPROACH AS I MADE MY WAY INTO THE RESIDENCE, BELIEVING THAT MY BEST COURSE OF ACTION WAS TO SURPRISE THE SUBJECT.

IN THE LIVING ROOM, WHICH SITS IN THE SOUTHEAST CORNER OF THE RESIDENCE, I COULD MAKE OUT TWO FIGURES WRESTLING IN THE AREA NEAR THE COUCH AND COFFEE TABLE.

AT THAT TIME, I HOLSTERED MY WEAPON AND PROCEEDED TO GO HANDS ON WITH THE SUBJECT FROM BEHIND. I DID MANAGE TO PULL HIM OFF OF THE VICTIM, MS. MORRIS, AND DID ENTER INTO A PHYSICAL CONFRONTATION WITH THE SUBJECT, KNOWN TO ME PERSONALLY AS BRENDEN MARKS.

DURING OUR STRUGGLES, WE TRIPPED OVER THE VICTIM AND ENDED UP ON THE GROUND. MARKS WENT FOR MY FIREARM, WHICH WAS NOT PROPERLY SECURED IN MY HOLSTER, AND A FIGHT ENSUED AS HE WAS ABLE TO GAIN CONTROL OVER THE FIREARM.

THE FIREARM IN QUESTION IS A GLOCK 22, .40 CALIBER, DEPARTMENT-ISSUED GUN.

MARKS WAS ON TOP OF THIS OFFICER IN THE FINAL MOMENTS OF THE STRUGGLE. A LIGHT WAS TURNED ON IN THE KITCHEN AREA BEHIND MARKS, AND A MOMENT LATER A GUNSHOT RANG OUT, AND MARKS COLLAPSED FORWARD OVER MY BODY.

I RETRIEVED MY FIREARM FROM MARKS AND PUSHED HIM OFF MY BODY. THE VICTIM, MS. MORRIS, WAS STANDING APPROXIMATELY TWELVE FEET FROM MY LOCATION AND HOLDING A FIREARM POINTED IN MY DIRECTION. THERE WAS SMOKE COMING FROM THE BARREL OF THE WEAPON.

AT THAT TIME, TWO OTHER OFFICERS ARRIVED ON LOCATION AND TOOK CONTROL OF THE SCENE.

AFTER CHECKING ON THE WELLBEING OF MS. MORRIS, I HANDED THE FIREARM OFF TO SGT. COVEN WHO ARRIVED ON LOCATION. I ALSO HANDED OVER MY DUTY WEAPON AND WAS ASKED TO REMOVE MY SHIRT AS IT CONTAINED BLOOD EVIDENCE OF THE SCENE.

MS. MORRIS WAS TAKEN BY AMBULANCE TO RUTHER'S MEMORIAL HOSPITAL TO HAVE HER INJURIES EVALUATED. AT THE TIME SHE LEFT, SHE REPORTED TRAUMA TO HER HEAD, NECK, AND SIDE OF HER FACE. THERE WAS APPARENT BRUISING ON THE RIGHT SIDE OF HER FACE, AND A LACERATION OVER HER LEFT EYE THAT WAS BLEEDING.

AT 2245 HOURS I WAS CLEARED TO LEAVE THE SCENE AND RETURN TO THE STATION FOR A FORMAL INTERVIEW AND TO COMPLETE MY REPORTS. I HAVE BEEN PLACED ON ADMINISTRATIVE LEAVE PENDING THE OUTCOME OF THIS INVESTIGATION.

END OF REPORT.

POLICE INCIDENT #30PJ140013968

LOCATION: 615 PERRY DRIVE, EAGLESVILLE

REPORTING OFFICER: DETECTIVE JERRY SANDOVAL

AT APPROXIMATELY 2145 HOURS I WAS CONTACTED VIA CELLPHONE BY OUR COUNTY DISPATCHER AND ADVISED OF A

SHOOTING, POSSIBLY INVOLVING ONE OF OUR OFFICERS. I DID ARRIVE ON LOCATION AT 615 PERRY DRIVE AT APPROXIMATELY 2215.

THE NEIGHBORHOOD IS RESIDENTIAL; THE HOUSE, VICTORIAN. THERE IS ONE PERSONAL VEHICLE IN THE DRIVEWAY AND THE FRONT OF THE HOUSE FACES NORTH TOWARD PERRY DRIVE. AT THIS TIME, THE PERIMETER HAS BEEN ESTABLISHED AND TAPED OFF.

SGT. COVEN GAVE ME A RUNDOWN OF THE EVENTS AS HE UNDERSTOOD THEM AND ALSO EXPLAINED THAT SGT. BROOKSFIELD IS CURRENTLY IN AN INTIMATE RELATIONSHIP WITH THE VICTIM, MS. TRINITY MORRIS. HE EXPLAINED THAT THE EX-HUSBAND HAD BEEN RELEASED FROM PRISON A FEW DAYS PRIOR AND HAD ABSCONDED FROM THE STATE OF TENNESSEE IN SEARCH OF HIS FORMER WIFE.

AT THAT TIME, I PHOTOGRAPHED THE OUTSIDE OF THE RESIDENCE AND WORKED MY WAY INTO THE PRIMARY CRIME SCENE, TAKING PHOTOGRAPHS AS I PROCEEDED.

IN THE ENTRANCE WAY, THERE ARE TWO BAGS OF GROCERIES LYING ON THEIR SIDES. A PUDDLE OF WHITE IS UNDER ONE BAG AND UPON FURTHER INSPECTION FIND IT IS VANILLA ICE CREAM. A PAIR OF WOMEN'S HIGH HEEL SHOES ARE LYING DISCARDED IN THE ENTRANCEWAY. IT IS UNKNOWN IF THEY WERE MOVED FROM ORIGINAL POSITION WITH THE TRAFFIC IN AND OUT OF THE SCENE.

ON THE ENTRANCEWAY TABLE IS A STACK OF MAIL. IN THAT STACK IS A LETTER MARKED 'URGENT' FROM THE PRISON IN ANDERSON COUNTY, TENNESSEE. THIS ENVELOPE IS UNOPENED. PHOTOGRAPHS WERE TAKEN OF THE FRONT AND BACK, AND THE LETTER WAS OPENED. INSIDE REVEALED INFORMATION ABOUT THE RELEASE OF BRENDEN MARKS FROM THE PRISON. THE LETTER WAS COLLECTED AS EVIDENCE AND MARKED AS ITEM #3.

AT THE REAR OF THE HALLWAY, IT INTERSECTS WITH THE KITCHEN/DINING ROOM AREA. OFF TO THE RIGHT IS THE FAMILY/LIVING ROOM. THERE ARE ITEMS SUCH AS MAGAZINES AND PILLOWS STREWN ABOUT THE AREA. A MALE BODY IS FACE

DOWN ON THE CARPET IN THE CENTER OF THE ROOM. A #1 EVIDENCE MARKER SITS ON HIS BACK. A FIREARM IS SET, SLIDE BACK, LOADED MAGAZINE BESIDE IT ON THE FLOOR APPROXIMATELY THIRTEEN FEET FROM THE BODY. IT HAS BEEN MARKED WITH A #2 MARKER. THIS FIREARM IS A SMITH & WESSON, M&P SHIELD, 40 CALIBER, AND SAID TO BE THE WEAPON THAT WAS FIRED AND KILLED THE SUSPECT.

ON THE KITCHEN TABLE IS ANOTHER FIREARM, THIS IS A GLOCK 22, SAID TO BE POLICE ISSUED TO SGT. BROOKSFIELD. THE SLIDE HAS BEEN LOCKED BACK AND THE MAGAZINE REMOVED. IT HAS BEEN MARKED AS #4. BESIDE THE FIREARM IS A POLICE UNIFORM SHIRT. THE NAME PLAQUE ON THE SHIRT READS, SGT. BROOKSFIELD. THIS ITEM HAS BEEN LABELED #5.

THE CASING FOR THE FIRED ROUND WAS LOCATED UNDER THE KITCHEN TABLE AND WAS LEFT IN PLACE AND MARKED #6. BLOOD SPLATTER ON THE WALL ABOVE THE DECEASED WAS MARKED WITH #7.

THE VICTIM'S HANDS HAD BEEN TESTED FOR GUNSHOT RESIDUE BEFORE SHE WAS REMOVED FROM THE SCENE. IT HAS BEEN MARKED #8. SGT. BROOKSFIELD'S HANDS WERE ALSO TESTED FOR GUNSHOT RESIDUE AND IT HAS BEEN LABELED AS ITEM #9.

A SINGLE BULLET WAS RECOVERED FROM THE BASE OF A LEATHER RECLINER. IT WAS MARKED #10.

AN INITIAL INTERVIEW WAS CONDUCTED WITH SGT. BROOKSFIELD AT THE SCENE, WHERE HE EXPLAINED THE EVENTS OF THE INCIDENT. HE WAS RELEASED FROM THE SCENE AND ESCORTED BACK TO THE STATION BY ANOTHER OFFICER TO COMPLETE HIS REPORT AND ALSO AWAIT A FORMAL INTERVIEW.

AT APPROXIMATELY 2320 HOURS, THE BODY OF THE DECEASED WAS REMOVED FROM THE SCENE BY THE CORONER'S OFFICE. THE CORONER STATED THAT IT APPEARED A BULLET HAD GONE THROUGH THE BACK OF THE DECEASED'S HEAD AND STRUCK THE SPINAL COLUMN, KILLING HIM INSTANTLY. HE STATED THE AUTOPSY WOULD BE SCHEDULED FOR NOON THE FOLLOWING DAY.

AT APPROXIMATELY 0010 HOURS, THE SCENE WAS RELEASED FROM POLICE CUSTODY AND TURNED OVER TO A FAMILY FRIEND TO CLEAN AND SECURE FOR THE VICTIM.

AT APPROXIMATELY 0035 HOURS, I DID RESPOND TO THE HOSPITAL AND MET WITH THE VICTIM, TRINITY MORRIS, AND OWNER OF 615 PERRY DRIVE. TRINITY WAS WILLING TO SPEAK WITH ME, BUT STATED THAT SHE WANTED HER BUSINESS PARTNER AND DOMESTIC VIOLENCE ADVOCATE WITH HER WHILE SHE DID.

THE INTERVIEW TOOK PLACE IN HER HOSPITAL ROOM WITH BROOKE PATTERSON PRESENT.

MS. MORRIS WENT THROUGH THE EVENTS THAT TRANSPIRED, FILLING IN THE GAPS OF WHAT TOOK PLACE BEFORE SGT. BROOKSFIELD ARRIVED. MS. MORRIS STATED THAT SHE HAD FIRED THE SHOT THAT KILLED HER FORMER HUSBAND WHEN SHE SAW HIM POINTING THE GUN INTO THE FACE OF SGT. BROOKSFIELD.

UPON ARRIVAL BACK AT THE STATION, I WAS INFORMED THAT THE ORIGINAL FAX HAD BEEN REMOVED FROM THE SHREDDER. THE SHREDDER IS A STRIP STYLE AND THE PIECES WERE ABLE TO BE PUT BACK TOGETHER. PHOTOGRAPHS WERE TAKEN, AND IT WAS PLACED INTO EVIDENCE AS #11.

CASE PENDING FURTHER INVESTIGATION.

Case SUPPLEMENT: September 16, 2014 - Autopsy

AUTOPSY REVEALED THAT ONE BULLET DID INDEED ENTER THE BACK OF THE HEAD AND STRIKE THE SPINAL COLUMN. THE CAUSE OF DEATH WAS LISTED AS GUNSHOT WOUND.

Case SUPPLEMENT: September 16, 2014 - Evidence

EVIDENCE WAS TRANSPORTED TO OUR LAB FOR PROCESSING.

Case SUPPLEMENT: September 17, 2014 – Evidence

I WAS NOTIFIED BY OUR CRIME LAB THAT THERE WERE TWO SETS OF FINGERPRINTS ON THE FIREARM. ONE THAT BELONGED TO SGT. BROOKSFIELD AND ONE THAT WAS FROM THE DECEASED.

I WAS ALSO INFORMED THAT GUNSHOT RESIDUE TESTS CONFIRMED THAT MS. MORRIS HAD MOST LIKELY FIRED THE WEAPON AS SHE HAD RESIDUE ON HER HANDS. SGT. BROOKSFIELD'S TESTS WERE NEGATIVE.

Case SUPPLEMENT: September 18, 2014 – Interview – Derek Wilson

A FORMAL INTERVIEW WAS CONDUCTED WITH OFFICER DEREK WILSON AT THE STATION. HE DID WAIVE HIS MIRANDA RIGHTS AND DID AGREE TO SPEAK WITH ME.

WHEN ASKED ABOUT THE FAX, HE DENIED KNOWING ANYTHING ABOUT IT. WHEN TOLD THAT HIS PRINTS WERE LOCATED ON THE PAPER, HE STATED HE WAS DONE TALKING AND WANTED A LAWYER. THE INTERVIEW WAS TERMINATED.

DEREK WAS PUT ON OFFICIAL UNPAID ADMINISTRATIVE LEAVE AND ASKED TO TURN IN HIS BADGE AND GUN BY THE CHIEF.

Case SUPPLEMENT: September 19, 2014 – Evidence

I WAS NOTIFIED BY THE CRIME LAB THAT THE BULLET RECOVERED FROM THE SCENE WAS MOSTLY LIKELY SHOT FROM THE SMITH AND WESSON M&P SHIELD THAT HAD BEEN RECOVERED AT THE SCENE. THIS FIREARM IS LEGALLY REGISTERED TO THE VICTIM.

I WAS ALSO NOTIFIED THAT THE BLOOD SPATTER FOUND ON SGT. BROOKSFIELD'S UNIFORM WAS CONSISTENT WITH THE TYPE OF INJURY THE DECEASED HAD RECEIVED. IT SHOWED THAT HE WAS PROBABLY INDEED UNDER THE SUSPECT AT THE TIME OF THE SHOOTING.

Case Supplement: September 20, 2014 – Information from West Tennessee State Penitentiary

INFORMATION WAS RECEIVED FROM THE PRISON THAT THE DECEASED, BRENDEN MARKS, HAD BEEN PLANNING ON LEAVING THE STATE AND FINDING HIS WIFE. A JOURNAL FOUND IN HIS CELL DEPICTED AN INTENSE NEED FOR REVENGE. HE DID STATE IN HIS JOURNAL THAT HE INTENDED TO TAKE WHAT WAS HIS ONE LAST TIME AND HE WOULD "MAKE HER SCREAM FOR IT" BEFORE HE KILLED HER.

THESE PAGES WERE SCANNED AND SENT TO ME VIA EMAIL. THEY HAVE BEEN ENTERED INTO EVIDENCE AS #12.

Case Supplement: September 20, 2014

AFTER REVIEWING THE SCENE, AUTOPSY, INTERVIEWS, AND EVIDENCE, IT HAS BEEN DECIDED THAT THIS WAS A SELF-DEFENSE SHOOTING.

MS. MORRIS DID FIRE THE WEAPON TO STOP THE DECEASED, BRENDEN MARKS, FROM SHOOTING AND KILLING A POLICE OFFICER, NAMELY SGT. GAVIN BROOKSFIELD.

IT HAS ALSO BEEN DECIDED BY THE DISTRICT ATTORNEY'S OFFICE THAT FORMER OFFICER DEREK WILSON WILL BE RELEASED FROM HIS POSITION WITH THE EAGLESVILLE POLICE DEPARTMENT AND WILL BE CHARGED WITH OBSTRUCTION OF JUSTICE AND CONSPIRACY TO COMMIT HOMICIDE.

THERE WILL BE NO CHARGES PENDING FOR MS. TRINITY MORRIS OR SGT. GAVIN BROOKSFIELD. SGT. BROOKSFIELD HAS BEEN NOTIFIED THAT HE CAN RETURN TO FULL DUTY ON HIS NEXT SCHEDULED SHIFT.

CASE CLOSED.

Epilogue

Two Weeks Later

Trinity

The grains of sand fell to the ground as they sifted through my fingers. The feeling was gritty but soft at the same time. The lull of the waves gently rolling up on shore drowned out the sound of footsteps behind me.

"Hey, sweetheart, you're up early," Gavin said as he lowered himself beside me in the sand.

I leaned my head against his shoulder as he wrapped his arm around me. "I couldn't sleep. Besides, I love to watch the sunrise. It always enthralls me that I lived to see one more day."

He kissed the top of my head. "You are going to live to see hundreds of sunrises. Scratch that, we are going to live to see them together."

I sighed. That sounded so wonderful. "You think so?" A seagull called out from behind us, and another answered up the beach a ways. "I'm so glad Taylor said we could borrow this place. It is amazing."

"It is amazing. He got it for a steal after a hurricane and has spent a few years fixing it up." He paused for a few seconds, and his body tensed slightly before he cleared his throat, "It would be nice to host a party here."

"A party? What kind of party?" I asked as I watched a seagull swoop down over the surface of the water.

"Maybe not a party, maybe more like a celebration." He shifted and pulled something out of his shorts pants pocket. "Like, maybe a wedding celebration."

I lifted my head off his shoulder as he held a dark purple ring box out in front of me.

"Open it," he whispered against the side of my face.

As he held the box, I cracked open the top and looked down at the most beautiful teardrop diamond engagement ring.

"Oh, Gavin!" I gushed as I stared at it.

He turned sideways so he could see my face, "Trinity Morris, will you please do me the honor of making me the luckiest man in the world by saying you will be my wife and the mother to my children?" He took the ring out of the box and dropped the box in the sand.

Tears rolled down my cheeks as I looked up into his face.

"What's wrong, sweetie?" His face looked shocked at my response.

It was at that moment that the events of two weeks ago struck me, and I realized how close I had been to losing the best thing that had ever happened to me. "Oh, my god. I almost lost you," I cried as I got to my knees and threw my arms around his neck.

My tears quickly grew to sobs, and Gavin gathered me into his arms and cradled me to his chest, rocking me slowly, "I know, sweetheart. I thought I had lost you that day, too." He whispered in my ear, "I love you, Trinity. I don't ever want to live a day without you."

I sobbed into his neck, holding him as tightly as I could as the fear and pain finally released.

It took me a few minutes to gather myself together and stop crying. During my entire meltdown, Gavin held me and cooed in my ear that he was never going anywhere, that we would always be together.

"You promise?" I asked him as I hiccupped, trying to regain my wits.

"I will promise, if you will promise to marry me."

Oh, damn! I had never answered him. "Yes! Yes, Gavin, I will marry you." I pulled back and kissed him, knowing that I looked a total mess, but knowing that Gavin wouldn't care what I looked like, and would even probably say I looked beautiful.

Gavin slipped the ring onto my finger, "This ring is the only tear you are allowed to have now."

I caressed the side of his face, "I love you so much, Gavin. How did I get so lucky?"

"I think I'm the lucky one. You did save my life, you know."

"No, I saved our lives." I kissed him again as another seagull hovered over our heads and squawked.

"I have one other thing I need to ask you," he said as he rested his forehead against mine.

"Okay," I said, wondering what else he could possibly want.

"How would you feel if I left the job?"

"What? You want to leave law enforcement?" I was shocked. I had never seen any inclination that he didn't like his job. "Where is this coming from?"

"With all that has happened these past few weeks, I have realized how much you mean to me. I don't want to be away from you at night, so I was thinking about giving up my position and maybe just going part time to keep my foot in the door, but I would be giving up my sergeant's position."

"But what would you do?" I was stunned and unsure what to say. I was important enough to him to leave a job he had been doing for over thirteen years? I was floored.

"Well, Taylor has been asking me for a while to go into business with him. He wants to expand a little bit, and I kind of thought that if I did, you would have someone on permanent retainer to fix things around the shelters."

"You would want to do that? Work with Taylor?"

"If it would mean I was closer to home, and I could be there for you and our family, yes. I would do it without batting an eyelid." He took my face between his hands, "I love you, Trinity, with all of my heart. I want to spend as much time as I can with you, and helping other people. Maybe I'll even get the nerve up to tell my story in public."

"Gavin, I don't know what to say, except that I love you, and I will support you in whatever decision you make. If you want to stay in law enforcement full time, I will support you, but if you want to step away and get a break, I will support you in that, too. Whatever you want, as long as you don't leave me."

"Never, Trinity, I'm never going to leave you. That's why I'm doing this, so that we can have more of a life together."

Eight Months Later

Gavin

Trinity and I stood hand in hand in front of our fifty-some guests out on the sand behind Taylor's beach house. An hour ago, we had said our vows standing in this same place. I pulled her close to my side and wrapped one arm around her back while the other hand rubbed her swollen belly. Trinity didn't get pregnant that first time we made love, but shortly after we got engaged, we decided that life was going to take its course and if a child was in our future, then it would come when it was time. It was only a matter of a few weeks later that we found out our first child was on the way.

I had stepped down at the department, despite some heavy talks with the guys trying to keep me in place. I knew that my family was the most important thing to me. I still did a shift a week to keep up with things, but tried to be home with Trinity as much as I could.

Wayne Drummond had finally seen his day in court, and with Brooke and Trinity at her side, Tabitha had testified against him. He was doing three years in prison.

Trinity had told me last week that the guy who had been breaking into the shelter was finally caught and charged with burglary, thanks to the video system that had been installed with Brenden's blood money—that's what Trinity called it anyway. I told her she should consider it what was owed to her.

My job with Taylor was working out better than expected. Between the two of us, we had more jobs than we could handle, and we had started hiring a few more guys. I even pulled a few of my cop friends in to work part time on their days off.

Trinity and I sold her house and found another one closer to her office, and a bit closer to my sister's. This one had no horrible memories and had never been tainted by Brenden's presence. It also had four bedrooms and plenty of room to expand our family.

I scanned the small crowd gathered to celebrate with us, and my gaze landed on my buddy Coven. He was out on the small dance floor with Marcy. Trinity and I had introduced them shortly after the incident, and they were going strong. He was staring down into Marcy's face in a very similar way to how I looked at my new wife.

I turned to her and took in her glowing face and was mesmerized by all the love that I saw shining in her eyes. That love was for me.

How differently she looked at me now as compared to eleven years ago when she had met my eyes in the courtroom. No longer was she broken and afraid. She was healed and loved. She was a woman who went out of her way for anyone and everyone, but always took care of her family first and wasn't afraid to say no if it affected them or herself.

She was my role model, the love of my life, and my wife—and I felt like not only had I helped her to heal and move forward in her life, but she had helped me. For the first time in my life, I felt complete.

I wasn't alone, either.

Books by Stacy Eaton

My Blood Runs Blue
Blue Blood for Life
Whether I'll Live or Die
Garda ~ Welcome to the Realm
Liveon ~ No Evil
Second Shield
Distorted Loyalty
Six Days of Memories
Barbara's Plea
Finding the Strength
Cured by Love
Tangled in Tinsel
You're Not Alone

About the Author

Stacy Eaton is a police officer by profession. Currently, she is working as the department investigator and enjoys digging into cases and putting the pieces of the puzzles together.

Stacy resides in southeastern Pennsylvania and is the wife to a police officer and the mother of two. She is very proud of her son who is currently serving in the United States Navy and equally proud of her younger daughter who works hard in her Tae Kwon Do studies.

When Stacy is not working her demanding job, or spending time with her family, she works on her business and volunteers with the World Literary Café. She is also on the Board of Directors of her local Domestic Violence Center. When there is time, she writes.

Be sure to visit www.stacyeaton.com for updates and more information on her books.